The Soulkeepers

G.P. Ching

Carpe Luna Publishing

The Soulkeepers: The Soulkeepers series, Book 1
Copyright © G.P. Ching, 2011, 2012
Published by Carpe Luna, Ltd., PO Box 5932, Bloomington, IL 61701
www.carpeluna.com

Fifth Edition November 2012

ISBN: 978-1-940675-02-2

Cover art by Adam Bedore at Anjin Design.
www.anjindesign.com

Photograph copyright Red Glass Sphere (isolated) © Kompaniets Tara and Handsome Young Man in Hood © Nejron Photo. Licensed through Shutterstock images.
www.shutterstock.com

Formatting by Polgarus Studio.
www.polgarusstudio.com

v 3.5

Books by G.P. Ching

The Soulkeepers Series

The Soulkeepers, Book 1
Weaving Destiny, Book 2
Return to Eden, Book 3
Soul Catcher, Book 4
Lost Eden, Book 5
The Last Soulkeeper, Book 6

Other Books by G.P. Ching

Grounded

For Aaron, Madi, and Hannah

Contents

Chapter 1
The Boy Who Died

D eath lived up to Jacob's expectations.

The day he died was sunny, as it was most days on the island of Oahu where he lived. Only a few miles away, bikini-clad tourists stretched out on the sand of Waikiki beach. While they toasted themselves golden brown, Jacob lay on a steel surgical table, broken and bleeding. He'd heard that when a person died they saw a tunnel that ended in a bright light. If the person moved toward the light, God or some already deceased loved one like a great-grandmother would meet them on the other side. Jacob didn't believe it. He'd accepted that everything would end in black nothingness and, for him, it did. What he didn't expect was that the end was just the beginning.

The light returned. His eyes fluttered open against bright white and a face emerged from the radiance, materializing from the void. A rumbling voice called him by name. "Jacob. Jacob, can you hear me?" Behind the voice was the *clink-clank* of metal hitting metal and a smell like a copper penny soaked in Clorox.

"I think he's coming 'round," the voice said from behind a green surgical mask. Soulful brown eyes came into focus. Spikes of pain stabbed through Jacob's head and chest and he realized the man in scrubs was shaking him. He wanted to tell the man to stop, but a plastic dome pressed over his face. As he fought against the plastic, the tubes connected to his arm slapped against the metal pole near the gurney.

"Relax, my man," the face said, pressing Jacob's arms to his sides. "The mask has to stay on. It's oxygen and you need it."

In his confused state, Jacob couldn't understand who the green man was. All he knew was pressure and pain, like he'd been torn apart and put back together.

"Jacob, take a deep breath. Come on, kid, breathe."

Of its own volition, the air went in. The air went out. The pain made the air rattle in his mouth.

"That's it. A few more like that, Jacob. Slow and deep. Can you understand me?" the green man asked.

"Yes," Jacob tried to say, but his voice was nothing but a rough whisper, muffled by the oxygen mask.

"Are you in pain?"

He tried to say yes again but the word dissolved in his throat. He nodded slightly, too, in case the green man hadn't heard.

"Okay, just relax. I'm going to give you some morphine." The green man held up a syringe with some clear liquid in it, and then locked it onto the tube in Jacob's arm. He pressed the plunger and Jacob felt a cold ribbon twist into his vein. The pain ebbed. The light dimmed. On the ceiling there were tiles, foam squares in a steel grid that he guessed hid the wires and pipes up there. He counted the squares as he floated away, thinking of the wires and pipes under his own skin carrying the green man's juice to all his fingers and toes.

When the darkness swallowed him again, all the thinking his exhausted, numbed-out, maybe-damaged brain could produce was a vague feeling that he'd forgotten something. The missing thought was an irritation at the back of his skull. The more he concentrated on it, the more the memory slipped from his grasp, an oily shoelace through languid fingers.

Chapter 2
The Uncle Who Wasn't

The sound of footsteps woke Jacob in his hospital bed. He was annoyed that the nurses kept waking him up. All he wanted to do was sleep, but as it turned out hospitals were not a good place to rest.

Without opening his eyes, he said, "I'm not hungry and I don't need another pain pill."

A gruff voice answered him from the side of the bed. "That's good because I don't have either of those things."

Jacob's lids flipped open. A stranger sat in the uncomfortable-looking chair next to his hospital bed, the pads of his fingers pressed together under his chin.

"Who are you?" Jacob asked.

"I'm your Uncle John. John Laudner," the man said. He leaned forward and extended a calloused palm.

Jacob did not take the man's hand. "You've made a mistake. I don't have an uncle and my last name isn't Laudner. It's Lau."

The man pursed his lips, his green eyes shifting to the hospital floor. He sat back in his chair, opening his mouth as if to say something and then closing it again. At last he lowered his hands, linking them at his waist. "There's no easy way to tell you this, Jacob. I am your uncle. I am the brother of Charles Lau, formerly known as Charlie Laudner. Your father changed his name before you were born."

Jacob licked his parched lips and reached for the cup of water the nurse had left him. He sucked greedily on the straw before speaking. "I've never even heard of you."

"It's a long story. You lived far away. After your father died, well, it never seemed like the right time to introduce myself."

"So why are you here now?"

"Jacob, do you remember anything about the accident?"

Jacob closed his eyes. The truth was, his brain did have an explanation for what had happened, but it was ludicrous. The memory was so far-fetched he could only believe his imagination had stitched it together to fill in the gaps. "No. I told the doctors, the last thing I remember was fighting with my mom that morning in our apartment. I don't even remember getting into the car with her."

"She's missing, Jacob."

"Missing?" he said, sitting up in bed despite the pain. "But she must've been in the car with me. How could they have rescued me and not her?"

"You were inside the car when they found it. She wasn't."

"But that doesn't make any sense."

"Your blood was on the inside of the car, Jacob. Hers was on the outside."

She'd had a gun. She'd been standing next to the door. He shook his head, ignoring the thought. It was a false memory, brought on by emotional and physical trauma. What had the doctor called it? Auditory and visual hallucinations: the brain's way of making sense of the damage it incurred when his skull collided with the windshield.

"How is that possible?"

"They think, maybe, you were driving."

"I don't have a driver's license."

John stood up and approached the bed. He unsnapped the arm of the hospital gown Jacob was wearing, pulling it down slightly. Then he tipped up the hideaway mirror on the overbed table. The bruise that arced across Jacob's chest looked like the top half of a large circle ... or a steering wheel. He traced the edge with his finger, a rainbow of purple-hued skin. A chill ran up his spine.

"Did I hit her?"

John returned the thin fabric to its place. "The police don't think so, Jacob. Her blood was on the passenger side door, not the hood of the car. You were found in a heavily wooded area of Manoa Falls. It's only a few miles from your apartment. They think, after the accident, your mom got out of the car to get help."

You'd followed her there. You'd had a fight and you wanted to apologize.

"I don't remember," Jacob said, but a more truthful answer would have been that the memory he had couldn't be real. It was nonsense.

"It's normal that you don't. The doc says people often block out extreme circumstances. It's your brain's way of protecting you from reliving the trauma."

"And then what? Where did she go?"

John's face contorted. His voice strained with emotion when he answered. "There have been abductions in the area. Nine women went missing in the last year; six were found dead. Murdered. There were signs of a struggle where they found you."

Jacob's blood froze in his veins. "Are you saying, my mom might have been abducted, or worse, killed?"

"They don't know for sure. I'm sorry, Jacob."

A tear escaped down his cheek and he wiped it away with his bare hand. It had been a long time since he'd allowed himself to cry. He wasn't about to start now. He'd survived by following two very important rules: don't feel anything and don't expect anything from anyone. To distract himself, he concentrated on the specifics of what happened. Why in the world would he have driven his mother's car?

The creature was coming for you. Your mom tried to fight it. He ignored the rogue thought. "What did I hit, anyway?"

John repositioned himself in his chair and folded his arms across his chest. "Nobody knows, Jacob. The front of the car is damaged like you hit a tree or something but they found the Toyota in the middle of the road. There wasn't anything in front of the car. They were hoping you could remember because no one has any idea what could've happened. They thought maybe the damage occurred earlier and then you drove to the scene ... but the car isn't operational and your wounds were fresh when they found you. "

"What happens now? Are they going to search for her?"

"Yes. There's already a group combing through Manoa Falls."

"I want to help." Only the irritating tug of Jacob's IV kept him from bounding out of bed.

"There's nothing you can do, Jacob. The doctor says you'll be in here for another week and then..."

"And then what?"

"The social worker says you need to come home with me."

"With you? I don't even know you."

"I am your nearest kin."

"Where do you even live?"

"Paris."

"Paris ... France?"

"No, a different Paris. Paris, Illinois. You have an Aunt Carolyn and a cousin, Katrina. They're waiting for us at home."

Home. The word annoyed Jacob. When he heard the word home, he thought of his apartment and the house he'd lived in before his dad died. He thought of how the smell of his favorite adobo chicken would fill the kitchen when his mom made it. He saw the faces of his mother and his father, bound to one another in some almost magical way. Home meant a sanctuary, as common and taken for granted as the sun rising in the morning. Wherever John was taking Jacob, it sure as hell wasn't home.

A wave of exhaustion overcame him. He took a deep breath and let it out slowly. "Do I have a choice about this?" he croaked.

There was a long stretch of silence. "No," the man said. The word was a guillotine.

It's for the best. You're not safe here.

Jacob closed his eyes. If he squeezed them shut tight enough, maybe his supposed uncle and the rest of the world would go away. A numb calm crept over him as he gave himself over to the future, unable to fight what would be, unable to care anymore. It crossed his mind that another person might pray in a situation like this, but Jacob didn't. Who would he pray to? If there was one thing his fifteen years of life had taught him, it was that there was nothing above him but sky. To believe in God would mean believing that He had allowed the tragedy that was Jacob's life in the first place.

He didn't want to know a God who made a war then killed off people's fathers in it. No, Jacob was sure he was alone in this. Alone with an uncle he'd never even met.

Chapter 3
The Memory

*J*acob lands in a crouch, knee deep in ferns and bromeliads, shoulder to shoulder with bamboo. Wet leaves brush against his arms and legs as he turns in a circle. There is no path here but he's familiar with the trees. He is sure he's been here before.

Dark clouds roll in overhead, faster than in real life, and the forest grows dim under their ominous bellies. Panic swells in his chest. Jacob launches himself into the forest. He darts through the trees, casting frantic looks over his shoulder.

Up ahead, the forest opens and Jacob watches a car climb a gravel roadway. It is his mother's. The faded blue Toyota Celica is unmistakable. From the driver's seat, she emerges, but she is not the woman he remembers arguing with that morning. He has never seen this Lillian Lau, a strong soldier of a woman in a long-sleeved black T-shirt and military pants. The hilt of a knife glints from a sheath on her leg. Her jet-black hair is swept up into a ponytail and her brown eyes are deadly serious. She is staring in the opposite direction, frowning at a particularly dark stretch of forest. She reaches across her body and draws a gun from a holster under her arm.

"MOM!"

"Jacob?" She turns toward him. Her face pales. Her eyes grow wide with terror. "Run, Jacob! RUN!" she yells, and that's when he notices it behind her. At first he can't actually see it but he can feel it. He can smell it—sulfur and something sweet. And although he doesn't know exactly what it is, he hates it with every fiber of his being.

"Behind you," he calls out. She moves to the front of the car and points her gun at the darkness that emerges from the trees, flowing forward like oil in water. It is a horrific abomination—scaly black skin, enormous leathery wings, and yellow eyes that lock on his mother. It's the sight of its talons that makes him run faster.

Crack. Crack. Bullets fly from the gun but the creature melts into the thick ripple it was when it oozed from the woods. It shifts right and his mom's eyes track it until it disappears again. Without lowering her gun, she feels for the knife on her leg. Jacob reaches the car.

"GET. IN. NOW," she commands.

He obeys, sliding in behind the steering wheel. That's when he realizes the car is still running. The keys dangle from the ignition.

Never taking her eyes off the woods, she backs toward the passenger side door. He thinks she will crawl in next to him and they will escape whatever this is.

Lightning-quick talons rip across her chest. Jacob screams as blood sprays the window … his mother's blood. Somehow, she is able to sink the knife into the shoulder of the beast before she drops. The creature backs away from her body with an ethereal howl that makes Jacob's hair stand on end.

It rears back in pain, placing itself in front of the vehicle. On instinct, Jacob slams the Toyota into drive and pounds on the accelerator. The hood crumples accordion style as he collides with the thing. He sees a flash of blood on glass ... his blood.

And then there is nothing but the tunnel, the light, and the man in the green mask.

Chapter 4
The Girl Next Door

Three weeks later, Paris, Illinois...

Jacob busied himself stacking wood in the shape of a pyramid within the brick walls of the Laudners' fireplace. The house smelled like dust and dried flowers. Building a fire was a welcome distraction but he also hoped the smell of burning oak would improve the stale air.

"That looks mighty professional. Where'd you learn to build a fire like that?" Uncle John said from behind him.

"My dad," Jacob responded.

"Wouldn't have thought there'd be much opportunity, growing up in Hawaii and all."

Jacob glanced toward John as he brought a match toward the kindling and watched the flames lick up the logs. He didn't respond.

"You can hardly tell you were in an accident anymore. Your hair covers the scar. How's the one on your chest?"

"Healing," Jacob said.

"It's a miracle you didn't break anything."

Moving from his place beside the flames to one of the two sage green recliners that faced the fire in the Laudners' living room, Jacob didn't respond to John's comment. While it was true from the outside he didn't appear injured, on the inside he was damaged. He wasn't sleeping well and sometimes the memory would come back as vivid as if it was happening all over again. The doctors said his symptoms could happen with a traumatic head injury, but knowing his condition was normal wasn't much of a comfort.

"I have some people cleaning out the apartment," John said, sitting down in the other recliner. "The boxes should be here in a week or two."

"A week or two?"

"Shipping from Hawaii to Illinois isn't as easy as you might think," John said.

John was pale with gray hair in a brush cut that reminded Jacob of the airmen at Hickam Air Force Base back home. But he was sure he'd never flown a plane because he had thick black glasses that made his eyes look bigger than they actually were. The sleeves of his red plaid shirt were rolled past his elbows, the tails tucked neatly into his blue jeans, cinched tightly under a black leather belt. He always dressed like that, like a lumberjack.

No one would have guessed Jacob was a blood relative based on appearances. Because his mom was Chinese he had the sort of skin that tanned fast in the sun. His hair was black and too long to make any adult comfortable but too short to be tied back, even if he'd wanted to. If there was any family resemblance at all, it was the eyes. Jacob had his father's pale green eyes and so did his uncle. His eyes were what seemed familiar to Jacob the day they met and were his only clue that John might be telling the truth about being his father's brother.

"I just want you to know you are welcome here for as long as it takes to find her. If something has happened. If she's ... passed on, you can stay with us permanently. There's no reason to worry about that. You'll always have a home with us," John said.

All at once Jacob was filled with the desire to throw something; his stomach clenched with his fists. His jaw hardened as he ground his teeth. In his head, he knew he should've been thankful to have a place to stay, but everything about this situation seemed wrong. He hated John for suggesting his mother might not be found. More than anything, he wanted to be back on Oahu helping to find her. And, worst of all, he hated what his uncle was about to say. He could feel it coming, those words so often repeated to him after the death of his father, those words he wanted to torch from the air before they could reach his ears.

"All we can do now is pray for your mom and trust that she's in God's hands."

Jacob thought he might explode. Pray was what people said when they didn't know what to say, when they couldn't offer anything else. Pray meant do nothing. His nails bit into the palms of his hands. He turned away from John and shoved the anger down deep, where it coiled like a snake in his gut. He closed the lid to it.

"Can I ask you something?" he said.

"Of course, what's on your mind?"

"You say you are my uncle, my father's brother, but your name is Laudner. My last name is Lau. My father's last name was Lau."

"There's a very good explanation for that Jacob. See, um, your father … he changed his name. He shortened it, from Laudner to Lau." John's face twisted before each word as if his brain was choosing the right one from a stack of thousands.

"Yes, you've said that before. But what I want to know is why," Jacob pressed. It was the first of many unanswered questions he'd asked without success. Why had he never met the Laudners? Why had his father changed his name? And, most disturbing to him, why hadn't the Laudners attended his father's funeral five years ago? It was more than not knowing John. It was not knowing of an Uncle John or any of the Laudner family. His parents had never even mentioned having family on the mainland.

John opened his mouth, then closed it again when a rotund woman with beady eyes and short brown curls entered the room from the kitchen. A sense of relief crossed his pale features as Aunt Carolyn interrupted.

"It's getting late," Carolyn said. She stared at John as if she were beaming her thoughts directly into his head. Her eyes flicked toward Jacob but seemed to find nothing to hold her interest and ended up resting back on John.

As always seemed to happen when Jacob brought up the topic of his parents, there was no time to talk. John became obsessed with how late it was, how he had to open the store in the morning, and how Jacob had better get his rest.

Once the goodnights were said, Jacob climbed the wooden staircase and passed through a hallway lined with portraits of Laudners throughout history. Some were so old their black-and-white images had a yellow tint beneath the framed glass. There were pictures of men and women, and multiple generations huddled on the front lawn. There were photos of men in military uniforms and newspaper clippings with Laudner names highlighted. Dozens of images lined both walls of the second floor hallway. Besides John, Carolyn, and their daughter, Katrina, Jacob didn't know the names or the faces. It was a hallway of strangers, even the few he recognized.

One thing was for certain: there were no pictures of his parents. No pictures at all. That's what bothered Jacob the most.

Near the end of the hall, Jacob passed by his cousin Katrina's open door and caught a glimpse of green eyes and curly brown hair. He began to say goodnight but was stopped mid-word when her foot shot out in a purposeful kick that slammed the door in his face. A road sign that read "Private Property" swung forward on its hook toward the tip of his nose.

"Goodnight then," he said to the door. He would have liked to be friends with Katrina. She was only two years older than him and the only person close to his age he knew in this town. But Katrina treated him like the plague, something to be avoided at all costs.

Suddenly, Jacob couldn't breathe. The walls billowed inward. The hall was too hot, too small. On his toes, he jogged down the stairs, lifting his coat from the hook near the door. His aunt and uncle's voices floated out from the kitchen and he hoped their conversation was enough to cover the click of the door as he pulled it closed behind him. He was desperate for air and some time to think.

Dodging left to avoid the kitchen window, he wrapped the wool coat around him and crept down the stairs into the dark driveway. Fluffy white flakes floated down from the night sky. Snow. He'd never seen it in person before coming here. He held out his hand as he walked toward the street, watching the cold, wet blobs melt in his palm: one second there, the next second gone.

"Just like my life," Jacob said to no one. The street was dark aside from the light of the moon. Enough snow had collected on the pavement to give it a luminescent sheen.

Once he reached the street, he glanced back for any sign the Laudners had noticed his departure. All was quiet. The Laudners' house was pale yellow with gray trim, a sort of long box with two windows that jutted out of the roofline on the second story like raised eyebrows. Katrina's room was under the left, Jacob's under the right. The house stood alone on the north side of the street.

Directly across the street, the only neighboring home was a looming gothic Victorian. He knew it was called a gothic Victorian because the building seemed so out of place here, he'd asked what it was. He'd thought maybe it was a funeral home or a museum or something. It was gloomy and gray with a black wrought-iron fence out front. Dead ivy crawled up one side of the place and wrapped itself around a tower the shape of a witch's hat. In the wetness and moonlight, the roof glowed like it was radioactive.

As he walked between them, he thought the houses were taunting each other with their stark differences. But then maybe the reason the Laudners didn't have more neighbors was no one would willingly join this architectural contest of wills. Of course Jacob wasn't used to any of this: the space, the cold, and other more important things he didn't like to think about.

Past the end of the Victorian's wrought-iron fence, Jacob gathered his coat around him. With nothing to break the wind out of the north, an icy gust blew right through him and toward the dead forest to the south. Ahead, shadows twisted, and the sounds of a winter night danced eerily around him. The shrill of an owl made him lurch back from the trees. Ice cracking off wind-bent branches had Jacob turning on his heels. But it was the scraping sound of wood on wood that sent a shiver through his bones. The whine of rusty hinges made the image of a coffin lid dart through his mind.

He walked faster. The swish-swish of his feet in the snow echoed in the night. Or was someone following him. He stopped. The footsteps stopped. He glanced behind him, searching the night. A ripple moved across the street. It was as if someone folded the sky and then quickly flattened it out again on the horizon. Something filmy and dark darted from one shadow to the next and the memory of the accident gripped his throat. There'd been a ripple in the woods, just like this one.

He launched himself down the Laudners' driveway, kicking up snow as he went. Heart hammering, breath coming in huffs, Jacob could feel the bruise on his chest ache by the time he reached the door. It was locked.

At first he panicked, lifting his fist to pound on the door. But then the warm light from the kitchen window caught his eye. Knocking would mean admitting he'd snuck out. From the safety of the porch, he looked back toward the street. Snow swirled over the pavement. Clearly the ripple was a trick of the moonlight. Of course it was. The memory wasn't real. It was a product of his damaged brain.

He took a deep breath and walked around the porch to the patch of yard beneath his window. A rose lattice ran the length of the wall. Good enough.

The icy wood was barely tenable but he dug his toes between the slats and climbed, gripping with throbbing cold fingers. When he reached his window he flattened his palm against the glass and pushed up with everything he had. The window opened with a bark and Jacob slid between the lace curtains, walking his hands across the rose-colored shag carpeting until his legs could fit through. As quietly as possible, he closed the window behind him and flopped onto the floral wingback chair.

Everything in his room was old lady pink. John's Aunt Veronica had lived there before they put her into a retirement home. John said he'd fix it up for Jacob someday but, until then, he had a pink room.

Jacob removed his jacket and moved toward the bed, ready to call it a night. That was when he heard the voices.

"John, I think this was a mistake. The boy is weird. He's not settling in. He's not like us." The voice was Carolyn's. It was a hushed tone coming from the vent on the south wall. Jacob crouched in front of the steel grate and listened. The position of the vent must have been just right to conduct her whisper to him. By the placement of the pink room, he assumed it connected to the kitchen.

"It's too late now, Carolyn. He's not a dog. I can't return him to the store," John said.

"I know. I'm just worried. What if he gets … violent?"

"Violent?"

"You know darn well what I mean, John. His people…"

"I do, Carolyn, but he's also our people. You know as well as I do that this boy is the last chance for our family. Hell, he doesn't even look…"

"He doesn't look German either."

"He is the last and only remaining Laudner heir. If we can't make this work, the most we can hope for…" John paused and Jacob leaned in toward the grate. "Over one hundred and fifty years of Laudner history will be lost. I can't let that happen. We can't let that happen."

"But what if he turns out like them?" Carolyn whispered.

"Jacob is young. We can raise him up right."

"It's a nice thought, but copper will never be gold, no matter how much you shine it. There are other ways ... Katrina?"

"Katrina isn't a male heir. You know the rules. Besides, Jacob is my brother's son. Don't tell me you haven't looked into that boy's eyes and seen Charlie's staring back at you."

"Well, yes, I suppose so."

"As sure as I am sitting here I am going to get to know that boy. I am not losing him the way I lost Charlie."

"John, he may look like Charlie but he's not Charlie. You can chase ghosts all you want but that ship has sailed."

"He's my nephew, Carolyn," John's voice strained to stay a whisper. "He's here to stay."

After a long pause, he heard a chair slide back from the table. "Then I guess there's nothing more to discuss," Carolyn said.

Jacob waited, ears trained on the vent. Silence. With a heavy sigh, he moved back toward the window, folding himself into the floral wingback. The conversation rolled through his head like a freight train.

Carolyn didn't want him here, that was for sure, but what was all that about being the last Laudner heir? What about Katrina? John had said something about a male heir. Jacob knew Paris was a small town, old fashioned even, but since when did women not inherit property? Certainly they didn't expect him to stay in Paris permanently. And if that were the only reason John had brought him here, what would happen when he refused?

The truth was, Jacob didn't care what had happened between his father and John. These people weren't family, not really. Whatever it took, he needed to get home to Oahu to find his mom. She was the only real family he had left. He didn't have time to worry about ancient family history or being a Laudner heir. What he needed was a way home.

He tried to watch the snow to clear his head but found he was more agitated than ever. The knot that coiled at the pit of his stomach seemed to grow larger as he dwelled on the conversation. It twisted within him. Almost midnight, he knew he should sleep.

No sooner had Jacob resigned himself to bed than he was distracted by something that stirred behind the icy wrought-iron fence across the street. He was pretty sure no one lived in the gothic Victorian. The lights never came on and he never saw anyone go in or out. But there was something in the yard now and it was big.

The thing moved, a massive black ball that rolled behind the fence spindles. The shadows made it impossible to see clearly from his window, even under the full moon. Sweat broke out on his palms and he swallowed hard. Jacob knew he was perfectly safe but the hair on the back of his neck stood up anyway. The dark mass seemed to divide, expand, and then fold in on itself just beyond view. Just as weird was how quickly it broke from this camouflage and crossed through the wrought-iron gate into the center of the street.

Surrounded by moonlight, he could see it was not an animal at all but a person in a long, hooded cloak. The shifting he'd seen had been the cloak becoming round and full in the gusty night. Hands emerged from the bell-shaped sleeves, thin and white, and pulled the black hood down to reveal the face of a young woman. Platinum hair cascaded from the hood and blew in the wintry wind, long and wispy behind her. The moon lit up the pale strands, eerily translucent against the dark cloak. Her skin was flawless and fair, as if she'd been carved from ice.

Jacob stopped breathing. She had to be a ghost the way she glowed and floated down the road toward him. For all the reasons he hated Paris, he had not expected the worst would be the town was haunted.

The ghost took a step forward and the bottom of her cloak split open. She was barefoot. Of course, a spirit would not feel the cold, which completely convinced Jacob she was supernatural. His arms broke out in gooseflesh. He wanted to look away, really he did. He wanted to scream or hide under the covers, but he didn't, because more than anything he wanted to watch. She was beautiful, bloodcurdling but beautiful. With an almost hypnotic grace, she moved to a patch of snow under his window. And then, to Jacob's horror, she leaned her head back and looked directly at him.

Within the whiteness of her skin and hair, eyes of palest blue pierced the night. The irises were barely darker than the whites, a color like thin ice over ocean. There could be no mistake; she was staring at him, or more accurately *into* him. Her gaze penetrated his skin, ricocheted off his internal organs, and caused his stomach to flip-flop. His heart paced behind the cage of his ribs.

She extended her arms, palms toward the night sky. Around her, the snow began to swirl, subtly at first but then with a purposeful force, as if she were producing her own gravity, defying the Earth and the natural order of things. The result was that she looked exactly like a figure in a snow globe, the ones you see at Christmas. Only, the darkness of her presence seemed oddly inappropriate for its charming effect.

And then she flew, lifting from the earth in a cyclone of wind and snow, until she hovered directly outside his window. Her black cloak billowed, the full moon a perfect circle behind her head. The corner of her mouth lifted, tugged upward by some well-kept secret. To look directly into her face was like sticking his finger into an electrical outlet. His skin tingled and tongue swelled.

She mouthed words through the snow at him. Jacob couldn't hear what she said but his mouth began to move, echoing hers. It was his own hushed voice he heard bouncing off the window, even though he was sure the words came from her.

Jacob, there is much to learn. Don't worry. I will teach you. I will help you.

It was useless to resist. If she'd said to leap out the window into her arms, he would have complied. But as he watched her, the realization that he still wasn't breathing came like a smoke alarm in the night, necessary but unwanted. Empty of oxygen, his lungs burned for air but he couldn't remember how to use them. His nervous system was simply paralyzed by either fear or beauty—Jacob didn't know which. The sensation of being sucked under thick water overcame him, a sinking feeling where the light from the window dimmed at the corners, became a constricting circle that narrowed to a pinpoint of light before extinguishing itself.

Suffocating. Drowning in her terrible beauty. His eyes rolled back in his head and he felt himself fall.

Her voice rang out, a dagger through the blackness, "I am coming for you." It sliced through whatever bound his chest and the air rushed in, a mighty gust of wind.

In the next moment, everything was pink. He was on the floor in front of the chair, in a rectangle of light from the window. The prickle of shag carpet on his cheek caused him to sit up and rub the stiffness from his neck. He was near the vent where he remembered listening to Carolyn and John's conversation. Had he fallen asleep on the floor?

Out the window, the blanket of snow that carpeted the ground as far as the eye could see gave no evidence, not a single footprint, divulging a nighttime visitor. The woman, he decided, must have been a dream, or more likely a hallucination, a creation of his damaged brain.

He shook his head. It was Monday and he was expected to attend Paris High School. He could already hear the clatter of Katrina getting ready in the bathroom across the hall. Jacob wished he could wake up from this nightmare, the one he was living, but this was no delusion. The really scary stuff started today.

Chapter 5
The Lows of Paris High

"You'll be okay," John said to Jacob's back. "I went to school here when I was a kid. Good people here."

Jacob scowled at the carved wooden sign that read Paris High School. The square brick building looked more like a prison than a school. He did not acknowledge John's comment but stared at the double doors and tried to remain numb.

"So, come to the shop after school. Just walk down Main Street and you can't miss it." Jacob could hear the note of frustration creeping into his voice. He didn't care. John could make him do this but he couldn't make him like it.

"Remember to check in at the office. I preregistered you but you'll need to get your class schedule from Betty."

Jacob nodded toward the school. His neck itched from the wool jacket John had given him to wear. He ignored it and took a slow step forward.

John sighed. "Okay then. See you later." The old blue pickup whined as he shifted it into gear. Jacob turned only when he saw, out of the corner of his eye, the flash of blue leave the school's circular drive.

Sure, it was only a matter of time until Jacob had to go back to school. He expected as much. Since it was the end of the holiday break and the beginning of a new semester, it made sense that he started now. But after all that had happened, he just didn't expect it would be so soon. Going to school felt settled and he didn't want to feel settled.

He joined a pack of students as they filed into the building, a machine of murmurs and sideways glances that churned to mustard yellow lockers. It wasn't a large school, maybe two hundred kids, but he had the oddest sensation of being in a fish tank—watched with curious indifference. He ducked through a windowed door under a black plaque with white font that read, "Office."

The short, mousy woman behind the desk typed vigorously, her square bifocals fixed on the computer screen. Her tight bun shifted slightly as she raised her eyebrows and turned toward him.

"Well hello!" she said in a high-pitched nasal twang. "Are you Jacob?"

"Jacob Lau. This is my first day."

"Welcome. I'm Mrs. Whestle, the school secretary. It's very nice to meet you."

"Yeah, uh, you too," he lied.

"Let me just find your paperwork." She thumbed through a pile of manila folders on her desk. "Here we are, Jacob Laudner."

"That's me but Laudner is my uncle's last name—mine is Lau."

"Yes, I see your uncle filled out these forms. John Laudner, such a nice man. He's been a friend of my husband, Herbert, for years. Anyway, here you are, Jacob Laudner." Mrs. Whestle squared the manila folder in front of him.

"Um, but my last name isn't Laudner, it's Lau. Can you change that on the paperwork?"

"But your uncle…" Mrs. Whestle's mouth pulled into a tight line. A nervous giggle parted her lips. "You are registered as Laudner."

It was clear to Jacob that Mrs. Whestle thought he was messing with her. Of course it didn't make any sense why his name was different than his uncle's. Hell, he didn't understand completely himself. But he wasn't going to let the circumstances rob him of his last connection with his real family. John and the social worker could force him from his home, but he was keeping his name.

"My name is Lau," Jacob said firmly. He could feel his ears getting hot.

"Okay, hon." Mrs. Whestle looked flustered and more than a little confused. "We can change it. Do you have a copy of your birth certificate?"

"Yes, right here." Jacob handed her an envelope. In order to enroll, John needed a copy of the original from Oahu. His name was Lau, legally.

"Well, here it is in black and white," Mrs. Whestle said. "Jacob Lau, son of Charles and Lillian Lau." Her brow wrinkled. "How odd," she added under her breath.

She turned back toward her computer and began to type, longer and more furiously than he would have thought necessary for a simple name change.

"Oh say, now this is interesting. It says here you're Chinese?"

"Yeah."

"You don't look Chinese."

"Well, my father was Caucasian," he drawled, thinking they'd just covered his family history.

"Do you know you are the very first Chinese person ever to attend Paris High School?"

"No. I didn't."

"Well, this is exciting!"

Jacob scowled. What the hell was that supposed to mean? Like he was Paris' token Asian? He wanted to tell her that the lack of minorities was only half as exciting as the overrun of idiots but thought better of it since it was his first day. Nonetheless, Mrs. Whestle seemed to get the hint. The smile drained from her face and she cleared her throat.

"Er … You will start in Mrs. Haney's class, classroom 208, for World History. She is right out that door, up the stairs and two doors to the left. Hold on a minute, honey, and I'll get Principal Bailey to show you the way. He's going to want to meet you."

The mousy woman left briefly and returned with a man who looked as though he had recently graduated high school himself. His brown hair was spiky and his skin, tan. Since it was January and there wasn't a sunbeam in sight, Jacob got the impression that Mr. Bailey tried hard to fit in with his students.

"Hi, Jacob. Welcome to our school," Principal Bailey said through a smile. He pumped Jacob's hand a few times. "Follow me and I'll show you to Mrs. Haney's." He pointed toward the door and Jacob led the way into the hall. "I think you will like Mrs. Haney. She is one of our more, ah, experienced teachers."

He climbed a short flight of stairs. Mr. Bailey paused at the top. "Jacob, I had a talk with your uncle about your unfortunate circumstances. I want to tell you how glad we all are that you're here. I certainly understand you might be feeling a broad range of emotions right now. That's totally normal in circumstances such as yours. I just want you to know, you can talk to me about anything, anytime."

Jacob blinked at the man and shifted uncomfortably. Why did everyone want to talk? There wasn't anything to talk about. His dad was dead, his mother was missing, and he was stuck in this freezing hole of a town. He couldn't think of anything to say about that to Mr. Bailey, so he just nodded stiffly.

"Well then, right through here." Mr. Bailey pushed open the door and strode to classroom 208. "You've got your schedule?"

"Yeah."

"Good. There's a map of the school on the back."

Jacob flipped the goldenrod schedule over and saw a blueprint-style drawing of the school.

Mr. Bailey motioned for him to wait while he poked his head inside the door. He repeated Mrs. Haney's name three times before she finally bellowed, "Mr. Bailey! How nice of you to stop by!"

"We have our new student, Mrs. Haney," Mr. Bailey yelled and opened the door wider. "Okay. Well, bring him in!" The words trickled out of her mouth between cackles. Jacob entered the room toward the decrepit old woman standing in front of the chalkboard. He was already sure she was half deaf. By the thickness of her glasses he supposed she was half blind, too.

"You must be Jacob. Class, this is Jacob Laudner, our new student. Jacob, you are the spitting image of Charlie! Do you know I taught your father here as well?"

"My name's not Laudner. It's Lau," he said.

"What dear?" Mrs. Haney turned to watch his lips.

"My last name is Lau," he repeated, louder this time.

"But aren't you Charlie Laudner's son?"

It would have been easier for Jacob to just go along, to pretend his last name was Laudner. Nobody there would've known the difference. But it was the principle of the matter. There were only so many things a person could lose before they clung to what they had left.

"I am, but my last name is Lau!"

The class and Mrs. Haney stared at him blankly. Mr. Bailey motioned to Mrs. Haney to step outside of the classroom and she promptly complied. Through the door, he heard Mr. Bailey attempt to discreetly explain what he knew about the name, which couldn't have been much more than what Mrs. Whestle had told him. Unfortunately, with her hearing as it was, Mrs. Haney was incapable of whispering and Jacob heard frequent and embarrassing outbursts from the conversation that left the class giggling in his direction.

Mrs. Haney reentered the classroom and apologized to the class for the interruption. "Jacob … Lau then, you will sit right here." She pointed to a desk at the front of the room.

As he sat down, the weight of fifteen pairs of eyes bore into him. Mrs. Haney turned to the board and continued a lesson on the French Revolution, pointing at a map and droning on about the civil constitution of the clergy. With her back to the classroom, the other students began to talk openly with each other. Jacob wasn't the only one who had figured out Mrs. Haney was hard of hearing.

"So, what kind of name is Lau anyway?" the boy next to him asked. He was big, built like a running back, but the gel in his brown hair made it look like he spent too much time in front of a mirror.

"It's Chinese."

"So what, you want people to think you're Chinese? Going for some Kung Fu rep or something?"

"No, my name is Chinese because I am Chinese."

"You don't even look Chinese."

"Well, you don't look like a prick either," Jacob snapped. "But I guess you can't tell a book by its cover."

The boy's expression melted into a glower.

"Dane Michaels, please come to the map and show us the area where King Louis XVI was arrested." Mrs. Haney turned toward the class, silence flooding the room like she'd flipped a switch. The guy rose, waiting until the last second to break eye contact, and walked to the board.

Jacob leaned back in his seat. "I think I've made a friend."

"It's best if you don't call attention to yourself," whispered a voice from behind him. Jacob turned to see the rich russet skin of an East Indian girl, a long black braid flipped over her shoulder. Her brown eyes connected with his and she raised an eyebrow. "You'll only make it worse." She looked down at her book as if it was the most interesting thing she'd ever seen.

The bell interrupted any ideas he'd had about talking to the girl. In seconds, she'd swept up her books and drifted into the hall. He checked his schedule and headed down to the gym for P.E.

The boys' class was playing basketball and by luck, or lack of it, Dane and a boy named Mike Gibbons were chosen as team captains. Jacob waited while everyone else was picked first and then ended up on Mike's team by default.

Mike was the kind of kid that looked traditionally bad at sports, thin and pale, like he spent too much time watching television. Jacob took the opportunity to step up his game. He'd always been a natural athlete and he thought winning might be a way to break the ice, maybe even make a friend. His team was ahead sixteen to twelve when Mike called a timeout.

"What the hell are you doing?" Mike said into Jacob's ear. He was standing in a circle of frowns—the rest of the team.

"I think I was winning the game for us," Jacob replied.

"Do you see that guy?" Mike said, pointing at Dane.

Jacob nodded.

"I don't *want* to beat that guy. Let him win."

He had to admit Dane was intimidating. Either the guy had filled out early or he was held back a grade. Dane was at least six foot and broad, maybe two hundred pounds of solid muscle.

"Look, this is real simple, Lau. Don't beat Dane." The rest of the team nodded.

But as much as Jacob wanted to, he couldn't force himself not to try. He held back and watched Dane score but at the change of possession, he took a three-point shot at the bell for the win. The P.E. teacher, Mr. Schroeder, gave him a knuckle bump as he headed for the locker room. But Mike flipped him off.

"You're a real asshole, Lau," he said.

The upside was that Dane looked furious, an outcome Jacob wasn't completely opposed to.

Biology was just as interesting. Since Jacob was starting in the middle of the year, everyone already had lab partners. Everyone except the Indian girl who sat at a table by herself. He pulled up a stool across from her and opened his book to a random page.

"Have you figured it out yet?" she asked, without looking up.

"Figured what out?"

"Obviously not," she said.

"What? Tell me."

Her eyes lifted to his. They were the color of melted chocolate and she smiled the first genuine smile he'd seen all day. "The people here have enough friends. They all know each other, grew up together. Well, everyone but us."

"I'm Jacob, Jacob Lau."

"I heard, in history." She nodded. "Can I call you Jake?"

No one called him Jake, but it sounded good when she said it. "Sure."

"I'm Malini ... Gupta."

"Can I call you—I don't know, how do you shorten your name?" Jacob grinned.

"I don't, but it's not hard. Say it MAHL-in-NEE"

"Malini."

"Good," she said, looking pleased.

"You're not from here, are you?"

"Ah, no."

"Me either ... obviously."

She giggled and Jacob could feel himself relax at the sound of it, like the knot inside of him had loosened a little. There was something about her that seemed honest and trustworthy. Maybe it was that she didn't wear any makeup and smelled clean like soap rather than the typical fifteen-year-old girl stench of cheap perfume. Maybe it was the way she squared her book in front of her and actually knew what page Mrs. Jacques would lecture on. Whatever it was, Jacob felt like he'd found a friend.

Mrs. Jacques began her lecture on the components of a human cell but he found himself phasing out. He reached over to Malini's notebook and wrote in big sloppy letters *lunch?*

Yes, she wrote back, beaming.

After a grueling lecture, the bell finally rang. Jacob noticed that Malini had taken three pages of notes on mitochondria, while his notebook simply had the word, *mitokondrea* misspelled at the top of the page. He didn't remember a thing Mrs. Jacques had said.

"Um, maybe we could study together?" Jacob mumbled.

"Sure," she said, a hint of pride in her voice. He stacked his books and followed her into the hall.

The cafeteria was an elongated rectangle of picnic-style folding tables, with orange trays stacked near the doors and two lines of students divided along the east and west walls. One line was for a salad bar and was made up mostly of girls, and the other was for hot lunch. Jacob couldn't see what they were serving but headed for the hot bar. Malini opted for a salad.

A group of guys cut him off and the orange tray he was holding slammed into his chest, eliciting a twinge of pain from his healing bruise. Dane and Mike glared at him, daring him to do something about it. Obviously his win in P.E. and the comment in history weren't going to be forgotten anytime soon. He let it go.

The tables were filling up fast and Jacob wondered where he and Malini would sit. Everyone else seemed to understand the social ecosystem of Paris High School, but Jacob wasn't speaking the language. Once he made it through the line, he was relieved that Malini had already sat down and there was plenty of room at her table. Plenty of room as in it was totally empty besides Malini and her tray.

"I hope you don't mind. This is my usual spot."

"No, not at all."

"Good. So, what do you think of your first day?" she asked and for the first time he noticed a hint of a mottled accent. He started to answer but was distracted by voices behind him. The group of people at Dane's table spoke in half-hearted whispers.

"Looks like P.S. has a new friend," Dane said.

"Awww. Now she doesn't have to sit alone anymore," Mike said.

"Right. She can sit with kung fu wannabe," Dane added with a laugh.

Jacob squinted at Malini. "Why did they call you P.S.? What does that mean?"

"I'd rather not talk about it," she whispered.

"Like, who does he think he is?" a girl's voice said. Jacob glanced over his shoulder and saw a tall girl with long brown hair whisper incredulously into Dane's ear. "Come on, he doesn't even look Chinese."

"Amy, I know, and what's with that shirt? It's all like 'surfer dude,'" a blonde girl said, holding up her thumb and pinky finger.

"Don't listen to them. They're all idiots," Malini said. She grabbed Jacob's arm. "I like your shirt."

As soon as Malini touched him, he felt warm to his toes. He caught himself staring at her and compensated by looking down at his shirt, suddenly self-conscious. It was his favorite from home—a red Matsumotos's Shave Ice T-shirt. It wasn't appropriate for the January weather but he'd layered it over a black turtleneck and some heavy jeans.

"Who are they?" Jacob asked.

"The one with the brown hair and the big forehead is Amy Barger. She goes out with Dane. Mike Gibbons is on his left and the guy on the other side of him is Phillip Westcott. They pretty much hang together all the time. The blonde who looks like she ladles her makeup on in the morning is Missy Hatfield."

"So, what is it with these people?" Jacob asked. But the voices interrupted again.

"I heard from Rob that he's actually related to the Laudners but his dad changed his last name to Lau," the one called Phillip said.

"Why wouldn't he just use the name Laudner? I mean it's like he wants people to know he's a gook." It was Dane's voice this time.

Malini's eyes pleaded with Jacob to ignore the racial slur. His jaw tightened until he thought he might snap his own bones.

"Did they just say what I think they said?" he asked her.

"Yes, but let it go. It's not worth it. Trust me."

The blonde girl's voice again ... Missy, "I don't know. He's got nice hair."

"Well, he's not bad looking, but who wants to date an egg?" Amy replied.

"An egg?" Dane asked.

"You know," she lowered her voice, "white on the outside and yellow in the middle."

The table burst into laughter. Jacob shot a glance at Dane and his hands tightened into fists. Malini grabbed his arm again, her delicate fingers on his wrist draining all aggression out of him. For some reason, he didn't want to make a scene in front of her. He was afraid if something happened, a fight, she might get hurt. Plus, she seemed above all this, and he wanted to be too. He turned back toward her.

"Are they for real?" he asked Malini.

"Hmm. I'm afraid so."

"I guess, where I'm from ... in Hawaii, no one would ever use that word."

"I know. Not where I'm from either."

"Where are you from?"

"All over really, but London last. I was born in India."

"I don't get it, Malini," Jacob said. "I mean these people act like it's 1950. They don't even know me."

"Most of these people have been here since well before that."

He laughed but then realized she wasn't joking. "What do you mean?"

"Well, take Dane Michaels, for example. His family settled here around 1900. His family has lived on the same land for over a hundred years. And Amy Barger, her family has lived in the same house for four generations. This town is like an island; all they know is each other. They grow up in the same houses, doing the same things as their parents."

"You've got to be kidding."

"No. Think about it. Who would move to Paris? I mean besides us, and we didn't have a choice. There's not much here. Logically, if you grow up here and you are open minded, you go to college and never come back. If you like it here, which means that you are happy living in the same house, with the same people, with the same thoughts and ideas as the generation before, then you stay. If you stay, you marry someone just like you. It's like inbreeding."

"How do you know all of this, Malini? I mean about the town history."

"My dad. He's the only insurance agent in town. Houses, cars, life insurance policies, you can learn a lot about people by what they insure. That's why we're here. State Benefit decided to embrace diversity and hello Paris, Illinois. You know, he took over because the last State Benefit agent died."

"He died?"

"Yeah. He was ninety-six years old and still working. Died in his office. Weird huh?"

"Weird."

"But good for us. There's no competition so, whatever these people think, if you want insurance in this town you see Jim Gupta."

Jacob opened his mouth to respond but was drowned out by the sound of the bell and the subsequent clatter of trays and chairs.

"Do you want to study later then?" Malini asked.

"Definitely. Bring your notes," he said, "please."

She gave the proud smile again, lifting her tray and carrying it to the conveyor belt near the kitchen. Jacob collected his things and turned to follow. He was halfway there when something hard pegged him in the back, knocking him forward. On the floor near his feet, pieces of hard-boiled egg lay broken. He whipped his head around and met Dane's cold gray eyes. A red tide of anger washed over him.

Jacob glared at Dane with wordless hate and, as he locked eyes with the guy, he thought of ten different ways he could attack him. The fork on his tray had promise. He could do it; tear off the lid to this thing coiled inside of him and loose it on Dane. He might even enjoy it. He may not be as big as Dane but he was fast and he knew how to fight. More importantly, he had nothing to lose.

Then he thought of Malini. She lingered by the door, watching the drama unfold with her books clutched against her chest like a shield. What would she think of him if he started something?

No one moved. The cafeteria was so quiet he could hear the ice machine running. Time seemed to slow as Jacob stared, unblinking, at Dane. Finally, one of the lunch ladies cleared her throat, breaking the silent tension and Jacob backed down. The thing in his stomach coiled tighter like an unsatisfied hunger as he made for the door.

No sooner was Jacob's back turned than the cafeteria burst into laughter.

He had to find a way home. If he didn't, this might be the longest year of his life.

Chapter 6
Dane

Dane Michaels wandered through the forest at the back of his family's farm. He knew better than to call her name. Man, she could be a bitch when she wanted to be. She was beautiful though, way cuter than Amy.

He wasn't sure why she always insisted that they meet out here. He was sick of it. It was always on her terms, her rules. Sometimes she even blew him off entirely. She never gave any excuse, just didn't show up. Today though, he wanted her there. He needed what she had more than before and he hoped she would give it to him quickly.

Snow drifted down from the pine needles and stung his exposed skin. The wind blew right through his wool coat. He raised the collar around his ears and huddled into the thick fabric. He hated winter.

"You've come alone?" she said. Her voice was smooth and as cold as the bitter air.

Dane's head snapped right. She was standing so close to him, close enough to touch, but he hadn't heard her coming. Her platinum hair blew back from her face in the uneven gusts. Eyes, like blue ice, cut through him. The cold didn't seem to bother her. In nothing but a blouse and plaid skirt, she leaned up against one of the lanky pines.

"Yeah," Dane replied. "So."

"I told you, I want to meet your friends."

"Damn ... I've been bringing people back here all year. You've met everyone."

"Don't lie to me." Her face was suddenly inches from his, the line of her mouth a grim warning.

"You've met everyone in my class that's worth meeting," he spat.

"Then, who is not worthy?"

Dane looked away. This was so not his idea of fun. "Whatever," he said under his breath. He turned for home. Her hand shot out, so fast he didn't see it coming. Fingers sank into his forearm, tightening like a vice. The pain was immediate.

"Oww! God ... stop! Let go!" Dane yanked his arm toward his body but her grip was like steel. The pain was intense, bone crushing. "Please!"

That's when he smelled her, a spicy, sweet scent that reminded him of fresh-baked pumpkin pie. It surrounded him, weaving into his nostrils and flaming out across his body until every part of him was salivating for it. He met her eyes again and a wave of pleasure washed over him like a warm bath.

"Who have I not met, Dane?" she cooed. Her voice was soft now, soothing. She loosened her grip.

"There are two kids that I don't hang with much. A girl and a boy."

"Their names?"

"Malini and Jacob."

"You will bring them to me. I want to meet them."

"Why?" he asked, but his voice cracked, weak and unsure.

"I have my reasons. Bring them here, at this time of day, in one month."

Dane rolled his eyes. To get Lau here, he would have to either overpower the kid or pretend to be his friend. Neither would be easy but the thought of the second made him ill. He considered telling her he wouldn't do it but then the smell came to him again, stronger.

"Do you have more of that stuff, from before?"

A thermos appeared in her hand and she held it out to him. Dane wondered for a fleeting moment where she'd gotten it. He hadn't noticed the container before and she didn't have a bag or a coat. She cracked the lid and the smell of cinnamon wafted out. All at once he stopped caring about where it came from and snatched it from her hand.

He took a deep swig. The stuff burned, from his lips to his toes, but then the rush he was waiting for came on full force. Power. Pure liquid power coursed through his veins. In that moment, he was enough. He was bigger than this farm, this family, and this town. There were no boundaries to what he could do or what he could be.

He reached into his pocket for a cigarette. Maybe he *could* do anything for this.

"Tell me more about these two," she demanded.

Dane lit the end of the cigarette and took a deep drag. "I think, maybe, I could tell you a couple of things." He rubbed his arm.

For some reason, it felt sore. As he started to talk, he couldn't remember how he'd hurt it. But he had no problem remembering everything he knew about Jacob and Malini.

Chapter 7
Excavation

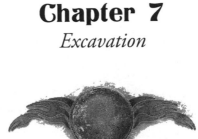

Two boxes. Everything from the apartment, all the material evidence that he'd ever had a family before coming to Paris, fit into two moving boxes. Jacob walked into the gaping mouth of the Laudners' two-car garage and stared at the brown rectangles wrapped in packing tape.

Strange, the thumping in his chest and the way his throat ached when he swallowed. He needed to open them, to go through his mom's things. Uncle John said it would give him closure. But he hesitated. The truth was, he didn't want closure; he wanted to believe she was alive. He refused to give up on her. But he also knew it was important to check that everything was there. To make sure, that when they did find her, all of her things would be accounted for.

He pulled a pair of gardening shears off their hook on the wall and sliced through the tape at the top of the first box. It was filled with items wrapped in brown paper. Jacob reached in and unwrapped one—a glass. He grabbed another—a soap dish. Kitchen and bathroom items, all of it. He guessed the flat ones on the bottom were plates and the things on top were mixing bowls and drinking glasses.

When Jacob sliced through the tape on the second box, white stuffing burst from the incision. The shears had sliced too deep, into the pillow that used to be his mother's. He pinched the hole and pulled the pillow out. Her quilt was underneath it, folded neatly on top of her clothes and a short wooden box. He caught the scent of cherry blossoms, the smell of her favorite lotion.

Resting his elbows on the sides of the box, he allowed his head to loll forward. With his eyes closed, Jacob could picture them there, sitting cross-legged on the quilt, playing crazy eights with a deck of cards so old you could tell the eight of spades from the fingerprint worn into the pattern on the back. Whatever happened to those cards?

Jacob opened his eyes. The brown corner of the wooden box peaked out from under his mother's salmon-colored sweatshirt. Was it a jewelry box? Did his mother own a jewelry box? He'd never, ever, seen her wear jewelry. If she'd had any before his dad died, they would have sold it a long time ago. Jacob absolutely did not remember the box. He reached in and pulled the shiny wood from under the linens.

Koa wood, inlaid with a pale carving of a phoenix, the box looked much too expensive to have belonged to her. He tried to lift the lid but it was locked. The gold keyhole was small, like a diary lock.

Jacob set the wooden box aside and dug deeper for the key. The moving box was an awkward height and the cardboard buckled under his weight. He swept his hand around the bottom and tried to feel for something that might contain small items. When nothing presented itself, he found a relatively clean section of concrete and unloaded the items one by one. The glasses, the plates, even the mixing bowls he freed from their paper cocoons. Everything was there, everything he remembered from the apartment. It looked like a rummage sale spread out across the driveway.

There was no key.

It wasn't a complete loss though. Near the bottom of the bedroom box, he'd found a framed picture of his family, the one that had hung on the bedroom wall. Smile lines creased the corners of his father's green eyes, serenity lingered in the curve of his mother's mouth, and Jacob was missing teeth but nothing else. This was a picture of a family that didn't exist anymore—a family extinct.

The cold bit into him as he rewrapped and packaged the items back into the boxes. For more than an hour, Jacob worked to replace everything except for the picture and the jewelry box. He set those aside to bring inside. When he was done, he pushed the boxes into a corner of the garage and turned to leave.

Across the street, the Victorian loomed black and blue, a bruise on the horizon. The wind rattled the ivy on the fence and knocked some icicles free. They fell like knives, slicing the snow-covered yard. Dead leaves swirled behind the wrought-iron fence. For a second, just a fraction of a moment, Jacob could've sworn he'd seen a face staring at him through the front window. He closed the garage door and hurried inside.

Chapter 8
Ancient History

Days of school turned into weeks, then months, hours carved out of a forced routine. The weather was cold, school was hard, and Jacob got very good at coming up with reasons to avoid getting too close to the Laudners.

The one light in an otherwise dismal winter was Malini. He ate lunch with her every day because he wanted to, not for the obvious reason that he couldn't have sat anywhere else. She was the only thing he looked forward to most days.

"You know, Jacob, I never told you what P.S. meant," Malini said as she picked at her French fries, eating only the brown crispy ones. Friday was always hamburgers and fries. The burgers were leathery Frisbees but the fries were tolerable.

"Yeah. I hear them calling you that. I haven't asked you because it's pretty obvious it's not a term of endearment." He reached across the table and dipped a fry into her ketchup.

"It means push start. They're making fun of me because I'm Indian. You know how some Indian women wear a bindi?"

"The makeup on their forehead?" Jacob said, touching himself between his eyes.

"Yes. Well, Dane and his friends seem to think a better term for the women who wear them is push start or P.S."

Jacob was speechless. "That's the stupidest thing I've ever heard."

"You have to consider the source."

"Is that why you don't wear one?"

"No. If I wanted to wear one, I wouldn't let those morons stop me. I don't wear it because it's sort of a Hindu thing and I'm Christian. I know that people now just wear them as makeup and it doesn't mean what it once did, but I've never gotten into the habit. Most of the time I don't even wear mascara." She laughed and then shifted her attention toward the corner of her orange tray.

"Effing idiots," Jacob said. The knot in his stomach tightened. Malini was joking about this now but he knew how it must feel. It wasn't right. He forced himself to smile for her sake. "Do you want me to pound them for you?"

"Yeah sure, right now."

He faked to stand just long enough for Malini's eyes to grow wide and her face to flush, then fell back into his chair, laughing. She clocked him on the shoulder. The truth was, Jacob thought he could take Dane and he had it coming, but taking on all of them in the cafeteria would be suicide. It wasn't the right time. But someday, someday soon, Jacob was going to teach that guy a lesson.

"Malini, what are you doing after school today?"

"Walking home, as always."

"Do you want to study together again? I'm supposed to meet my uncle at his shop but then we could go to McNaulty's."

"Sure."

McNaulty's was a six-table family restaurant next to the Peterson's Clothier up Main Street. Malini and Jacob had gone there a couple of times after school. It was usually empty on the weekdays and Mrs. McNaulty let them sit at a table for hours sipping free refills of soda.

After school, they made their way down the cracked squares of concrete along Main Street. Malini pointed out the green necks of crocuses sprouting in the muddy patches on either side of the walk. The snow had melted, but Jacob had to take her word for it that spring was coming. The cutting wind seemed to disagree.

"You know, my father says your uncle's shop has been here since Paris was settled."

"Really?"

"Your family has been in Paris over one hundred and fifty years, Jacob."

"Wow, a hundred fifty years and I didn't know they existed until just after Christmas."

"What?" Malini turned toward him, but Jacob ducked inside the shop. The last thing he wanted to talk about was the Laudners. But Jacob noticed for the first time the crumbling red brick around the entrance, the worn marble floor, the hand-carved sign: Laudner's Flowers est. 1858.

"Jacob, is that you?" Katrina's voice called from the back room.

"Yeah, Katrina. Is John around?"

Katrina emerged, large clippers in her hand. "No, he had to go on a delivery."

"Could you tell him Malini and I are going to McNaulty's to study?"

"Tell him yourself. You're supposed to stay and help out this afternoon. They've got the Harrington wedding tomorrow and need fifty feet of fern garland."

"Sorry, Katrina. Can't."

"Whatever. I'll just tell him the truth. You're completely useless." She rolled her eyes.

Jacob was out the door before Malini could introduce herself to Katrina. He heard her beating feet down the sidewalk trying to catch up to him. He opened the door to McNaulty's for her.

"What was that all about?" she asked.

"My uncle keeps trying to get me to work in his shop."

"Well why not? It doesn't sound so bad."

"It's a long story, Malini. Just don't ask. You don't want to know."

"If you say so, but I would love to have my own money." She slid into a booth by the window.

Jacob crossed his arms over his stomach. He'd been accepting spending money from his uncle for lunch, his cell phone, movies, and of course his new cold-weather clothes. Jacob hated taking the man's money, but it couldn't be avoided. He would have to get a job eventually if he ever wanted to earn a ticket back home, but he figured if his dad disliked the Laudners enough to legally change his name, then he wasn't going to work in a shop by that name. It just didn't feel right.

"Can I ask you something, Jake?" Malini leaned forward across the table. "That first day, in school, I heard you say that your father was Caucasian and your mother was Chinese, but your last name is Lau. Why wouldn't your dad just take your mom's last name? Why shorten Laudner to Lau?"

"The sad thing is that I don't know. Three months ago, I thought the only last name my father ever had was Lau." He stirred his soda with his straw, watching the trail of bubbles circle the glass.

"What happened to your parents?"

"They're gone. My father died in Afghanistan, and my mother is missing."

"I'm so sorry. How awful. Is that why you never talk about Hawaii, or when you were a kid?"

"I don't want to talk about my parents."

Malini made a small choking noise and Jacob could see he'd embarrassed her. A blush crawled up her neck. He opened his mouth to tell her it was okay, but she cut him off.

"You don't have to talk about it, Jake," Malini said, her hand on his arm. "We have Biology." She held up her book and smiled.

Chapter 9
Heads Will Fly

Sleep was the enemy. Jacob wrestled with it every night, the endless rush of thoughts that no amount of tossing or turning could lay to rest. The guilt that he hadn't done enough to help find his mom mingled with his anger toward Dane and his friends. Together, the emotions created the world's best anti-sleeping pill. The alternative was worse. If he fell asleep, he'd dream weird, vivid dreams, the kind that made you sweat and scream in your sleep. Sometimes it was the false memory replaying in his head. Other times he saw the ghost at his window. He might dream of being chased or showing up to a test without a pencil but all of his dreams were alike in one important way. He was helpless in them. Absolutely helpless. So, as the first rays of sunshine cast dappled shadows across his desk, he was already awake.

In his hands, he turned the jewelry box that he'd found among his mother's things. How could he have missed it in the tiny apartment? He needed a way to open it, something that wouldn't damage it. If he could just see what was inside, maybe something would explain why she was different those last weeks, and why she'd gone to Manoa Falls that last day.

He lifted the box higher, heavy even with two hands, and inspected the bottom. There was a label, the white kind that you see on the tabs of manila folders. Hurried but familiar, it was a phone number, nothing more, but it was definitely in his mother's handwriting. Jacob set the box down carefully and copied the numbers onto a yellow sticky note. Then he grabbed his cell phone off the dresser and crept down to the kitchen.

In front of the bay window, at the heavy pine table, he sat with the number in one hand and his phone in the other. What would he say? Do you sell jewelry boxes? Do you have any extra keys? There wasn't much time before the Laudners woke up and he didn't want to explain who he was calling. Not wanting to waste another minute, Jacob plugged the numbers into the phone, still unsure what he would say, and listened to the ring, once, twice, three times. Finally, he heard the familiar static of an answering machine.

"You have reached Red Door Martial Arts." The voice was male, rich, and deep. "We are not available at the moment but if you please leave a message, we will call you back."

Jacob snapped the phone shut. Of course they wouldn't have answered; it was the middle of the night on Oahu. He reread the sticky note. Had he dialed the wrong number? He dialed it again and got the same message. Why would his mother have the number for a martial arts business on the bottom of her jewelry box? It didn't make sense.

He leaned back in his chair and stared across the street at the Victorian. The vines on the wrought-iron fence were beginning to green. He tried his best to concentrate on the color and to forget where he was and why. The world outside was a rolling sea and he was on a raft without a paddle. There was nothing to anchor him and no way to shore. He had to think. He had to find a way back to his life.

The floor creaked. Jacob turned in his chair. Katrina stood in the archway to the family room, a wry grin lifting the corner of her mouth. She cocked her head sideways when their eyes met. The expression reminded him of a rat. How long had she been looking at him like that?

"What do you want?" he asked.

"I was just wondering if you were hungry," Katrina said. She flipped her curly brown hair behind the shoulder of her sweater. One of her blue suede boots rested on the wall behind her. Her gray tights and suede mini skirt reminded him of doll clothes, too perfect, too pressed.

"No, not really…"

"Because, if you were hungry," she interrupted, "I would be happy to make you some eggs. That is what you like isn't it? Eggs? You know, you are what you eat." She laughed callously.

The knot in Jacob's stomach tightened to a point he'd never experienced. It was a point of pain, of looking out from his loathing as if it were a cocoon that had served its purpose. His ears felt hot. His heart thundered in his chest.

"Just wanted you to know your cafeteria adventures have made it all the way to the senior class." With a smirk, she held up her cell phone.

It was too much. Everything here was wrong: the people, the weather, the box that didn't make sense, the house across the street that gave him the chills, the pink room. He couldn't breathe. He couldn't move. The muscles in his chest and stomach had tightened to the point of self-suffocation. The events of the last four months flashed before his eyes: the accident, finding out his mom was missing and maybe dead, Dane, Paris, learning his father once was named Laudner. At every turn there were walls and those walls were closing in. He didn't belong here. But, most of all, Jacob would not allow his suffering to be Katrina's entertainment.

Air rushed into his lungs. It was an involuntary thing, a reflex. The breath filled him until something snapped. It was as if each event had been a rubber band wrapped around the last, winding tighter and tighter. This new air, this new breath of oxygen, had broken the outer band. All of them were unraveling at once, snapping and rolling within him.

The lid was left open and the snake was set free.

Jacob sprung to his feet. He vaguely felt himself ascend the stairs and enter Katrina's room. It took only seconds to decide. The glass case made it all too obvious that they were precious to her, perfectly adorned in frilly outfits, certificates of authenticity displayed behind each one. In one smooth movement, he picked up her desk chair and brought it crashing down on the case. Glass exploded all around him. It sliced his arm open but he didn't feel it. Jacob reached through the shards and ripped the five antique dolls from their stands.

It took both hands to carry them all but he cruised down the front steps two at a time, shoving through Katrina's best attempts to stop him. Jacob ran out the front door and dropped the dolls in a heap in the driveway. A moment in the Laudners' garage and he'd found what he was looking for: a lead pipe and a spool of twine.

Katrina must've filled John and Carolyn in on what had happened because the three glowered at Jacob from the front window while he quickly tied the dolls to the Laudners' white picket fence. A vengeful grin that felt unfamiliar crawled onto his face. Then, as he watched the Laudners move toward the door, Katrina's horror evident in her open-mouthed expression, Jacob heaved the heavy lead pipe over his right shoulder and swung.

CRACK! The first dolls head left its body and slammed into the oak tree in the middle of the Laudners' front yard, bursting into a million china pieces on impact. The pipe came around and hit him in the back. The pain, the sound, the anger, the vibration in his hand, it was all a wonderful release. It was like feeling sick all day and then finally throwing up. Jacob let the sick escape his body in a dark laugh that he would have sworn was someone else's if it wasn't coming out of his own mouth.

"Stop!" she screamed from the open door. "They're antiques!"

Jacob swung again and a blonde ponytail went bouncing into the street. He was disappointed this one didn't shatter. It must have been made of something else.

"YOU WANT TO MESS WITH ME, KATRINA!" Jacob yelled and moved down the fence.

"Stop! Jacob, they are worth hundreds of dollars—you must stop!" John bellowed.

Nothing they could do but watch. The metal pipe swung with such force and abandon that Katrina cringed as it whistled through the air and Uncle John stood frozen in the doorway. The strange laugh bubbled out of him again as the pipe made contact with doll number three. Blood from the cut on his arm had trickled down to his hands. Drops of it bloomed in the air around him on impact, peppering the explosion of glass with splashes of bright red.

"OH MY GOD! JACOB, YOU WILL PAY!" Katrina was hysterical now. She bawled into the arms of her mother and huddled behind John in the frame of the front door. Jacob glanced in their direction, twisted his body, and launched a round head with a black bob across the road. His skin tingled, his heart thumped, the blood drip-dripped onto the grass. As Jacob approached the fifth and final doll, he was vaguely aware John had joined him in the yard.

John was yelling but, although he could see his mouth move, he couldn't hear him. The only sound was the blood that pounded in his ears. His only thoughts were wrapped within the snake, the coil of anger he'd kept knotted in his stomach for so long, no longer in its cage but in his skin. It was an anger that filled him, that set every cell in his body on fire.

Jacob refused to be a victim for one more day. He refused to accept what life had handed him without a fight. His name was Jacob Lau, L. A. U. And if anyone had a problem with that, he had a lead pipe.

Time slowed. He approached the red curls of the last doll and wielded the lead pipe with everything he had. His wrists turned over as he connected. Blood sprayed across the white picket fence. The pipe came around and hit him in the back.

Jacob had played some baseball when he was a kid but he wasn't exceptionally good at it, which is why the flight of doll number five came as a shock. The dolls head sprang from its neck with astonishing force, the mouth molded into a tiny "o" that took on new meaning as it rotated through the air and arced over Rural Route One. For what seemed like forever, he could feel the vibration of the impact in the cold metal pipe clutched in his hands.

His mouth fell open as the wind lifted it higher than its original trajectory, higher and higher still as if it were gaining speed with distance, unaffected by gravity. The Laudners had stopped yelling and were staring wide-eyed at the amazing flight. Until, to his horror, it dove and with a disturbingly loud crash shattered a stained glass window of the neighboring Victorian.

In a hundred years, Jacob would never have guessed a doll's head could have inflicted that kind of damage. He stood in awe, staring at the undeniable wreckage around him. There was nothing left to hit and no reason to continue. The sick was gone.

Jacob dropped the pipe.

"You evil bastard!" Katrina charged at him across the lawn.

"You called me an egg!" he screamed in her face, pushing her hard in the chest. The fight didn't last long. John inserted himself between the two, holding them in opposite directions. His fingers hardened around Jacob's shoulder.

"Ho! What is this all about? What's going on here?"

"Dad, what do you mean? You saw what he did! Punish him!"

"Jacob," John said in an amazingly calm voice, "what is this all about?"

"She called me an egg!" he snapped.

"What does that mean?" John asked.

"White on the outside and yellow in the middle. I'm sick of people in this town calling me names. You're all bigots! Why don't you just send me back where I belong?"

At the look on her father's face, Katrina interjected, "I didn't call you—I just repeated it. Everyone's saying it at school. I was just letting him know, Daddy."

John turned the full force of his stare on Katrina. "I am too tall for you to pull the wool over my eyes." He squared his shoulders between them. "Now listen up, both of you. Jacob is a member of this family and will be treated like one. Katrina, if I ever hear you call Jacob a name again or in any way degrade him, you will deal with me. Jacob, your behavior is inexcusable. Those dolls were antiques given to Katrina by her grandmother. They were worth hundreds of dollars each. You will help me repair them. The ones we can't repair you will pay to have repaired or replaced."

"I don't have any money."

"You'll earn the money," John boomed. His thumb pointed at his chest. "My way."

Katrina turned back toward the house in the arms of her weeping mother. Aunt Carolyn shot a look at him that was meant to cut deep. But Jacob wasn't sorry—not at all.

He rubbed his shoulder where John had released his grip.

John shook his head and turned away. "Collect the bodies and heads and put them in my workshop. I need to talk to Dr. Silva. Someone's gonna have to pay for that window."

He walked away, moving down the driveway and into the street. He didn't need to go far.

"Dr. Silva?" Jacob muttered.

The door to the Victorian opened. A woman in a floor-length black coat descended the stone steps. The wind circled her, the dead leaves framing the billow of her cloak as she descended. Wisps of platinum-blonde hair floated around her as she moved. She was tall and thin, a runway model, a goddess.

She was exactly the woman Jacob had seen out his window.

The last doll's head dangled from her fingertips. She crossed the yard and met John in the street, a grim expression on her face. Jacob watched her lips move but couldn't hear what she was saying. Uncle John responded with an occasional head nod.

Panic rose like bile in his gut. She was horrifically beautiful, just as he remembered, and she was looking at Jacob. He remembered the drowning feeling. He remembered falling under the weight of … those eyes. The color of a winter sky, they pierced his flesh and his knees began to shake. John's head bobbed. They had come to some kind of an agreement and then the woman came for Jacob.

She left John's side and closed the distance between them with unworldly grace. The cloak she wore concealed her feet, giving her the ethereal appearance of floating over the pavement. When she was upon him and at an angle where John couldn't possibly see her expression, her scowl melted into a crooked smile and her brow arched.

The smell of freshly baked cookies surrounded her, like her pockets were full of chocolate chips and brown sugar. Jacob inhaled deeply and knew it was a weird thing to do. He was sure it wasn't polite to smell someone you just met. His palms began to sweat. Zaps of electricity ran the course of his body, a feeling he didn't quite understand. He was equally tempted to kiss her as to run.

Even as Jacob felt it, this strong attraction, he knew it was wrong. She looked young, maybe twenty-six, but he knew she must be older. John had called her "Doctor Silva." Jacob tried not to think about how she made him feel. He tried not to think about anything.

She laughed at him, a hollow sound like frozen wind chimes. Over the heap of bodies in his arms, she dangled the fifth doll's head. She tilted her face slightly as she dropped it on the pile.

In a voice that oozed over her lips like warm honey, she said, "I believe this belongs to you."

Chapter 10
A Possible Life Sentence

If there were a contest for the worst possible time to have to urinate, Jacob would've won. Once the surge of adrenaline had passed, the awkward bandaging session with Aunt Carolyn had begun. All of the glass was picked out of his arm, which was now covered in ample amounts of gauze. Then he was instructed to sit in the living room because Uncle John wanted to talk to him about his punishment. Jacob wasn't sure how long he'd waited in the sage green recliner, but it was long enough to make him feel like he needed to pee at the exact moment the man sat down. Based on the frown on Uncle John's face, he decided not to get up.

"So, here's how it's gonna be," Uncle John began. "I think we can fix three of the dolls by hand. We'll snap their heads back on and touch them up with some fresh hobby paint. The china dolls are obviously beyond repair. You will help find replacements and earn the money to buy them for Katrina."

Jacob nodded. Even though he felt Katrina got what she deserved, he knew there would be consequences. It was time to pay the piper. As he saw it, the good news was that the way he earned the money to pay for the dolls could become the way he earned a ticket home. Even working in the shop a few weeks would be worth it, if it got him out of Paris.

"Now there's the issue of the window. I've spoken to Dr. Silva and she thinks insurance will cover it, but you will have to pay her deductible. It's one thousand dollars."

"A thousand dollars?" Jacob winced.

"Jacob, that house was built in 1850. That window was leaded glass. I was as surprised as you were that it broke, but it did and it was expensive."

"What do I have to do?"

"Dr. Silva has a garden out back and a greenhouse. Usually this time of year she hires some help to spread fertilizer, plant seeds— that sort of thing. It's really more of a hobby but she has a large collection of rare and unusual plants that she's amassed during her tenure."

"Her tenure?"

"She's a professor of Ethnobotany at the University of Illinois."

"I don't even know what that is."

"Ethnobotany is the study of how people around the world use plants as part of their culture. She told me once that she found a root in Tibet that was used there for centuries to cure headaches. She brought a piece of it back to the United States, analyzed it, and a pharmaceutical company thinks they can make a new migraine medicine from it. She's really, um, fascinating." John's eyes twinkled and Jacob wondered if Dr. Silva had the same effect on his uncle as she did on him. What was it about her? Yeah, she was beautiful, but he'd seen plenty of gorgeous women on the beach where he came from. It wasn't like she was showing skin or in any way acting suggestively. So, why did he feel such an intense physical attraction toward her? It was like ... magic.

"She has an extraordinary garden," John continued. "It's too much work for one person. So, this year she'll have you."

Jacob's skin went clammy.

"She's agreed to pay you seven dollars an hour for your labor and will employ you until such time as you pay off your debt or longer if you agree to it. It's actually a great opportunity. Her work is known throughout the world. You may get to see some of it firsthand."

Jacob shifted in his seat. He was trying to be mature about this, but the truth was he was terrified of the woman. He was sure she was a witch or something. He wondered if the night he'd seen her out his window was a hallucination at all.

"A professor, huh." Jacob searched for the words. "She seems really ... young."

"You noticed. They say she's brilliant. Graduated college top of her class at seventeen. I think she's around thirty now. She moved here about ten years ago. Mostly keeps to herself."

"So, what's with the black cloak? It's ... creepy."

"Yeah, I guess she's a little eccentric. I mean, I can see why you might think that with the way she dresses and all. But if she makes you uncomfortable, you should have thought of that before you broke her window." John's eyebrows arched and the muscle in his jaw tightened. He pushed his plaid sleeves up to his elbows and threaded his fingers over his stomach. "You know, I knew her grandmother. She lived there before Abigail moved in. She was quite a looker. Even when she got old, really beautiful." John was staring toward the fireplace, not looking at anything in particular.

Jacob searched his brain for something to say, any excuse to escape having to work for Dr. Silva. But nothing came to him. It was as if his brain were hiding in a corner of his head, inaccessible, a blank slate, and no help at all.

"You start Saturday." He got up from the chair and turned toward the staircase. "Oh, and Jacob, you and Katrina will apologize to each other. I'm going to talk with her right now. This thing between you two has got to stop. You are part of this family now—that goes for you and that goes for her. You two have got to start treating each other like family or this is going to be hell on Earth for all of us."

As John jogged up the stairs, Jacob rose from the sage green recliner and headed for the bathroom. On his way, he crossed in front of the large bay window. The world beyond was disguised as an early spring day but he knew it was as turbulent as ever. Why hadn't John used this as an excuse to force him to work in the Laudners' flower shop? That Jacob would have expected, but not this. This smacked of disaster.

There was definitely something odd, if not dangerous, about Dr. Abigail Silva. Jacob caught sight of her across the street, lying upside-down on a rocking chair on her front porch. Her bare ankles were crossed where her head should have been and her fingers dangled above the porch floor. At once, he realized she was looking at him, those blue eyes searching his face across the distance. And then, as if she had more muscles and joints than the average human, she planted her hands on the blue wood of the porch and flipped her feet over her head, landing easily on the balls of her feet. Jacob watched as she rose to her full height and leaned over the porch rail. Distance and glass couldn't mellow her effect and the spice of terror and longing filled him, a confusing concoction that made his whole body clench.

She grinned, like the cat that was about to eat the canary.

Chapter 11
Moon Tea And Somali

As agreed, Jacob met with Dr. Silva the following Saturday to discuss his new responsibilities. He dreaded the encounter to the point he had to force himself up each of the inlaid stone steps, his shaking knees betraying his fear as he knocked tentatively on the heavy wooden door. But the Victorian was full of surprises. For one, the inside was as warm and cozy as the outside was cold and foreboding. Dr. Silva had welcomed him into a room she called a parlor near the rear of the house, decorated in honey-brown leather and burgundy plaid with a lively fire burning beneath a gold mantel. Dr. Silva's cat, a large red Somali that looked like a fox, took an unnatural interest in Jacob, following at his heels and guarding his every move. Dr. Silva said it was the breed; Somalis were known for their loyalty and Gideon, as the cat was called, was not accustomed to strangers.

But perhaps the greatest surprise was that despite Dr. Silva's casual manner and that she'd forgone her black coat for a sweatshirt and khaki pants, Jacob remained horrified by her presence. The touch of her hand when they greeted one another was enough to send a charge of electric current coursing through his body, and set every hair on end. It was embarrassing, but Jacob felt powerless to fight it.

"Before we get started, I think it would be a good idea for us to get to know each other." Dr. Silva lowered her chin and stared at Jacob until he felt a bead of sweat drip down his temple. "Would you like some tea?"

He nodded. As if he had any other choice but to say yes. She moved like grace personified, practically gliding to the kitchen. In less time than it would've taken him to walk there and back, she returned with two steaming cups. He took a sip with shaky hands, trying his best not to spill any on himself. Around the flavor of oolong tea, he could make out a trace of mango twisted with cinnamon and coconut. The aftertaste was—what was it? Pumpkin. Clearly, pumpkin.

"Do you like it?" she asked.

"Yeah, it's really good," he said honestly.

"It's my own secret recipe. It has over seventeen distinct ingredients. I call it moon tea because it takes a month to make, a full cycle of the moon. I use pumpkins from my garden. Imparts a unique flavor, wouldn't you agree?"

Jacob nodded. Something about the warm tea and the way the light of the fire flickered across the wood grain coffee table was helping him feel more like himself. Dr. Silva looked him directly in the eye and smiled, but he didn't feel the same electric tingle as before. He felt … normal, like he might have felt around any adult. She was still stunning but her beauty wasn't overwhelming.

"That's better," she said, but Jacob didn't know what she meant. She couldn't possibly know how attracted he'd been to her before.

"You look tired, Jacob. We don't have to start in the garden right away. Why don't you just rest awhile and tell me about yourself?"

"Well, I am a little tired," he replied. To Jacob's surprise, he began to speak, more openly than ever before. The words poured out of him as if he were a bag of sand that she had slit open, releasing every grain of thought he'd ever had. Jacob told her about his parents and growing up in the little house on Oahu. He told her about his father's death in the war and then about living with his mother in the family car. He described in detail the public housing apartment he eventually moved into. Jacob admitted that Malini was the only friend he'd had in a long time. But what would upset him the most, later when he'd had the chance to think about their talk, was that Jacob admitted to her that his living situation had cost him friends, and how he wondered, somewhere deep inside, if his mother had meant to abandon him. It was a private thought, not meant to be shared with anyone, but he'd said it just the same.

It didn't bother him while he said it. Every word was a weight, rolling off his tongue, leaving him lighter than before. It was so easy, to cast the weight aside. When every event his brain could remember was laid out on the table, he leaned back in his chair, feeling as light as a feather, and closed his eyes. If she minded, Dr. Silva did not say so or anything about the silence that ensued.

It was warm here, relaxing. Jacob didn't care if he ever started work, or if he ever left.

He was on the edge of an irresistible sleep. But just as the feeling threatened to overpower him, he forced his eyes open one last time. He looked across the coffee table at Dr. Silva, her empty cup in hand, and suddenly felt rude for doing all of the talking and none of the listening.

"What about you, Dr. Silva? Tell me about yourself."

Dr. Silva sat up straighter, her eyebrows arched in surprise. She shifted in her chair, looking uncomfortable.

"Well there's not much to tell really," she began. Her eyes flicked from her cup to Jacob. "My father kicked me out of his house a long, long time ago, and I have been trying to get back home ever since."

She may have continued but Jacob didn't hear. He was fast asleep.

Chapter 12
A Girl Worth Fighting For

When Jacob woke up, Dr. Silva was in the same chair. He had no idea how long he'd been asleep, but the weather had changed and rain pelted the window in angry bursts. Self-conscious, he ran the back of his hand across his mouth to check for drool. Had she been watching him sleep?

Dr. Silva explained that he was done for the day, but Jacob would be expected to work every Saturday morning. She would be waiting for him in the back of the house a week from today. He agreed, straightened his shirt, and followed her to the door.

Spending a morning with Dr. Silva made Jacob feel like he'd survived skydiving or bungee jumping. What was it she'd said about herself? Something about her father kicking her out of the house when she was young? He couldn't remember.

Why had he told her all of those things about himself? After all, people had been hounding him to talk since he'd arrived here: Principal Bailey, Uncle John, and even Malini would have loved some info. Why did he pick the one person he feared the most and trusted the least to share his most private thoughts? There was no explanation. Jacob broke out in gooseflesh just thinking about it.

The Laudners' front door was unlocked and he let himself in. He didn't mind the rain so much, but he was anxious to put another door between Dr. Silva and himself. Plus, it was cold, Paris cold. In his haste, he almost whacked John, who was standing just inside the door, scowling at a list in his hand.

"Jacob! You're back. Are you done for the day?" John's eyes were annoyingly hopeful.

"Yeah, she said we would start next Saturday, so…"

"Probably can't do much today with the rain and all, huh. So, do you have a few minutes to help me with something?"

"Uh, sure. What is it?"

"Good! I need you to come into town with me. Aunt Carolyn needs some groceries but I have some things to do at the shop. I was hoping you could pick 'em up while I'm working."

"Sure." Jacob needed to get his mind off of what had happened with Dr. Silva and he wasn't excited about hanging out in the house alone with Katrina.

"Let's take Big Blue."

Big Blue was a monster of a Chevy with rusted-out wheel wells and robin's egg blue paint that barely adhered to the metal. The engine was loud and the seats were torn, but John often said, "Still runs great!" Aunt Carolyn refused to ride in it. Jacob guessed that was an added incentive for John to keep it around.

They headed into town on Rural Route One, the uncomfortable silence not overcome by the hum of the engine.

"Have you heard anything about my mom?" he asked.

"Yes and no," John sighed. "I was trying to find the right time to tell you this. The police have stopped the active investigation. The case is still open but nobody is going out on it anymore."

"Do you mean they've stopped looking for her?" His voice was louder than he'd intended and it filled the small cab.

"I don't want to upset you, Jacob. The case is still open but they just don't have any leads. There were no fingerprints and the only blood they found was hers. They are not actively looking because there's no place left to look … unless more evidence pops up somewhere."

Jacob had suspected as much. It had been months. But it didn't make it any easier to hear. "Do you know … can I have what was in her purse? I mean, there were pictures and things in her wallet," he said, but what he was thinking was that somewhere, near the bottom, there might be a small key: a key that might open up a jewelry box, a box that might hold a clue to her last days. He couldn't say that to Uncle John though because the box was his mother's secret, a secret she'd kept even from him, and Jacob would keep it from everyone else, until he knew what it was and if it could help find her.

"I honestly don't know. I think all of that stuff is locked up as evidence. I'll ask though."

John parked in front of a chain of Paris businesses with decorative wooden signage. The town had a policy against electronic or neon signs in favor of hand-painted wood. It was one of the few things Jacob liked about Paris. Another great thing about Paris was that anywhere you parked you could reach everything else within a couple of blocks. That was the end of Jacob's list of things to like about Paris.

"Meet me at the shop when you're done," John said before darting out into the drizzle.

Exiting the truck, Jacob jogged through the rain to Westcott's grocery. He ducked inside the door and dug into his pocket for Carolyn's list. Great. Scented hand soap and hair dye along with a bunch of other stuff. This could take a while. John had given him an envelope full of cash for the purchases. The money seemed to get heavier in his pocket and he was tempted to skim a few dollars off the top. He dreaded his next workday with Dr. Silva and any amount would make his time with her shorter. Even as he thought about it, he knew he couldn't do it. All Jacob had was himself and he knew deep down he wasn't a thief.

He absent-mindedly thumped and sniffed a cantaloupe. How did you tell if a melon was ripe? He had no idea.

A flash in his peripheral vision brought his head around. He watched her duck behind the dairy section, her hair down today in long layers that fell around her face and down her back. Jacob dropped the melon and turned the corner to follow. She was working her way down the cereal aisle. He pursued, riding the grocery cart like a scooter to make up for lost time. He caught up with her in front of the Cocoa Crispies.

"Malini?"

"Jacob! Hey, it's good to see you." She smiled and tucked a strand of hair behind her ear. Her eyes lit up. "What are you doing here?"

"Shopping for my Aunt Carolyn." He frowned. "I'm not exactly a pro at this. How do you tell if a cantaloupe is ripe?"

"You've come to the right place, actually," Malini said, taking the list from his hand. "I'm a natural. Leave it to me. You do have money for this?"

"Of course."

"Good. No problem then." Malini walked ahead while Jacob pushed the cart.

For some reason, he became concerned about the wrinkles in his shirt and the fact that he'd forgotten to use a comb after falling asleep at Dr. Silva's. Behind her back, he ran his fingers through his hair, over his face, and down his shirt. Malini's slender fingers reached for a cantaloupe and he noticed the soft pink crescent of her nails against the silky bronze of her skin. Funny, he'd never noticed before.

"Don't you have your own shopping to do?" Jacob asked.

"No. Not really." She blushed. "I sometimes come here when there's nothing else to do."

"Don't be embarrassed. I understand. You don't like it here either."

"Not particularly. It's a bit rural for my taste. I miss the culture of London."

It came as a sudden surprise to Jacob how little he knew about her personally. He spoke with her every day. They ate lunch together and studied after school. But it seemed like their conversations had hovered around their classes and the people of Paris. He'd neglected to ask Malini about herself.

"Is there anything you like to do here, in your free time?"

"I read, listen to music, that sort of thing. In the summer, I water-ski. I used to play soccer, at my old school. They don't have a soccer team here."

"Soccer's cool. I play soccer."

"Really?"

"No. Not a lot. I've played before but I'm no good."

She smiled and reached for a roll of paper towels.

"What type of music do you like?" she asked.

"The hard stuff: alternative, metal, rock. It just has to be fast and loud."

"Hmm. Don't you ever just want to relax?"

"Sometimes, but then I don't listen to music. You?"

"A little of everything. I just like music that takes me to a different place. If it does that, it doesn't matter what it is." She dropped a loaf of bread into the cart and squinted up at him. "What's your favorite book?"

"I'm not a big reader. You?"

"Silas Marner."

"What ... the classic?"

"Yeah, I know it's nerdy but it's my favorite. I just love how Silas ends up with everything he ever wanted even though he never knew he wanted it." She had stopped shopping and was twisting the list between her fingers. "You really don't read?"

"For school, that's about it."

Malini looked disappointed.

"I've read Silas Marner though," he added quickly. "We had to, for school. And, I liked it. I really did."

She smiled and continued down the aisle, tossing items into the basket. She had an innate ability to decipher Aunt Carolyn's cryptic writing and, too soon for Jacob, they were headed toward the checkout.

He watched as Malini unloaded the cart onto the belt. She was wearing form-fitting jeans and a clingy pink sweater that showed off her figure. He wasn't up on fashion but her outfit seemed like something she'd brought from London. It didn't fit in here, more like what you'd see on TV or in a big city.

It occurred to Jacob then how beautiful she was. Up until then, he'd thought of her only as a friend, a study partner, and a co-conspirator. Today, though, as the light filtered in through the windows at the front of the store, he felt an odd sort of fluttering in his stomach. He guessed it was because, for the first time, he realized she was a girl.

But he knew he shouldn't *like* Malini, not in that way. If he messed up their friendship, he could lose what he cared about most in Paris—her. Life here might be intolerable without her.

Jacob reached down to help her empty the cart and their fingers brushed. Malini's eyes shot up, warm chocolate with flecks of gold and red that danced in the sunlight. He caught himself staring for seconds too long. He swallowed hard.

"What, Jacob? I've got it." She placed a loaf of bread on the conveyor belt. "Are you feeling okay?"

"Oh. Yeah. Sorry."

"That'll be eighty-six eighty," the woman behind the counter said. Jacob counted out the money and then lifted both bags into his arms before Malini could try to help. He led the way out into the parking lot, stepping over the large puddles that had collected from the storm that now rumbled harmlessly in the distance.

"I can help you with that," she said, pointing at the bags.

"No, no, I've got it. I was supposed to meet my uncle back at the shop but we were so fast I'm not sure he'll be done. Do you want to hang out at McNaulty's if he's not?" Jacob asked this absently because the unusual movement of a puddle at his feet distracted him. The water swept toward him to one side of the dip in the parking lot, as if it were blown by the wind. Only, there was no wind. In fact, there wasn't even an incline. The weirdest thing was that he could hear it; the water seemed to hum as it moved, as if the molecules were whispering to him.

"Do you hear that?" he asked Malini.

"Hear what?" Malini's eyebrows scrunched as she saw the water run out of the hole and flow between his feet toward the grocery store. "That's odd," she said.

They turned their heads to see where the water was flowing and saw Dane Michaels and Phillip Westcott saunter toward them. Dane looked bored, but when he spotted them his expression morphed into something like relief. Why Dane would be relieved to see him and Malini, Jacob didn't know, but he didn't like it. The two boys were smoking and Dane took one last drag on his cigarette before flicking it at the pavement.

"If it isn't our two special friends, P.S. and Kung Fu," Phillip said.

Dane slammed a fist into Phillip's shoulder. "Don't be rude, Phil," he said.

Phillip looked confused but shut his mouth.

Dane scanned Malini from head to toe and then raised an eyebrow in Phillip's direction. Jacob wasn't a mind reader but he was fairly sure Dane had just realized Malini was a girl, too. If looks could kill, Dane would have fallen over dead right then because Jacob didn't like his sudden appreciation of Malini. He didn't like it at all.

"Dane," Jacob said. It sounded less like a greeting than a threat.

"Hey, we were just on our way to my house. Why don't you guys come hang out with us?" Dane said. His expression was stiff.

"I don't think so, Dane. We're busy," Jacob replied.

Dane ignored him and snaked his arm around Malini's waist. "Malini, come hang out with me," he said softly.

"Don't touch me." She pushed him away. "Have you been drinking?"

Jacob could smell it too, a faint spicy sweetness that hung in the air around the two boys.

"Oh, come on. You can't be having much fun with Lau. Come with me." Dane pressed his hand into the small of Malini's back.

Malini slapped his hand away. "Go home, Dane."

Phillip laughed. "Looks like she wants to go with Jacob, Dane. Guess you're not enough fun for her."

And that was the end of the fake politeness. Dane's face warped into rage.

"Is that it?" Dane moved toward Malini again, grabbing her wrist. "You wanna have more fun? I can be fun." Malini tried her hardest to push him away but Dane dug his fingers into her like he had something to prove, turning her skin red around his grip.

"Come on, Dane, that's enough. Back off," Jacob said. He set the groceries down. His fists clenched and he took a step forward.

"What's wrong, Jacob? You don't want Malini to have any fun without you?" Dane leaned forward and ran his tongue up the side of Malini's face. Phillip laughed hysterically but Malini looked like she might vomit as she struggled to free herself.

Jacob didn't wait to see if she would succeed. His fist shot out toward Dane's jaw and he threw his weight into it. Dane's head snapped back, forcing him to retreat a step. His hand reflexively shot up to the point of impact, wiping away the blood that bubbled out of his split lip. Malini didn't miss the opportunity to free herself and lunge behind Jacob.

Phillip stopped laughing.

"You are going to wish you never set foot in Paris, freak," Dane said.

And then, the side of Jacob's jaw exploded. Before he could recover, Phillip's hands were on his shirt, and then holding his arms. Dane pummeled his stomach and chest. With each hit, pain radiated and the taste of blood filled his mouth.

But Jacob wasn't giving up. He knew how to fight. It was the one benefit of the time he'd spent living in public housing. He turned his body sideways, shoved his shoulder into Phillip, and sank a sidekick into Dane's knee. But Phillip was stronger than Jacob hoped and he couldn't get his arms loose to block Dane's punches. He took one to the face and felt his lip split open. Another and his eye started to swell. The hurt wasn't as bad as the loss of his full range of vision.

Jacob could hear Malini screaming as he took blow after blow, the pain driving him toward the edge of consciousness. What he worried about most was Malini. If he passed out, what would Dane do to her? He had to protect her. No matter what happened to him, Jacob couldn't let them hurt Malini and somehow he knew they would. With everything he had left, he turned his face toward her and mouthed, *Run*!

That's when he heard the hum again from the water at his feet. It was like when he was little and he would place his hand on the speaker of his father's stereo. The buzz would tickle his fingers. Only now, the hum made his whole body prickle.

His thoughts became clear and quick, so quick that everything around him seemed to move in slow motion. Dane's arm retracted. Malini's mouth opened as if to scream, and Phillip's head nodded at Dane, but whatever sounds they made didn't reach Jacob.

His body was a string map. Every finger and toe was the end of a string that was tied to the center of his chest, right over his heart. The strings were tight and when he strummed them with his mind they played a note, the same note as the water. In that moment everything felt connected. Using the hum was instinctual. It was like knowing what to do with his kidneys. He didn't have to understand how they worked, they just did.

With a new strength, he wrenched his arms free from Phillip's grip. As Dane's fist neared his head, he gathered the hum tightly inside and then let go. His arms flew out toward Dane, to push him away. But he missed. Jacob's hands stopped short of Dane's chest, but those strings inside of him released.

Like a slingshot, the hum shot toward Dane, but instead of a stone flying loose, the rain started again—sideways. Not from the sky but from everything wet: the pavement, the trees, and the tops of the cars in the parking lot. It came from behind Jacob, like someone had turned on a fire hose. In a mighty gust, the water washed Dane and Phillip against the wall of Westcott's grocery. Jacob stared in shock. The impact was so strong he hoped the boys weren't dead. The water fell to the pavement as abruptly as it had come.

After moments of painful silence, he was relieved to hear a sharp intake of breath from the two boys, followed by plenty of coughing and spitting. He didn't press his luck. He grabbed the groceries and Malini's hand.

"Let's get the hell out of here," he said.

"What the hell was that?" Malini gasped, falling into step. They hurried up the sidewalk toward Laudner's Flowers and Gifts.

"I don't know. I guess … weather."

"No, Jacob. That was not weather. That was some kind of miracle. Did you see the water wash those two away when you pushed Dane?"

"It was a coincidence. It had to be."

"Were you just there? Did you not see Phillip fly over your head? He was behind you, Jacob! The water washed him away. And look at me! I'm dry as a bone. If it was the weather, why am I not wet?"

"I don't know … I don't know."

"What?"

"I don't know what happened, okay? Let's just forget it ever happened."

Malini narrowed her eyes and filled her cheeks with air. Her body stopped moving. He pulled her hand gently but she stood her ground.

"I'll tell you one thing, you are not going to be able to forget about *that* anytime soon." She pointed at his face.

Jacob turned to see his reflection in the window of his uncle's shop. His left eye was a swollen red slit and blood from his lip oozed down his chin. He dabbed it with his finger. The door opened and John stepped onto the sidewalk, his mouth twisting into a grimace.

"Aw hell, Jacob! Could you possibly make my life any more difficult?" John lifted the groceries from Jacob's arms. "Your Aunt Carolyn is going to have a field day with this. Get in the car!"

He did as he was told.

John asked Malini if she needed a ride somewhere but she insisted she was meeting her dad at his office. He didn't ask twice.

As John pulled away, Jacob watched Malini through the window of the truck. She remained standing, on the same spot of sidewalk, staring after him with her lips parted slightly. Her expression was unforgettable, like she had just seen a ghost ... or a miracle.

Chapter 13
The Not-So-Ordinary Sunday

Every day with the Laudners was bad but, for Jacob, Sundays were the worst. The Laudners were Catholic, which meant they dressed up in their nicest clothes and attended church every Sunday morning at nine o'clock. They had a specific pew where some Laudner had sat in their Sunday best for one hundred and fifty years. Apparently, they had never missed Mass, but as the story goes, twenty-five years ago a visiting family unknowingly sat in the pew before the Laudners arrived. The priest politely asked them to move.

Jacob struggled to understand the meaning of this Sunday ritual. His family had never practiced any religion. He'd met religious people on Oahu, but he filed the whole concept of religion in the same part of his brain where he kept information on

Greek mythology and Santa Claus. It wasn't that he thought people were stupid for believing, he just thought they were naive.

The worst part was remembering all of the rules. None of the Laudners ate breakfast before church in order to keep the sacrament of Holy Communion sacred—whatever that meant. He wasn't allowed to take communion because he wasn't Catholic, but he was also not allowed to eat breakfast. So, stomach growling and head nodding, he'd endure the hour-long service and try his best to tolerate the stand, sit, and kneel routine.

After church, John would pick up Aunt Veronica from the Paris nursing home for brunch. Aunt Veronica's daughter, Linda, son-in-law, Mark, and their two twin daughters would drive from Morton to have brunch with the Laudners. Linda insisted that they couldn't possibly pick up her mother themselves with the added travel from Morton and John said he was more than happy to do it.

Everyone would finally join together around the large pine table around one o'clock. By that time, Jacob was starving and regularly snuck food from the refrigerator when no one was looking. A slice of ham was his favorite because he could shove it all in his mouth and swallow in a matter of seconds.

This particular Sunday was exceptionally stressful as the fallout from his fight was still fresh. His eye was an obnoxious purple and his lip was puffy and probably infected. John had tried to back him up—turns out Dane had a reputation for trouble—but Carolyn wouldn't hear it. She hadn't punished him exactly, just yelled long tirades until Jacob felt small and tired. Carolyn had never acted as if she liked Jacob. The fight didn't help.

This Sunday, he was determined to keep a low profile and go with the routine, not an easy task considering Aunt Veronica didn't like him either. She'd never told him so. Actually, she never told anyone anything. Dementia had rendered her mute years ago. But she would point at Jacob and hiss if he got too close. He was pretty sure that wasn't affection spraying out from between her teeth. Luckily he could smell her coming. The old lady stench was warning enough to beat feet.

He'd legitimately inhaled several pieces of fried chicken when his cell phone began to vibrate in his pocket. Carolyn looked positively bewildered as she glanced at John and then around the table.

"It's my phone," he offered.

"Who could that be?" she asked him with a sharp look.

Jacob slid open the phone and read a text message from Malini asking him to dinner. When he raised his head, Carolyn was glaring at him, like a predator ready to pounce on its prey. He wasn't thrilled about being the prey.

"My friend, Malini, is inviting me to dinner at her house tonight. Can I go?"

Carolyn's head shook and she began to say no, but John interrupted, talking over his wife as if he couldn't see her obvious disapproval, "Of course, Jacob, I'll give you a ride."

To say he was surprised at John's concurrence would have been the understatement of the year. After an awkward silence, everyone went back to his or her food. The rest of the table began a conversation about the fried chicken recipe.

"Was that Malini I saw you with yesterday?" John asked quietly.

"Yeah. But she had nothing to do with it," he whispered. "I just know her from school."

"She's Jim Gupta's daughter," John said. It wasn't a question. The town was too small to not know the one Indian family who lived there. "He lives right by his office. I know just where it is."

At quarter to six, John and Jacob excused themselves from a lively conversation about why Linda and Mark didn't visit Aunt Veronica more often to drive to the Guptas. He thanked John as soon as he climbed into Big Blue.

"It's no problem, Jacob. I'm glad to hear you're making friends. I want you to feel like you're at home here. It's about time you settled in."

He nodded to be polite, but cringed when he thought of settling in to Paris. This was a resting point, a waiting room until he could save enough money to go to his real home.

"I need to tell you, I asked about your mother's things. The police won't release them because they're considered evidence. I'm sorry."

Jacob stared out the window at the blur of trees racing through his reflection. He would just have to find another way.

* * * * *

Four fifty-five Front Street was a beautiful, brick, two-story. The Gupta residence, like all homes in Paris, was enormous by Jacob's standards. Even without leaves on the trees, the yard looked manicured and the house could have appeared on a postcard.

John yelled through the window to call when he wanted to be picked up and backed out of the driveway. Jacob approached the house, nervous about meeting Malini's parents. A gust of wind blew the large American flag that flew from a brass pole near the front door and the striped material swallowed him up. After unwrapping himself, he rang the bell. Malini must have been waiting by the door because it opened almost immediately.

"Jacob, come in. It's good to see you!"

Jacob stepped into the beige marble foyer, his footsteps echoing off the cathedral ceiling and around the crystal chandelier above his head. A man with stylish hair and a black turtleneck extended his hand.

"Jacob, this is my father, Jahar. He goes by Jim," Malini said.

"Malini, why don't you just introduce me as Jim?" he said, shooting Malini a hard glare. "Hello, Jacob. Welcome to our humble abode."

Jacob returned the handshake, wondering if he should call him Jim or Mr. Gupta. He decided on Mr. Gupta. It seemed the most respectful.

"Malini told us about your accident. You must be more careful next time. That eye looks terrible."

Jacob glanced at Malini and she lifted the corner of her mouth. Well, if her story was that he was in an accident, he wasn't going to argue.

"And this is my mother, Sarah," Malini said.

"Hello, Jacob." Mrs. Gupta's accent was more pronounced than her husband's. She wore the traditional long braid and bindi he associated with Indian women. However, her manner of dress was as American and sophisticated as her husband's: tan slacks and a red sweater set. "We are so happy you could join us tonight. Malini says you like Indian cuisine?"

"Yes!" Mr. Gupta chimed in, clapping his hands. "What is this? I thought young people enjoyed hamburgers and pizza, but Malini insisted on an Indian meal."

"Yeah, I've been craving Indian food," Jacob said. "I'm sure Malini has told you I grew up on Oahu. The food is different here. I really miss the variety my mom used to make."

"Can I offer you something to drink?" Malini asked, after Mrs. Gupta elbowed her in the side.

"Yes, thank you. Water would be great."

"While Sarah and Malini get the drinks, let me take you on the tour," Mr. Gupta said.

The home was suspiciously vacant of anything Indian. In fact, it was the most American home Jacob had ever seen. Even the Laudners had vases made in China and rugs from Pakistan. The Gupta home was decorated entirely from items made in the Americas. This was not something Jacob would have normally noticed, but Mr. Gupta made a point of it as they walked from room to room. In the den, he showed off a small antique writing desk that was used by Abraham Lincoln.

"Can you believe it, Jacob? Abraham Lincoln! I couldn't be happier to have this in my house."

Malini, who had entered with the water, looked at Jacob and rolled her eyes.

After some light conversation, the family gathered around a long cherry table and Mrs. Gupta served the food. There was yellow curry with chicken, lamb vindaloo, pineapple chutney, and mounds of jasmine rice. He ate like he hadn't seen food in a month.

When dinner was over, Jacob followed Malini through a glass-paneled door, down a flight of stairs, to a large game room. A polished pool table was at the center of the room. Behind it, he spotted a foosball table and ping-pong.

"Wow, your basement is awesome," Jacob said.

But Malini turned to him at the base of the stairs, a panicky look on her face. "Now tell me what happened yesterday. What's going on with you?"

"I told you, I don't know. It was some freak … weather coincidence."

Malini shook her head. "No. It wasn't. You did it. You made it happen."

"No. I didn't."

"Then what happened, Jake? What explanation could there possibly be?"

"I can't explain. Can we just forget about it? To be honest, it gives me the creeps."

"No. We can't. You ... hosed Dane and Phillip to the wall. It was like you made the water move. Has anything like this ever happened to you before?"

"No."

"Do you have a family history of controlling the elements? Levitation maybe?"

"You can't be serious."

"Okay, maybe I went overboard with the levitation thing, but you can't honestly believe it was nothing."

Jacob turned from her and walked deeper into the room, resting his backside against the foosball table. He crossed his arms over his chest and shook his head.

"Listen, I've been in this town for two years," Malini said. "It's like I told you: people who have been here all their lives ... it's like..."

"Like they have enough friends," Jacob finished.

"Then you show up, out of nowhere, out of the clear blue sky. And, I like you, Jake. I really like you. I just can't help but think that fate brought us together for a reason, you know?"

"I don't really believe in fate, but I like you too. I'm glad we met."

"This, this miracle..."

"Coincidence," he interjected.

"Maybe I'm supposed to help you figure out what it is, what it means."

"Maybe it was a fluke and doesn't mean anything."

"So, you're sure, it never happened before or since?"

"I'm sure. No."

"And, you haven't noticed any other unusual abilities: superhuman speed, the ability to read minds…" She was smiling, but only half joking. Malini was so open and believing, her eyes wide with utter confidence that something supernatural had happened to them yesterday.

Jacob shook his head, a cynical grin on his lips.

"What about any odd dreams?" Malini asked.

His grin faded. He looked at the floor.

"That's it, isn't it? Dreams?" Malini shook his arm excitedly.

"Not exactly. Before I came here, before I met you, I was in a car accident. I've had some really vivid hallucinations but the doctors told me I might. I hit my head and they said I might see things or hear things. Some things that happen in them, they seem to happen for real. But I know it's just my subconscious working things out. It's just a coincidence that it happens the way I hallucinate it."

"Or it could be a symptom. Maybe something bigger is happening to you?"

"If I agree, can we talk about something else?"

"For now." Malini looked disappointed.

Jacob walked over to the air hockey table and switched it on. Malini fell in at the other side and served him the puck. It took all of fifteen seconds for her to sink her first goal.

"I guess you've probably noticed that my dad really loves America," Malini said, serving the puck again.

"Yes, I've noticed." He grinned. "But there's nothing wrong with that, is there?"

"No, I guess not. It's just I wish we could remember where we came from now and then. Do you know this was the first Indian meal we've had in six months?"

"You're kidding. Why? The food was spectacular."

"I know, right? It started with simple excitement that we'd become U.S. citizens. It's a real difficult process and we were all ecstatic when it was official. "

"Congratulations."

"Thanks, but then Dad insisted that we act like real Americans. I think part of it was this town. He needed to be accepted here, for his business. He has, you know. He's very successful. But the thing is, Jacob, we still have family in India. I mean, I haven't lived there since I was six, so maybe I don't know what I'm talking about, but … I mean, the food here, the clothes, everything is different and not necessarily better."

Understanding swept through Jacob and would change the way he saw Malini's family forever. He knew too well what she meant. The irony was that both of them had been robbed of their culture: he by the absence of his parents and her by their presence. It wasn't that where they were was so bad; it was that where they came from was important even when everyone else said it wasn't.

"I'm sorry, Malini, I bet India is beautiful."

"It's not just India." She sighed. "It's everywhere—everywhere I've been. It's part of who I am and I don't want to forget it. I don't want to lose it, you know?"

"Yeah, I think I understand," he said.

Malini sunk another goal.

"So much for the possibility of superhuman speed," he said.

Malini giggled.

"Would you like to see a dance I learned in India? It's been a few years, well, almost a decade I guess, but I think I remember."

"Sure."

Jacob sat back against the wall and Malini pulled a couple of chairs to the side to clear a makeshift stage. She placed a CD in a small player in the corner of the room and took her position in the center of the cleared patch of rug, her fingers delicately positioned near her shoulders.

As he heard the first sounds of a stringed instrument, Malini's wrists began to roll. Her arms became snakes, coiling around her sides. As the drumbeats joined the melody, her feet rose and stomped in a dance as beautiful and threatening as a looming thunderstorm. Her hands twisted intricate circles around her body, her back bending with the music, her hair sweeping against her shoulders.

She was exotic—brown and lean. Most importantly, she was open, as different and lost here as he was, and for the first time since coming to Paris, he felt connected.

Jacob stood. She was spinning but stopped when she noticed him rise. The thick black layers of her hair whipped against her neck and fell to her right shoulder. Her breath came in huffs as she looked at him. There was a question in her eyes that he couldn't read, but he desperately wanted to be the answer. He wanted to be the thing that made this world better for her.

Without thinking, he reached for her hand. Stopped. Reached again. He linked his finger into hers at an awkward angle, fearful his sweaty palms would gross her out if he held her hand properly. His heart thumped in his ears and his mouth went dry. She walked toward his chest and on instinct Jacob moved his other hand to the small of her back. Bending his neck in a series of light but erratic movements, his lips came within a fraction of an inch of hers. He waited. He wouldn't make the decision. He wouldn't cross the line without her.

He didn't have to wait long. Malini rose up on her tiptoes, grabbed the back of his head, and kissed him. Jacob was more than happy to return the favor. Everything seemed to melt away, the feel of her lips against his drowning out the world. He wanted to remember every moment, every feeling. It was his first kiss, but as she moved in closer and pressed her body into his, Jacob hoped it wouldn't be their last.

Chapter 14
The Other Garden

Jacob never expected his punishment to be so, well, punishing. After their first meeting resulted in tea and a nap, he was disappointed that Dr. Silva was no longer concerned if he looked tired. Nor did she ask him to talk. She simply expected him to work.

The first two Saturdays, he worked in the greenhouse. He repotted saplings, watered row after row of plants, and moved pots around for no apparent reason but Dr. Silva's whim. When he was done, his back ached and his fingers were permanently stained. The working conditions were humid and cramped.

That was child's play compared to this.

The pile of compost in front of him was three feet high and smelled like mushrooms. Jacob watched bits of brown crud blow off the top and swirl in the air around him. Although the sun was shining, the wind cut through his gray hoodie and chilled him to the bone. Six o'clock on a Saturday morning and his workday had officially begun.

"Add another two inches of this to each of the raised beds and rake it in," Dr. Silva said, handing him a shovel.

Jacob responded by hoisting the wheelbarrow and heading toward the half acre of sixteen-foot-long cedar rectangles. He wasn't afraid of the work and the faster he started, the sooner he'd finish.

"When you're done, I have something else in the greenhouse for you to do," she said, leaning casually against a garden bench. Gideon rested atop the back of the bench, flicking his fluffy red tail as Dr. Silva's long nails compulsively raked the cat's neck and shoulders.

Jacob began shoveling. As cool as it was, it didn't take him long to work up a sweat and by the time he headed back to the pile to refill the wheelbarrow, he was tempted to take off his sweatshirt. He paused when he noticed that Dr. Silva was still watching him.

"Am I your entertainment, too?" he asked. Since their first meeting, when he'd had tea with her, she didn't have the same effect on him as before. She was still as beautiful, but his skin didn't tingle when he saw her and her eyes didn't cut quite so deep. But it was awkward having someone watch him shovel. If she wasn't going to help, the least she could do was not stare.

"Well, looks like you've got everything under control here," she said, an edge to her voice as if his comment had caught her off-guard. She dusted her hands off against the sides of her cargo pants. "I have some things to do in the orchard. I'll check back with you later about the work in the greenhouse."

Jacob was relieved when she finally left. She wandered off into the maple trees, the big red cat following close behind.

The first hour wasn't bad. He glanced at his watch only twice and was making good progress. The second hour became increasingly tedious. His hands began to blister. He caught himself checking the time every ten minutes and stopping often to count the remaining beds in the field.

Refilling the wheelbarrow proved more difficult than he anticipated. If he loaded it up as much as he could, it became so heavy that the handles cut into his hands. But if he filled it only halfway, he would tire himself out making multiple trips. He tried a combination of both approaches, leaving his whole body sore and covered in compost dust.

At least he had something good to think about while he worked. Malini. Amazingly, she was his girlfriend now. He thought often of their first kiss and those that followed. The memory never got old.

By the time he hoisted the last shovel into the last bed, the sun was high. He felt dirty, tired, and, more than anything, thirsty. He was supposed to be done in an hour. Jacob wasn't sure if Dr. Silva would even want him to start the next project, but he decided to track her down to find out.

As he approached the threshold of the orchard, he noticed the maples were covered in buds. They lined up on the east of the property like a skeleton army. Fog had settled among them, under the shade of the entangled branches, creating a border between light and shadow that he stepped over to follow Dr. Silva's general direction. Mist slithered in wispy tendrils around his ankles, the ground beneath him squishing under each step. Layer upon layer of fallen leaves decomposed below his feet. A musty smell like dirt and maple syrup lingered in the air.

Jacob tried not to think about how creepy the orchard was. The trunks of the trees were scarred with knots and hollows. Cobwebs stretched from limb to trunk. He ran into a few and wiped his face repeatedly to make sure it was free of spiders.

"Dr. Silva?" he called. There was no discernable path, no footprints to follow, but the terrain sloped gradually downward. He wasn't worried about getting lost. When he needed to find his way out, he could simply walk uphill.

He was thinking about how thirsty he was when he almost walked into a hedge. It wasn't so much a traditional hedge as it was a thick garden wall, at least ten feet high, which made it even more embarrassing he hadn't seen it until his face had practically met greenery. How he couldn't have noticed it was beyond him, but he felt a strange type of disorientation, like walking into a room and forgetting why he had entered it. Maybe he was dehydrated. Maybe exhausted.

"Dr. Silva?" he called again and began walking along the wall.

A break in the privet revealed a wrought-iron gate, similar to the one at the front of the house, as if the iron had grown out of the hedge itself. Ivy interlaced itself among the gate spindles, making it almost impossible to see anything behind it. Across the top, a vine of red roses grew, its thorns reminding him of barbed wire.

The roses surprised him. In Hawaii plants bloomed all year round, but since he'd come to Paris he was painfully aware that the deciduous plants here died off in the winter and gradually came back in the spring. This plant was bright green and leafy, the crimson roses open and bright. The vine seemed to defy the brown stick branches of the maples. He wondered if Dr. Silva had used some kind of special fertilizer to make these plants come back sooner than the rest.

"Dr. Silva, are you in there?" he yelled through the overgrown bars.

Silence.

He reached down and tested the handle but the gate was padlocked with an antique iron lock. This did not surprise Jacob. It was perfectly matched to the wrought-iron gate. What did surprise him was that someone had left the key in it.

"Gaaah!" He jumped at the flash of red that moved beyond the gate. Through a gap in the ivy he'd seen Gideon; the red fur was unmistakable. Dr. Silva must be behind the gate after all. Gideon was always with her.

Jacob was struck suddenly by an urge to go home to the Laudners. The gate was locked, key or no key, and going through without permission was risky. It didn't seem like he was supposed to be here. Besides, it may have been the dehydration, but his heart was racing and his gut twisted. Something told him to turn back, to give up. If he left, he could just talk to Dr. Silva about it another day or make up the hour next week.

But when he thought about the Laudners, he remembered his eye and lip, healed now but not forgotten. Uncle John had put himself on the line to shield him from Aunt Carolyn's fury but it was horrible anyway. As much as he hated staying with the Laudners, he was sorry that his actions had proven Aunt Carolyn right in her eyes. She had feared that he would act out violently, that he was somehow deranged, and he had proven her right. Jacob didn't want to spend any extra time with her right then.

Swallowing hard, he reached for the lock and tried to ignore the slight trembling in his hands as he turned the key. There was resistance as the mechanism engaged. He turned harder, stepping closer to the device to take advantage of his center of gravity. The lock finally sprang and he removed it from its metal ring. The gate swung open and he stepped forward, over the threshold, releasing the ivy-covered metal behind him. With a head-splitting clank, the gate slammed shut.

It was hot, rainforest hot. At least thirty degrees warmer than the other side of the gate. He stripped off his sweatshirt and rolled up his pants before reaching through the ivy and placing the lock back on the gate handle. Dr. Silva must have had a reason for doing this and he thought it was a good idea to leave things the way he found them.

Following the overgrown trail, he was amazed at the variety of plants he encountered. John had mentioned Dr. Silva's rare plant collection and Jacob was beginning to appreciate its significance. There were rubber trees, bamboo, palms, and others he couldn't name. The plants were huge and thriving in an environment he could hardly believe existed in Illinois.

When he turned the corner, a sickly sweet smell met him head on, causing him to gag and bury his nose in his elbow. He wished he hadn't left his sweatshirt by the gate and could tie it around his face. The stench made his knees quiver. He recognized it for what it was. The smell of death.

In the back of his mind he hoped Dr. Silva didn't have anything to do with the smell. Was she capable of killing? He wasn't sure. Jacob had to admit finding a dead body out here wouldn't have surprised him.

A row of gigantic flowers, six feet tall, lined the bend in the trail. They were purplish black and covered in beetles. He followed the pebble pathway toward them, searching the ground for the source of the odor. The smell became more intense, almost unbearable. He forced himself to continue down the path and the smell gradually faded.

The corner of the gate's iron frame was barely visible now. The ivy seemed to be growing around it as he watched, covering what was left of the gate in thick green leaves. Once he turned the next corner, he would lose sight of it completely.

Jacob thought again about turning back. There was an odd feeling in his stomach, like he was at the top of a roller coaster, when you can't see anything but air and you know at any moment the cart is going to fall out from underneath you.

"Jaaacooob," a female voice sang from behind the trees. He whipped his head toward the giggle that followed and saw only a flash of flesh color between the green branches, followed by a rush of red fur.

"Dr. Silva?" he called, but the voice didn't sound like hers. It was higher, younger.

"Go back, Jacob," a deep male voice reverberated around him.

"Who is that? Who are you?" he said, turning in place.

Up ahead, farther down the trail, he saw the flash of flesh again, a hip, maybe an arm. Jacob couldn't tell what part of the body it was through the dense foliage but he knew it was a woman, a naked woman.

The female voice called to him again from the trees. "Don't listen to him, Jacob. Come this way. Don't you want to know?"

"Know what?" he called back. "Who are you? How do you know my name?"

There was no answer. A streak of red followed where the flesh color had been.

The smell of pumpkin pie wafted over him from up ahead and he found himself walking, only half conscious, toward the voice. Whoever she was, he wanted to know her. He wanted to see her. He felt pushed and pulled at the same time, a compulsion that forced one foot in front of the other instinctively.

The pebbles gave way to a narrow strip of stepping-stones, so grown over Jacob had to push aside branches to work his way through. In a normal garden this might not be a difficult task, but this was anything but a normal garden. Thorns the size of his hand grew from some of the plants. Bright colors and strangely shaped leaves made him tentative to touch others. The thick canopy allowed only pinpoints of light to filter down from above.

Everything about the place seemed wrong. For one, the size of the plants shouldn't have been able to fit within the boundaries of the property as he could see it from the street. He wondered if it was an optical illusion, the sloping terrain and winding trail making the garden seem bigger than it was. But that couldn't explain why it was at least ninety degrees. He tried not to think about it as he pushed a vine out of his way and stepped to the next stone.

A broad mass of spiky yellow needles, like a cactus but with no green trunk, bordered the trail. Jacob balanced on the far edge of the stone and slithered to the next. From this stone, he could see a vine with what looked like a two-foot cucumber growing from it on his right. It wouldn't have been as remarkable if it weren't fuzzy and blue, with a texture like mold and a middle that rippled like a jellyfish. The rippling was hypnotic and, as he continued down the path, he glanced back several times to watch.

The distraction caused him to trip over a root grown across the trail. The momentary illusion of flight gave way to a painful meeting of hands, knees, and stone.

"Crap!" he cursed. The fall had gashed his knee and blood ran down his calf.

"Have a nice trip! See you next fall," the girl's voice said with a giggle. He looked around but couldn't see anyone.

"Where are you? Who are you?" he called.

"Keep going and you'll find out."

He removed one of his socks and tied it tightly around the wound. Bending and unbending his knee, he tested if anything was broken. He got to his feet and tried to put some weight on it. Pain shot up his leg. There was no way he could go any farther. He decided to head back to the Laudners and talk with Dr. Silva later.

"Good, Jacob. Go home." The man's voice again.

As he moved to step over the pool of blood on the stone, Jacob reconsidered. What was the man's voice trying to keep from him? What was Jacob missing at the end of the path? If he left, he would never know.

Besides, going back was looking a lot more difficult. On both sides of the path a sprawling mass of flowers waved. Their heads looked like yellow snapdragons but their foliage was exotic like some type of orchid. The heads were slapping the bloody stone. If he continued this way, he would have to push past them. That was a bad idea: first, because they were moving without the benefit of any type of breeze and second, because they were licking the blood from the stone. The flowers were drinking his blood.

Jacob flinched as one of the flowers reached for the bloody sock around his knee. Its teeth latched onto the blood-soaked cotton. He backed away and a piece of the sock ripped off in the flower's jaws. "What the hell?" He turned and ran down the path to dodge the remaining swinging heads. What was this place? He leapt over a snapping yellow flower and bounded stone to stone toward a stream of light ahead. The forest opened.

From the shaded stepping stone path, Jacob emerged onto a delta of sand where the trees and plants ended. Panting and exhausted, he stooped forward with his palms on his knees and the sun on his back. Calling out for Dr. Silva wasn't an option. His mouth was too dry and, besides, he was sure he'd reach the back of the garden soon anyway. How big could this place be? There was no turning back now. His only hope was to find her.

Forward he trudged through what seemed like an acre more of meadow before the sandy path ran directly into a dune. The climb to the top left his muscles burning and his mouth dry as a stone. But from the top of the dune he could see the back wall of the garden. The ten-foot privet was a natural blockade to the skeletal forest beyond. In the valley between the dune and the back privet, a labyrinth of spiky cacti went on for miles. At the center, he could make out the twisting branches of a gigantic tree.

His head hurt. Where was Dr. Silva? Why had he come so far? Had the voices he'd heard before been a figment of his damaged brain? Exhausted and dehydrated, he suspected he was in trouble and was sure that if he sat down, he would never get back up. If he died here, would anyone ever find him?

He closed his eyes, longing for the Laudners' sage green recliner.

When he opened them again, he was surprised to see Gideon sitting in the sand by his feet.

"Where did you come from?" he croaked.

The cat gave a low growl.

"I don't suppose you know where Dr. Silva is?" he said to the cat. The animal stared at him for a long time. If Jacob didn't know better he would swear that Gideon was thinking something through. After some time, the cat blinked slowly, then started down the dune toward the maze. Jacob followed to the mouth of the labyrinth but the cat was too fast and by the time he entered under the thorny arch, Gideon was nowhere to be seen.

Instinctively, Jacob knew which way to go. It was the pulling feeling again, like he was navigating each bend on autopilot, trusting his gut with the labyrinth's twists and turns. He was disappointed not to hear the girl's voice again, but she had probably been a hallucination to begin with. It didn't matter. The important thing was finding Dr. Silva and then getting out of there before he collapsed.

When he reached the center of the maze, he was disappointed that Dr. Silva was not there, just the tree he'd seen from the dune. The gnarly, twisted trunk gave way to corkscrew branches that reached in all directions. The trunk was as wide as he was tall with layers that looked like multiple trees had grown together. The leaves of the tree started near the ends of the branches, allowing the sun to shine through the small green clusters. A thick layer of moss grew over the bark.

He'd never seen a tree like this before. But then, he was sure there'd never been a garden like this before. Just then, Gideon entered the center of the maze and sat down between the tree and Jacob.

"Where'd you come from?" he said to the cat, but then returned his attention to the tree. The moss on the bark looked soft and inviting. He took a step forward. It wasn't a conscious choice, more like riding on a conveyor belt.

Gideon leapt from his seat and knocked him to the sand.

"What's wrong with you?" Jacob yelled, pushing the cat off his stomach and standing back up. Gideon repositioned himself, growling. The animal looked absolutely deadly, all teeth and claws. But Jacob only cared about the tree. The twisting bark was so alluring. He wanted to run his hand along the moss and climb the twisting branches. He reached out and took another step toward the trunk.

Gideon leapt again, sinking his teeth into his wrist.

"Ouch! What the hell?" Jacob yelled, flinging the cat aside. It took more muscle than he expected. The cat had to weigh thirty pounds or more. Gideon rolled and moved to take another swipe, but this time Jacob didn't hesitate. He reached out.

His fingers connected with the roughness of the tree and everything slowed down. The bark climbed up his arm, as if the tree were swallowing him. Like he was changing from a liquid into a solid, every cell in his body hardened from animal to plant. Inside the tree looking out, he became the tree. A butterfly fluttered by as quickly as a jet plane. The air buzzed around him in a dance of gravitational pulls.

Looking up through the branches, he saw the clear blue sky above and slid up those corkscrew arms into the air. Then he was the sky. He was an ageless power in connection with something infinite.

Too soon, he was falling, sliding down through a new branch, turning inside out like his stomach was lurching through his belly button. Only, his stomach wasn't a stomach but layers of wood growing one on top of the other. Until, the last layer hit the air and his bark became skin. And then he was only touching the bark.

Jacob was human again but he was not in the cactus maze.

In front of the tree that was not the tree in Dr. Silva's garden but a tree on the edge of a wild jungle, he finally collapsed. His body could take no more and his knees buckled underneath him until his butt was firmly planted at the base of the tree. Propped against the trunk, he stared across a large open plain. A purple, white-capped mountain rose up beyond a sprawling savannah.

It looked a lot like Africa.

He shook his head in disbelief but watched the heads of a pod of giraffes bob as they ran across the plain, a spotted machine. He licked his lips. Hallucinating. He was hallucinating. But the more he attempted to free himself from the delirium, the more real it seemed.

The grasses parted unevenly a hundred yards ahead, no more noticeable than a gentle breeze. A lioness crept forward from the greenish brown savannah, yellow eyes locked onto him. She was hunting Jacob and he was easy prey. His legs felt like rubber bands. Whatever magic had brought him there had drained every ounce of energy he'd had left. All he could do was watch in fear as the predator inched closer, and hope that she was a figment of his dehydrated brain.

The lioness pounced, teeth flashing.

Claws sank into his back, but they were not the claws of the lioness. A hand grabbed him by the shirt, pulling him backward, plunging him into the tree's slowing sensation. As he was absorbed into the bark, he saw the lioness fall to the earth in fast-forward before experiencing the funny inside out feeling again, but backward. Then he was sliding down a branch and folding into a tree trunk. Until, finally, he was Jacob again, lying on a patch of sand looking up into the sky.

No ... he was looking up into two sky-blue eyes.

Dr. Silva's face hovered above him, her frown stern and resolute. She glanced at the tree, which now appeared normal in its cactus habitat, and then back at him on the sandy mound.

"Well," she said with a sigh, "I see that you've found Oswald. Jacob, it is time we had a serious talk."

Chapter 15
The Root Of The Problem

"There's no sense hiding it from you now. I'm going to need your help keeping this a secret. Let's go back to the house and get you cleaned up. I'll explain everything over lunch." Dr. Silva reached for his elbow and helped him to stand.

Jacob's knees wobbled. As hard as he tried, he couldn't get his mind to form coherent words, his thoughts a jumble of images lost in translation. Without asking permission, she grabbed his arm and rolled him onto her back, piggyback style.

"Don't worry, the feeling should clear up in a half hour or so," she said. Dr. Silva navigated the cactus maze with astounding speed considering his added weight. He could already see the sand dune.

"It's amazing that you made it through the cacti unharmed. Some of them are quite poisonous—even deadly. Of course, I planted them myself to keep people out. You can see why, I'm sure. There could be ... complications, if Oswald was accessible to the wrong people." She stepped down the stone pathway, between the snapdragons and past the blue cucumber.

"That bloody knee has my *Dracaena Daemonorops* in a state." The plants swayed violently and he could feel Dr. Silva accelerate across the stones, dodging the yellow heads. When the teeth of one succeeded in latching onto the bloody sock again, she casually reached into her pocket and pulled out garden shears. Without missing a step, she clipped the flower at its neck and the head dropped to the stone walkway.

Moments later, he was overcome with the stench of rotting flesh. He buried his face in his arm to escape it.

"Yeah, that will bring you around." Dr. Silva laughed. "They are *Amorphophallus titanum*—very rare. The smell is to attract flies and beetles, which pollinate the flowers. Totally harmless but, again, meant to deter. Apparently, you were not to be discouraged."

She bounded through the gate, carefully unlocking and locking it behind her. Before he knew what was happening, he landed on his backside beneath the shady maples, a mass of achy joints and throbbing temples. She handed him a bottle of water from a pocket in her cargo pants. He drank greedily, his blood bounding in his veins. A moan escaped his lips as he broke contact with the bottle to catch his breath.

"Right. Keep drinking. I've heard it feels like altitude sickness ... to your kind." In her hand was his sweatshirt. She wrapped it around him, pursing her lips against the puff of compost that escaped the fabric, and helped him get his flaccid arms into the sleeves. He noticed she was wearing a sleeveless black T-shirt but didn't seem the least bit cold. She tucked the empty bottle into her pocket and hoisted him onto her back as gracefully as if he were her cape.

When they reached the sunroom off the kitchen, she dumped his body into a rattan chair.

"What the hell?" he stammered.

"Now, Jacob, relax and listen to what I have to say. There's a logical explanation for all of this. Wait here, I'll be right back." She left the room and returned several minutes later with a tray of pita bread, hummus, cheese, and assorted fruits and vegetables. "I hope this is all right. I'm a vegetarian." She poured them both a tall glass of water and settled into the chair across from him.

Hunger is a powerful motivator. Jacob started in on the tray with no regard for manners. "I'm listening," he said between bites.

"It was a mutual love of plants that brought Oswald and I together," she began, and as she did she turned her head slightly and stared at a spot on the wall. "I was a graduate student studying the plants of India when I made the most remarkable find while visiting the Bengali marketplace. It was an amazing specimen that any horticulturalist would be proud to display. The seed of the Coco de mer can be found naturally only in the Seychelles, a group of islands off the coast of Madagascar. It was a truly incredible find, easily forty pounds or more, and I was haggling with the shopkeeper for it. I can be very persuasive. The seed was as good as mine.

"Oswald swept into the shop and recognized my prize immediately. I would be lying if I told you I wasn't immediately taken with him. He was quite an attractive man, my husband. But I was more concerned at the moment with acquiring the find of my career. In perfect Bengali, he told the shopkeeper he would pay whatever he asked and proceeded to buy the seed right from under my nose for the equivalent of fifty U.S. dollars. I followed him out of the shop, of course, demanding that he return the seed to me at once.

"'Lady,' he said, 'I know that you probably want this as a decorative mantelpiece but I will have you know this is a—'

"'—A priceless seed! It is the largest in the world. A truly remarkable botanical find,' I said.

"We agreed at that moment to join each other for dinner, to discuss who was the rightful owner of the seed. I learned he was a young professor and also from the United States, California specifically. After spending two weeks together in India, Oswald gave me that seed as an engagement present. We returned to the United States and I convinced him to move here, to my house.

"Our marriage was one adventure after another. We traveled all over the world, you see, studying plants of all sorts and discovering new species. At one point we had the largest natural seed collection of anyone in the United States. But he died, as all men do."

Jacob stopped eating at "died." Her face was different as she talked about Oswald and he could tell this was a difficult memory for her. "I'm so sorry. That must have been horrible. What did you do?" he asked softly.

"Once I confirmed he was dead, I buried him in the garden."

"Wha—excuse me?" Jacob spit out a bite of pita and looked Dr. Silva in the eye.

"I buried him in the garden," she said again. "It was what he always wanted. It was in his will. He loved plants. He wanted to be part of nature, eternally."

"But didn't you have to go to the emergency room or call the police or something?"

"Jacob, this isn't TV, it's Paris. I called the coroner, he was pronounced dead, and I buried him. That's all. No fanfare, no funeral, no autopsy. It wasn't required back then."

Jacob sat back in the cream futon and raised his eyebrows. The only thing he could think to say was "okay," which must have been enough because she continued.

"I did the best I could to bury him. It was probably not deep enough. Not as deep anyway as they bury you in a cemetery, but he was my first grave. I buried him in the fall. The ground froze over that winter and I trudged through the snow to visit his grave. In the spring, I was ecstatic to find a sapling growing there. I knew then that his blood had unlocked deep magic."

"Magic? Are you a witch?" he blurted.

"No. I. Am. Not." She held up a finger in front of his face. No further explanation was offered. She continued with her story.

"As the year progressed and the tree grew faster than any, I realized that the air around the tree was always warm and humid, no matter what the temperature. I began planting some of our collection of rare seeds around Oswald. Everything grew, faster and larger than possible. It is always around eighty-five degrees there, three hundred sixty-five days per year. I took precautions—the hedge, the corpse plants, the cacti maze—to make sure that I was the only one who knew the secret of the garden.

"Even I did not learn of Oswald's greatest secret until later. I was transported the first time in the summer, when Oswald had reached his full height. I was lucky to be found by a medicine woman. She was a Healer and an elder of the Achuar tribe of the South American rainforest. See, they have none of the preconceptions about time and space that we do. She just assumed my presence was a sign from the spirit world and took me in. She showed me what I needed to know. That's when Gideon came to me." She looked across the room at the cat. "I've been traveling with Oswald ever since."

Jacob blinked. Was she serious? "So, you can travel anywhere in the world through the tree?"

"Well, to anywhere there are trees. They are connected … spiritually."

He didn't really understand but nodded his head anyway.

"But, Jacob, that's not the most important thing I have to tell you."

At that moment, Gideon rushed across the room and jumped into the chair next to him. A growl escaped his throat. Jacob rubbed the bite mark on his wrist. He was beginning to think the cat was downright moody.

"Oh, Gideon, it's time he knew. How long do you expect me to wait?"

Jacob interrupted. "There's something you have to tell me that's more shocking than the news that you've buried your dead husband in the garden and his body has grown a magical tree?" Saying it out loud sounded even more ridiculous than hearing it.

"Yes. It's about you, Jacob. About who you are and who you are becoming."

"Me?"

"You. See, my garden, the other garden, is enchanted. Only a spiritual being can find Oswald. Spirit finds spirit. A normal human being would wander aimlessly, if they ever managed to get through the gate at all."

"But that's me, normal human being." He waved his fingers, just to make the point.

"Really? Nothing has ever happened to you to make you think you might be something more?" Dr. Silva raised an eyebrow.

Jacob looked into his glass. The fight with Dane at the grocery store came to mind, but he didn't answer.

Dr. Silva's eyes bore into him.

"Admit it or not, your genealogy is written in records that are not of this world."

"Huh."

"Here, look at this." Dr. Silva poured a drop of water from her glass onto her saucer. "What do you see here?"

"A drop of water."

"And what do you know about water."

"You drink it."

"No, no. That's not what I mean. How do I start? I guess I should just say it. Water is alive, Jacob." She touched the water with her finger and watched it roll down her hand to her wrist. "In every drop of water live over one hundred thousand microbes, so, it is quite literally alive. It is the universal solvent, required for all life. It is the beginning of all things. Water is strong enough to wear down mountains but agile enough to move through the tiniest crevice. Your body is two-thirds water and every cell in it responds to that water."

"Yeah, uhm, it's amazing," Jacob said. He reached for his glass and gulped down half of it, then wiped his mouth with the back of his hand and belched.

Dr. Silva's mouth pulled into a straight line.

"A long time ago, there were two people, a man and a woman, the first two people who ever walked the Earth. I think you know them as Adam and Eve."

"Uh, yeah, I've heard of Adam and Eve."

"Then you know that the serpent persuaded them to eat the fruit and as their punishment God cast them out of the Garden of Eden."

"So?"

"God knew they would need help resisting the temptations of the Serpent, of the evil that existed on the Earth. He allowed some of the water from Eden to run out of the garden, down to where Adam settled. The water was made to be undetectable to all but those who had a sincere desire to devote themselves to ridding the world of evil. When the pure of heart drank the water, it changed the drinker. That water infused into the person's cells, changing their DNA, changing their blood. It gave them gifts, power they could use to defend themselves against evil."

"Uhuh. Right. Gosh, I gotta go." Jacob looked at his watch, and then pushed his chair back from the table.

"They spread out across the globe, Jacob, doing the will of God." Her voice was frantic now, anxious. She stood and was behind him in the blink of an eye. Her hands pressed into his shoulders, keeping him in his seat. "They kept the balance between good and evil in favor of good. But they married and had children and, as they did, the water became more and more diluted and the children became more and more human, their gifts diminished."

"Damn, the bad luck," he said and tried to stand, but her nails dug into his flesh.

"Hope found a way. When a descendant of a brother and a descendant of a sister married and had children the two halves became whole again. The water became more pure. The power returned. And now, today, there are among us the descendants of those the water changed, charged with carrying on the work of God. You are one of those descendants, Jacob. You are a Soulkeeper and you have the power to combat darkness. The power to fight evil."

"What power?" he laughed nervously.

"Every Soulkeeper has power as individual as a fingerprint but each is an integral player in the battle between heaven and hell. You've probably heard of people with the gene for a certain type of disease. The gene is always there but the person may or may not get the disease. Something happens, a stressor, and the gene flips on. This is the same. People like you carry the gene. You've always had it, since you were born. But it takes something big to turn it on: something like losing your parents or being attacked in a parking lot."

"How do you know about that?"

"It's a small town. Word travels fast."

"But nobody saw but Malini."

"I didn't have to see, Jacob. Not in the way you do. Why don't you tell me what happened and we can get started?"

"Started with what?"

"I am your Helper. I've been assigned to help you discover your gifts. I can help you discover your true purpose."

"You're crazy." Jacob squirmed from her grasp, knocking the chair to the floor. Pain shot through his knee as he stood. "This is nuts. Why are you saying these things to me? I don't even believe in God."

"Don't believe in God?" Dr. Silva's face twisted into a scowl. "Do you believe in the atom? In the air you breathe? How can you deny the very fabric of who you are?" She shook her head. "Believe or not, Jacob, I am your Helper. You are my assignment and I will help you discover what you were sent here to do."

"I don't believe any of this," he said in a whisper, shaking his head and backing toward the door.

"The memory you told me about last Saturday, the vivid one, did it ever occur to you that it wasn't entirely normal? Awfully odd how close to real life it played out, isn't it?"

"How do you know about that?"

"You told me. And, what about that black eye, Jacob? It's already happening." She grinned. "Just like osmosis, the goodness in you will always attract evil. Have you ever wondered why trouble always seems to find you? You are discovering your power. Now all you need to do is allow me to help you figure out how to use it." Her voice was breathy, almost hypnotic. She walked over to Jacob and reached for his hand.

He jerked away, mind reeling. None of this made sense. All he wanted to do was get out of this house and never come back. Continuing toward the door, he saw alarm sweep across her perfectly carved features.

"Don't go," she said, and the edge was back in her voice. The smell of fresh baked cookies washed over him like a fog, and his skin tingled.

"What are you? What are you doing to me?" He forced himself to keep backing up even though the electric sensation, the attraction, hit him full force. He turned toward the door and reached for the knob.

"Your mother! I can help you find your mother." Dr. Silva's voice was high pitched and quick.

Jacob wanted to leave. He wanted to never come back. Dr. Silva scared him and he thought she was crazy. But months ago he'd made a choice to not give up on his mom no matter what. He couldn't let this go, no matter how unlikely it was to be true.

"Can you? Can you find her? Can the tree … take me to her?" He turned from the door and met her icy stare. The temptation was too great. If there was any hope, any hope at all…

"Oh, it doesn't work that way. You have to know exactly where you want to go and then concentrate on the longitude and latitude. Date and time have an effect. It's not like boarding an airplane. It's taken me decades to master."

"Decades?" Jacob looked at the woman in front of him. She looked to be in her late twenties but clearly after all she had told him she must be much older. "How old are you?"

"Another time, Jacob. I'll explain everything in time. There is much to learn. But right now, what you want is to find your mother. And what I want is for you to work with me, to allow me to be your Helper."

"Will you take me to Oahu then, to look for her?"

"Jacob, where would you stay? Where would you even begin to look? Who's to say she's even there? She could be dead."

Jacob rubbed his temples. He didn't know the answer to her questions and was feeling awfully tired. Gideon weaved between his ankles. The soft fur was oddly comforting and his shoulders relaxed a little. Still, he couldn't find his voice.

"We could visit the medicine woman," she offered. Her hand reached toward him, cautious, nervous, as if her life depended on his answer. "You could come with me and we could ask her. Maybe, she could tell us where your mom is. If you agree to train with me, I will take you to her and we will find out."

Jacob dropped his fingers from his temples and looked Dr. Silva in the eye. "Okay. I still don't believe what you're telling me, but if you help me find my mom, I'll do it."

"It's a deal!" she said. A smile crossed her face, like she'd just won the lottery.

As she pumped his hand, up and down, up and down, he wondered what she had in store for him. His gut instinct was to run and never look back.

Jacob regretted the agreement, even as he made it.

Chapter 16
Oswald's Rules

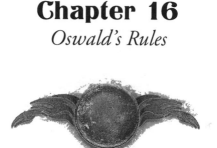

While the hope of finding his mother comforted Jacob, he was disappointed to learn he'd have to be patient for his journey to meet the medicine woman. Dr. Silva explained certain locations were possible only on certain dates. The next time the tree was connected to the South American Amazon was June 10th, the day after Jacob's sixteenth birthday, and two months away.

Later that night, he lay on the pink bed thinking about what Dr. Silva had told him about his blood. There was no way Jacob believed it. It didn't make any sense. Still, he was sure that what happened with the tree was not a hallucination. The hardest part would be keeping it all from Malini. Ever since the incident with Dane, she had desperately jumped at any clue to what had happened that day. He cared deeply for her but he knew if he told her what Dr. Silva had said, she would believe every word. The last thing Jacob wanted was any more pressure to believe the impossible.

Plunk

Something skimmed across his window. He glanced at the clock: 11:30 PM. He cringed when he thought of Dr. Silva visiting his window weeks ago and hoped it wasn't her.

Cachink

A stone skipped across the glass and he decided it was more human than anything he'd expect from Dr. Silva. It was, after all, a stone and not the glowing skull of a dead husband. He stood up and looked out into the front yard. Malini was waving from the lawn, her hand full of rocks. Jacob opened the window.

"I need to talk to you," she whispered.

He pointed to the rose lattice on the side of the house. She scaled it with ease and he reached out to help her inside.

"Nice room," she said with a grin.

Jacob had never hated the pink room more.

"Long story." He closed the window behind her. "How did you get here?"

"Drove." She held up a set of keys. "I know I won't be legal until September but all those driving lessons should count for something. I had to see you."

"It's great to see you too, but what's going on?"

She leaned against the floral wingback. A sigh escaped her lips. "I just needed to talk to someone."

"Why? What happened?"

"We were sitting at home tonight. I was just watching TV, you know; it's not like there's a ton to do in Paris on a weeknight."

"Right."

"Well, the doorbell rang and my dad answered it. It was a deliveryman from Paris Pizza. Jacob, they sent ten pizzas to my house."

"Who?"

"I can only guess it was Amy or Jessica."

Amy was Dane's girlfriend and Jacob suspected the reason for the prank. Although his lip and eye had healed, the animosity had not. None of them ever talked about what actually happened that day at Westcott's grocery, but everyone at school knew there was something. Only, somehow, all of the speculation had Dane coming out on top.

"Dane. Dane was behind this," Jacob said.

"What makes you so sure?"

"I just know. Tell me what happened next."

"My dad just shook his head and said we didn't order any pizzas. The driver said that Malini Gupta ordered them. So, my dad calls me to the door, right in front of this man, and asks me why I ordered the pizza. I tell him that I didn't. But my dad keeps asking me over and over, 'Why are there ten pizzas here?' Meanwhile, the driver is looking for his money. He says we owe like a hundred dollars. My dad is having a fit and finally, I say to him, 'Dad, I think this is a prank, the girls from school, again.'"

"So what did he do?"

"It was the weirdest thing, Jacob. He reached into his wallet and paid the man. After the driver had delivered all ten pizzas to our kitchen counter, my dad turned to me, looked me straight in the eye, and said, 'Tomorrow, you tell the girls thank you for the pizza. You all laugh and try to be friends.'"

"What?"

"He just doesn't get it. He thinks this is all normal hazing, that it will somehow get better once people get to know me. We've

been here two years. They hate me. They will always hate me."
Malini's warm chocolate eyes glistened wet in the moonlight.

Jacob moved in close and kissed the top of her head. "Bastards."
He took her hand and led her to sit on the edge of the bed.

"You're the only one who understands, Jake. I don't know what
I would do without you."

He swallowed hard and looked at the floor.

"What was that? What were you thinking about just then?"
Malini asked.

"Nothing."

"You're keeping something from me."

"I…" He searched for the right words. "Malini, if I could figure
out a way to get us out of here—out of this town—would you
come with me?"

"You mean, like, permanently?"

"Yes."

"That's it, then. That's what you've been hiding. You're
thinking of running away."

He nodded. It wasn't really a lie. He was just leaving out some
information about using a tree that grew out of a dead guy to get
there.

"You can't go." Malini's arms crossed over her chest. "I can't
go. We're fifteen, Jake. How would we survive? I mean, believe me
I know, I want to go as much as you do, but this is temporary. We
just need to graduate from high school first and then we can go to
some college somewhere and leave this town in our dust. It's the
only way that makes sense."

Her hand was so small in his. He rubbed her knuckle with his
thumb and thought about leaving without her. Could life get any
harder than this? And then, as if in answer to his question, her lips

were on his, her fingers were in his hair, and he was falling back on the pink comforter, her full weight stretched out on top of him.

"Don't leave me," she whispered into his ear.

Jacob kissed her cheek, breathing in the clean smell of her skin. Then he met her lips again.

She was the only girl he'd ever kissed, and the experience was still new. He didn't think he would ever grow tired of the softness of her lips or the way her hair fell against his face. Before he could really think about what he was saying, he replied, "I won't."

"Good," she said and crawled off the bed. He grabbed her thigh and looked up into her eyes, the moon reflecting yellow circles in the brown.

"So that was it? All you wanted from me was a promise to not leave you in Paris by yourself?"

"No," she said, a smile creeping impishly across her face. "I also wanted the kiss."

"Lucky me."

"I better get back." She walked toward the window and then suddenly turned toward the box that sat on his desk.

"What's that?"

"A jewelry box. It used to belong to my mom. I haven't been able to get it open though. It's locked."

Her fingers found her hair and pulled out the bobby pin that was holding her bangs back. She reached for the box as a chunk of hair fell over her right eye.

"You don't have to do that," he began, but before he finished his sentence the box was open. Without looking under the lid, she handed it back to him.

"You should do the honors," she said.

He took the box and peeked inside. The blood rushed from his face and Jacob felt his hands grow cold. The box snapped shut between his fingers.

"This must be hard for you," she said. "You miss your mom. Do you want me to leave you to your thoughts?"

He nodded. Jacob set the box down and moved with Malini toward the window. With his hand under her elbow, he helped her climb out.

"McNulty's tomorrow after school?" she asked.

"Sure."

She was down the lattice and smiling back at him from the yard in a few lithe moves. He waved as she moved toward her car.

When she was out of sight, he returned to the box on the bed and lifted the lid. It was not a jewelry box at all. Inside there were three indentations in blue velvet. The first two were filled with knives. Double-sided blades with polished bone hilts glinted ominously in the moonlight.

The last indentation was empty.

Chapter 17
The Fight

"LAU," Dane Michaels barked from the end of the row of mustard-yellow lockers.

Jacob turned but did not respond. He was waiting for Malini to finish talking to Mrs. Jacques about a job working in the Biology lab. It was the end of the day, and the hall was empty.

"Lau, I'm talking to you." Dane spread his hands like he was surprised Jacob wasn't responding, as if they talked every day.

"What do you want, Dane?"

"I want to show you something. Can you come with me, outside?"

"No."

"Come on, Lau. There's someone I need you to meet." Dane looked agitated. He had dark circles under his eyes and Jacob could smell that spicy sweet stench on him again, like a combination of cigarette smoke, alcohol, and coffee breath.

"Why would I go with you, Dane? What? Are a bunch of your friends going to jump me as soon as we're outside?"

"No. It's not like that. Listen, Lau, I met someone who wants to meet you. I don't know why but it's important. Just come with me, all right?"

"No way. I'm not going anywhere with you. If you're going to do something to me, do it right here. And, don't think I don't know you were behind what happened to Malini last night." He pointed a finger at Dane's face.

Dane chuckled. "Hey, that was just a joke. Besides, it was Amy, not me. Now stop messing around and come on." His hand shot out and grabbed Jacob's shoulder.

"Let go of me," he said, yanking free of Dane's grip.

Dane looked frustrated. He opened his mouth as if to say something else but then seemed to give up. Instead, he sank his shoulder into Jacob's gut and tried to lift him from the floor. Apparently if he wasn't willing to come voluntarily, Dane was prepared to force him.

Jacob sank a knee into his chest and with a twist freed himself. Thinking fast, he sprinted toward the office. No way would Dane pursue him there. But he was wrong. Something hard hit his ankles and his forearms slapped the linoleum floor with such force, pain shot up both elbows. He clenched his teeth to avoid yelling out. Paris High School had a zero tolerance policy. If he was caught fighting with Dane, they'd both be suspended regardless of who started it.

Dane's body weight was on top of his calves from the tackle. There had to be something he could do to fight him off. But every time he pushed himself up off the floor, Dane pulled his legs back, flattening him to the linoleum. The worst part was he knew Malini would be coming out of Mrs. Jacques' room any minute. If Dane hurt her…

In an army crawl, he pulled Dane toward the wall. If he could just get some leverage, he might be able to flip himself over. He reached for the pipes of the water fountain across from the office. The silver tube hung down from the porcelain bowl, almost level with his head, and he desperately gripped the cold steel. The humming started again, the same as that day at the grocery store. He could hear the water, calling to him from the pipes. Everything slowed. He tried to gather the hum inside, like he'd done before.

The door to Mrs. Jacques' room opened. It was now or never.

The release reverberated inside his chest. Water sprayed from the fountain toward Dane's face, not a gentle spray but like hail that formed in the air. The sharp pieces pegged Dane in the forehead and he released Jacob's ankles to block his face with his hands.

"Ahh! Crap!" Dane yelled from behind his forearms.

Jacob flipped onto his feet, leapt over Dane, and headed for Malini, who was emerging from the science lab.

The fountain stopped, just as Principal Bailey stepped out from the office door.

"What's going on out here?" he asked. His eyes moved from Dane to the puddle of water on the floor, which was all that was left of the hail, and then toward Jacob. He stood at the other end of the hall, completely dry.

Dane stood on wobbly legs, holding his head.

Principal Bailey gave Dane another once over and then turned back toward Malini and Jacob. Eyes squinting in their direction, he looked much older than the man Jacob had met the first day of school.

"You two move along," he said. He placed a hand on Dane's arm. "Let's have a talk in my office, Dane."

"We need to go," Jacob said to Malini. He took her hand and headed for the exit. As he held the door open for her, he looked back to see Dane seething with rage as he followed Principal Bailey into his office.

"What was that all about?" Malini asked.

"Dane."

Malini needed no further explanation. She nodded and walked faster toward Main Street.

* * * * *

"So what did he say to you?" Malini asked once they were safely nestled into their regular booth at McNaulty's.

"He wanted me to come with him. He said he wanted to, I don't know, introduce me to someone or something. It was really weird."

"What do you think he was trying to do?"

"It's obvious. He wanted to get back at me for that day at Westcott's. I'm sure a bunch of his friends were waiting somewhere to beat me senseless."

Malini took a deep breath, puffing up her cheeks before allowing the air to escape her lips.

"Don't worry about it," Jacob said. "School is almost over and I'm sure Dane will find something better to do than to torment us over the summer."

"I hope you're right."

With school winding down for the year, Jacob was looking forward to being free of Dane's clutches. As a bonus, Katrina would be graduating. She'd been accepted at the University of

Illinois. It would be a relief to not have her around next year. Of course, he hoped not to be there either. If all went well with Dr. Silva, he'd be back home on Oahu in a few weeks.

"What are you doing this weekend?" Malini asked.

"I have to work." He didn't attempt to hide the disappointment in his voice.

"That's right, you're still working for your neighbor to pay off the window."

"Yep. I have a feeling it's going to take a while."

"Is it hard work?"

"If you consider shoveling compost for five hours hard work."

"Ugh. Sounds awful. Is that woman nice to you?"

"Dr. Silva? She's all right, I guess," he said. There was no way he was going to try to explain his relationship with Dr. Silva.

"Hmm, because she gives me the creeps."

"You've met her?"

"Just once, with my dad. She came into his office to file the claim on her window. My dad started acting strange, like he couldn't do enough for her. She just kept staring him down. Have you noticed how she rarely blinks? How she almost always wears black? And, her house gives new meaning to the term Goth."

"Did you talk with her?" he asked.

"No. I wasn't feeling well, so I excused myself. It didn't stop me from hearing their conversation though. It was embarrassing the way my dad tripped over himself to help her. She was just, I don't know, odd."

"Yeah, you should see her cat. Creepy big and she doesn't go anywhere without it."

"Wow, so I was right. She's totally whacked."

"As far as I can tell."

The sound of the door opening behind him interrupted their conversation. Uncle John entered and walked up to their booth.

"Jacob, I'm done at the store. It's time to go," he said. "Hello, Malini."

"Hi, Mr. Laudner."

"Do you need a ride home?"

"No, sir, I'm meeting my dad at his office."

"Okay then."

"See you later," Jacob said, sliding from the booth to follow John out the door and across the pebble parking lot to Big Blue.

"How was your day?" John asked as he started the engine and pulled out onto Main Street.

"Fine," Jacob answered toward the window.

"Seems like you're spending a lot of time with Malini. She a nice girl?"

"Yep."

They sat in silence for a while, as John made the turn onto Rural Route One. Jacob stared out the window and hoped John wouldn't try to talk with him again. Without warning, the truck veered onto the shoulder and came to a rough stop.

Surprised, Jacob turned toward John. The man stared over the steering wheel, eyes blank. His foot rested on the brake.

"John?" he prodded.

"Jacob, do you know why I brought you here, to Paris?" he said to the windshield.

Jacob didn't answer. He didn't know.

"Do you think a person is only as good as the worst thing they've ever done?" John turned to face him as he said it, shifting the car into park.

Jacob thought about what his uncle said. Memories of all the things he'd done wrong in his life came rushing back: memories of

his father and mother punishing him for getting into a fight at
school, staying out past dark, and the time he tried unsuccessfully
to steal candy from the grocery store. He remembered his parents
explaining to him, loving him through his mistakes. He thought of
the day with Katrina's dolls, how angry he'd been. Then he
thought about his mother and the fight they'd had in the
apartment. If he believed she was only as good as the worst thing
she'd ever done, he'd have given up on her long ago.

"No, I think people make mistakes and learn from them. I
think most people get better after the worst thing they've done—if
they want to."

"Well, what happened with your dad was the worst thing I've
ever done." He rubbed the stubble on his chin and looked at the
floor of the car. "I brought you here because I lost touch with your
father before he died. You look so much like him, you know. Sure
your coloring's a little different but your eyes, the way you hold
your head ... What I'm trying to say, Jacob, is that I brought you
here because I want to know you. I want to know who you are."

"Why?" Jacob snapped. "I'm never going to be what you want
me to be. I'm not like you or the people here. This isn't home to
me."

"That may be true and you may only be here for the next three
years and then be off to fame and fortune, to never speak to a
Laudner again. But aren't you curious, Jacob? Doesn't even some
part of you want to know who your father was? I lived with your
father for eighteen years, you know. We were close for a long time.
Don't you want to know what he was like?"

Jacob couldn't look away from John's eyes. For the first time,
he saw in John what John had seen in him. John was Charlie's
brother. They shared the same chin, the same pale green eyes, and

more importantly the same history. He had to admit, what John said was starting to make sense.

"Jacob, this thing that you are doing. This, I talk to you and you do everything in your power not to talk back thing, it's not getting it done."

"I talk to you!"

"Only if you want something or if I ask you a direct question. Never because you want to. Nothing about this relationship is going to help either one of us keep the spirit of your father alive. If that's how you want it, then continue this attitude. But if you want something more—if you want to actually be part of your father's family, be here, really be here with us. I, for one, would love to have you."

John turned back to the steering wheel, threw the car into drive, and re-entered the road. The only sound in the car was the familiar roll of the wheels on imperfect concrete and pebbles clinking against the rusty trucks exterior. Mile after mile rolled by with John's words tumbling inside Jacob's head.

It wasn't until John turned into the driveway that Jacob decided.

"Okay," he whispered. "I'd really like to know more about my dad and his family."

That evening, Jacob spent hours going through Laudner family albums with John. He told John stories of the last years of his dad's life and John told him about the early years. By midnight, both of them knew each other better and started to piece together the life of the man who was both Charlie Laudner and Charles Lau.

Together, they picked out a picture from the back of one of the albums, his father in his army uniform, and hung it in the upstairs hallway. It had been a long time since Charlie's photograph had hung beside his brothers and sisters. The image looked at home there, now.

Jacob lay under the pink comforter that night and stared into the darkness. Although he still wanted to find his mom and he still hated Paris, he wasn't angry anymore. The last thought that entered his mind as he drifted off to sleep was the sensation that his dad was somehow watching over him. Somewhere, in the darkness, he was with him.

Chapter 18
No One Said Anything About Shots

Jacob's theory that Dr. Silva would take it easy on him because he knew about Oswald proved false, and he found himself sweating over some disgusting horticultural task every Saturday morning. It was just such a day, when he was weeding the seedling tomato plants in the raised beds, that Dr. Silva approached him with a smile that showed a few too many teeth.

"June tenth is just around the corner."

"Yes, I know. I'm excited to go."

"Yes, yes, I'm sure. But there are preparations to be made." She was standing with her hands behind her back.

He stopped digging and dusted the dirt from his pants. "What kind of preparations?"

"Roll up your sleeve."

"Why?"

"Oh for Pete's sake, just do it. Would it kill you to trust me just this once?"

Since she put it that way, he rolled up his sleeve. No sooner had he pulled his hand away than hers shot out and grabbed his bare shoulder. Jacob barely saw the glint of the needle before she thrust it into his muscle like a dart and pressed the plunger. It was over before he could say, "Owww."

"We are traveling to the Amazon. Immunizations—just in case." She held up the empty syringe.

"You could have just asked me," he said, rubbing his arm.

"It hurts more if you can see it coming, or so I am told."

"You've never had a shot, have you?" he asked.

"Don't need them," she said.

"I don't suppose you are going to tell me why?"

"It's not important. What is important is that we make all of the preparations for our trip."

"Okay. What else do I need to do?"

"Get a passport."

"I don't remember Oswald asking for a passport when he sent me to Africa."

"Jacob, this isn't like climbing on an airplane. It isn't a tested form of transportation for humans. If something happens to me, or we find ourselves in a place with no trees, you have to have a way to get back into the country."

"As luck would have it, I already have a passport. My mom always said it was important, just in case. What else?"

"We will have to stay overnight."

"Huh? Why?"

"We need the medicine woman to dream. There is a ceremony that has to be performed. This can only happen at night. The Achuar people are a culture steeped in tradition."

"So, what do I tell the Laudners?"

"I will tell John you are helping me do some research on a new species of plant and the procedure needs to be performed over twenty-four hours. I think he will allow you to stay. I can be very persuasive." She lowered her chin and looked at him through her lashes.

Jacob's heart skipped a beat and he internally slapped himself.

He thought about the ruse. It was a good story but not true. Over the last couple of weeks he'd gotten to know his Uncle John and lying to him suddenly felt wrong. He knew he couldn't tell him the truth but he wished he didn't have to lie. He wouldn't have had a problem lying to Aunt Carolyn or Katrina. They still treated him like an unwanted pet.

"I'm glad you are asking. I don't think I can lie to him."

"You are the loyal sort aren't you? Well, whatever works. I will ask him soon so that we don't have any problems on the tenth. I don't want John to come looking for you. That could be a disaster."

"Okay. Shots, passport, permission for overnight," he recited. "Anything else?"

"No. Just dress appropriately for the jungle," she said.

Jacob turned back to his work but soon the weight of her stare became distracting. "Is there something else?" he asked.

She ran her nails through Gideon's bushy red hair. "It's time for your first lesson."

Jacob rolled his eyes. That was the deal: a trip to see the medicine woman in exchange for going along with this delusion that he was a Soulkeeper. "What do I need to do?"

"Let's worry about what you need to know first, then we'll move on to do." She began to pace up and down the row between the flat beds. "There are people all over the world that work for good, ordinary people that do extraordinary things in the name of God. But there are also people like you. You and the others of your kind are not normal people. Your bodies are different because your blood is different. Your parents gave you abilities beyond the average human." Dr. Silva was digging through a pile of gardening supplies. She pulled out a large bowl-shaped liner, the kind she used in the planters at the front of the house.

"There are three types of gifts that Soulkeepers possess. There are Helpers, like me, who use their power to help others. This could mean anything from gathering weapons to helping someone learn about their gifts. For instance, training you. Every Helper has a specialty, and as you may have guessed, mine is horticulture."

"Yeah, horticulture on steroids," he quipped.

She handed him the bowl and walked to the side of the house. "Other gifted ones are called Horsemen. They are warriors. They fight evil by physical force, when all other interventions have failed. They are soldiers for God. King David, from history, was a Horseman. So was Moses." Pausing, she took a long look at Jacob, giving him the distinct impression she was sizing him up. "And then there are Healers. Healers are very rare. I've only ever met one personally—the medicine woman. They are the ones that can tell good from evil."

Jacob laughed. "Since when did it become a gift to tell good from evil?"

"Since the devil became the lord of illusions. It's very easy to do evil deeds when you are trying to do good."

"Hmm." He leaned against the garden bench and crossed his arms over his chest.

"Healers are leaders because they know what direction will lead to the greater good. Not only can they heal people physically, they can heal situations—solve problems. Noah was a Healer. He had to solve the problem of the Ark, of how to heal mankind." She smiled down at him.

"So, which one am I?" he asked.

"I don't know yet, but we are going to find out," she replied. Reaching out, she squeezed his upper arm at the place where she'd given him the injection.

"Owww!" he yelled and pulled away.

"You're not a Healer. If you were, that would have been healed by now. Tell me what you used in your fight against that boy at the grocery store."

Jacob remained silent for a minute or two, rubbing his shoulder. If he said it out loud he'd be admitting that some part of him believed he had caused the water to move. He wouldn't be able to tell himself it was a coincidence anymore. Of course, he hadn't believed it was a coincidence since the incident with Dane and the water fountain at school, but he'd never fully owned up to the power.

"Water," he said.

"Ah, as I thought. Let's begin."

She pulled a hose from the side of the house and filled up the bowl that was already in his hands.

"How did you know?" he said, staring at the bowl that she had handed him long before his confession.

"I didn't. I only suspected because of where and when the fight took place."

Once the water was turned off and the last drops had left concentric circles in the bowl, the liquid settled in his hands, calm and clear. Nothing happened.

"Now concentrate, Jacob."

"On what? What exactly am I supposed to be trying to do here?"

Dr. Silva rubbed her chin. Her mouth pulled into a pout that was so attractive Jacob had to look away.

"Ask the water to point out evil."

He opened his mouth but Dr. Silva held up her hand.

"Not with your voice. With your mind."

Jacob closed his eyes and pretended to play along. He was sure he couldn't make the water move again but didn't want to disappoint Dr. Silva. Not thinking about the water proved to be harder than he expected. Behind his closed lids he saw the scene in the parking lot, the water flowing out of the puddle, between his feet, toward Dane. He saw that afternoon at school when he'd saved himself from Dane using the water fountain. Why had the water done that? How had the water done that?

A familiar hum vibrated in his hands. The water shifted in the bowl. Opening his eyes, he was shocked to see the liquid spinning like a whirlpool, splashing over the edge. He concentrated on two words: find evil. The water slowed, then shifted to one side of the bowl, defying gravity.

The water pointed at Dr. Silva.

"Good, good!" she said. "Yes, I am in fact the closest thing to evil in the vicinity. That means it's working!"

Jacob frowned. "What are you?"

"Not now, Jacob. All in good time. We are just starting to make progress. But pointing out evil could mean anything. We need to know more. Now, ask the water to jump into your hand. Think of a weapon. Pretend you want to destroy me," she said, grinning as if the idea of him destroying her was preposterous.

Gideon, however, did not seem amused. Leaping between Dr. Silva and Jacob, he crouched and showed his teeth.

"Oh, Gideon, please!" she said with a small laugh. She picked the cat up and cradled it against her chest. "Let's go, Jacob. Show me what you've got."

He closed his eyes and tried to imagine Dr. Silva attacking him. The water moved again in the bowl, but all he could produce was a harmless splash that drenched his hand. "This is ridiculous. If I am truly a Soulkeeper, shouldn't I be able to walk on this stuff?" He threw down the bowl and turned his back to her. The water seeped into the ground.

"You have gifts from God, but you are not God. You just need to figure out how to use the power you've been given. There's always a trigger, something that allows you to access what's within you. You just need to find it."

"Right," he said, cynically. "And the purpose of these gifts would be what?"

All humor drained from Dr. Silva's face.

"To fight the Watchers," she said. "To stop the evil ones from taking human souls." Her lips were a straight line and her eyes as sad as Jacob had ever seen them.

"Who are the Watchers?"

"Evil creatures that thrive on the destruction of humanity. They are called Watchers because they are lazy creatures who sit back and watch the universe unfold, waiting until a person is at their most vulnerable before moving in and destroying them. Under the western world's lexicon, you would know them as fallen angels."

Jacob, who'd been listening intently up to that point, slapped his forehead with his palm. "You're crazy. You have had one too many cups of your own tea." He started walking toward the gate.

"It's in the Bible, Jacob. The Archangel Michael cast Lucifer and his followers from heaven and they fell to Earth. It's right there in Genesis. 'The sons of God saw the daughters of men and took of

them all that they chose.' They never left and it's up to us to hold
them back, to keep them from wrecking all of God's creation all
over again."

"Again?" Jacob stopped halfway out of the gate, the wrought-
iron latch carving a groove into his palm.

"Your first assignment is to read a Bible," she snapped. "Lessons
continue next week. Don't be late."

The gate slammed behind him. He didn't say goodbye.

* * * * *

What was good for the goose was good for the gander. At least
that's what Jacob told himself as he parked the big blue truck that
he'd borrowed from the Laudners around the corner from the
Gupta residence. He'd had to roll the beast down the driveway in
neutral; the engine was loud enough to wake the dead. But it was
worth the risk of getting caught if Malini had some answers.

Just after midnight, he crept below her window. Her room was
on the second floor with a small terrace barely large enough for a
lawn chair. Bright pink flowers bloomed in flower boxes on the
railing.

He picked out several small stones from the landscaping.
Unlike the Laudners, Malini lived in town, making his midnight
visit all the more dangerous as the street lights glowed brightly and
the neighboring homes were close enough to see clearly. But it
must have been late enough because he saw no evidence of life
behind any of the neighbors' windows.

Cachink

His first rock hit Malini's window and ricocheted back, rolling
out from between the slats of the terrace railing. It was louder than
he'd expected and he ducked behind a bush near the side of the

house. He waited but Malini's window didn't open. After scanning the houses for curious neighbors, Jacob came out from behind the yew branches.

He searched the wall of the house, looking for some way to climb up. The brick held no convenient rose lattice to rely on. But at the base of the house, directly under the terrace, there was a garden hose. Once he'd determined there was no other way, Jacob decided it was worth a try.

The puddle he formed on the side of the house wasn't very deep. The water sank into the ground almost immediately but he let it run long enough to make a twelve-foot circle of very wet grass. Then he turned the water off and placed himself in the middle of the soggiest portion of lawn. He closed his eyes and envisioned himself rising, surfing up to the terrace on a spray of water. Nothing happened.

Jacob concentrated harder, reaching out with his mind to listen to the hum of the water at his feet. He thought about how he'd felt when Dane had touched Malini, how the jealousy and anger had coursed through his veins, how he'd needed to help her. Something beneath his feet shifted. He concentrated on how he needed to get to the terrace. It was absolutely essential he get to her, to protect her. A wave of self-induced panic lurched in his stomach.

Whoosh

All of the water from the lawn rushed out in a geyser beneath his feet. He squatted a little for balance as the pressure shot him into the air and then abruptly let him fall. Jacob landed awkwardly on the terrace railing and had to circle his arms for balance before jumping down onto the small square of wood. The water had already returned to the lawn below.

"That was interesting," he said to nobody. For as much as he was desperate to believe Dr. Silva was crazy, he could no longer deny that this gift was very real—and very cool.

He knocked lightly. The lace curtain moved aside and Malini's face lit up behind the glass. She fumbled with the lock and threw open the window.

"Jake! What are you doing here?"

"Needed to talk to you. Can I come in?"

"Of course," she answered. Her arms snaked around his neck and she gave him a peck on the cheek. "How did you get up here?" She moved aside so Jacob could crawl through the window.

"Jumped."

"Very funny."

As his eyes adjusted to the inside light, he was surrounded with Malini. Every inch of wall was covered with a reminder of the vastness of the world. There were framed photos of Big Ben, the Eiffel Tower, the Coliseum, and European castles, but also pictures of a Bengali marketplace, African orphans pulling water from a well, aboriginal dancers, and an American Indian meditating on a red mesa. There were maps of the world, as well as more detailed ones of the Middle East and Asia. An oversized picture of Anderson Cooper hung beside the multicolored sari print of her bedspread.

It was exactly the type of room he would have expected Malini to have.

"Wow," he managed.

"Thanks."

A pang of jealousy and resentment of his grossly pink room shot through him.

"What's with the poster of Anderson Cooper?" he asked, trying to get his mind off his own self-pity.

"He's who I want to be when I grow up."

"You want to be a middle-aged white guy?"

"No!" she said, slapping his shoulder. "I want to be a journalist, a citizen of the world. I want to be someone who makes a difference, not just for one country but for everyone."

Jacob stared silently at her, wondering how so much good could be contained in one person's body. He wondered why God, if there was one, hadn't given Malini gifts like his. He was sure she would do something better with them.

"So, what's going on?" she finally asked.

"You're Christian, right?" Jacob asked, awkwardly.

"Yep, all my life."

"Do you have a Bible?"

"Of course." She pulled down a thick book from her shelf and placed the heavy volume on her desk. She turned on a small desk lamp.

"What can you tell me about fallen angels?"

"Hmm. You came to my room at midnight to ask me about fallen angels? You've got to be kidding."

"It's like homework, for Dr. Silva. She wants me to research fallen angels. I'm not sure exactly why but if it means I pay off my debt faster, fallen angels it is." He looked at his feet, hoping she would buy it. He hated misleading her, but wasn't ready to share what he'd learned so far.

Malini considered him for a moment, then resigned herself to whatever conclusion she had drawn and opened the Bible. She also reached across the desk and booted up her computer.

"I'm not sure where to start," she said, flipping to the back of the massive book.

"How about Genesis?" Jacob said, recalling the passage Dr. Silva had mentioned.

"All right." She flipped back to the beginning. "I've actually heard of this one before. It's very controversial. We spent an hour talking about it in my Bible study."

"Why? What's it say?"

"Genesis six, when men began to increase in number on the Earth and daughters were born to them, the sons of God saw that the daughters of men were beautiful, and they took of them all which they chose." Malini looked up from the page. "See it's controversial because not everyone agrees on what it means."

"What does it mean?" he asked.

"Well, there are different interpretations. See some people believe that the 'sons of God' were people descended from Seth." Malini paused at his quizzical expression. "You have no idea who Seth was do you?"

"No."

"The remedial version then."

He winced.

"Seth was a later son of Adam that was said to be exceptionally godly." She raised her hands and elongated the word *gaawdly*, like she found the term a little humorous. "Another interpretation is that it refers to leaders from neighboring countries: like how the Egyptians thought of their pharaohs as the sons of Ra. But the last interpretation is the one that applies to your research. It says that the 'sons of God' were fallen angels who married human women and had children by them."

"Why would anyone believe that one? The first two sound much more reasonable."

"You would think, but the biblical evidence actually points to the third interpretation. Look at this." She flipped to the index again and then back to a page in the middle. "Job chapter one, verse six, now the day came when the sons of God came to present themselves before the Lord—and Satan also arrived among them. See the 'sons of God' here is clearly referring to the minions of Satan—fallen angels. In fact every other passage in the Bible referring to 'sons of God' is about fallen angels. But the best evidence that the third interpretation is correct is not in the Bible at all. Well, not in this Bible."

She turned to her computer and typed something into the search bar.

"This Bible? Isn't the Bible ... the Bible?"

"Actually no. Different branches of Christianity have different books that they include. The book of Enoch, as it so happens, is a book in the Bible of the Ethiopian Orthodox Church, but no other Christian church recognizes it as anything but a prophetic writing." She turned the computer monitor toward him.

"Anyway, the book of Enoch comes right out and talks about fallen angels. It calls them Watchers. See what it says here, in chapter seven." She pointed to the screen. "Then they took wives, each choosing for himself whom they began to approach, and with whom they cohabited, teaching them sorcery, incantations, and the dividing of roots and trees. And the women conceiving brought forth giants."

"Giants?"

"You've heard of the story of how David slew Goliath?"

Jacob nodded.

"Well, the theory is that Goliath was a giant descendant. King David was battling a child of the fallen angels."

A chill ran up his spine. It was the same story Dr. Silva had told him.

"But if all this is true, Malini, don't you think someone would have noticed if angels and giants were here?"

"Well, the great flood … You know the story of Noah's Ark, right?"

He nodded again. Even he'd heard that one.

"God sent the flood to kill the giants and the humans that had turned to the angels' dark ways. Then He made it so that it couldn't happen again."

"How?"

"I think … I'm not sure but I think He made it so that they can't have relations—you know, sex—with human women anymore."

"That wouldn't have killed the fallen angels, though."

"I don't know. It isn't logical. That's why most people believe the other interpretations."

Jacob stepped back and sat on the multicolored bed, feeling overwhelmed. Was this what Dr. Silva wanted him to learn? Was this what she meant by destroying man again? Was the battle between good and evil really a battle between the descendants of the Soulkeepers and the followers of Lucifer?

It couldn't be true.

"Are we done with the Bible, now?" Malini asked.

"Oh, sure. Thanks for helping me," he said.

"No problem." She turned off her computer and her desk lamp. "I fully intend to extract payment for my services," she waggled her eyebrows and puckered her lips, "in kisses."

The next thing he knew, she was in his arms.

Chapter 19
This Might Be Cooler Than It Sounds

"Something else has happened, hasn't it?" Dr. Silva said, staring at Jacob in that unblinking way that made him think she was reading his soul.

"Yes," he replied. For the first time, he wanted to tell her what happened. He wanted to try it again. "I shot myself out of a puddle—about twelve feet, I think."

She clapped her long fingers together and laughed. "This is terrific news. Let's see if we can make that happen again and maybe stretch it into something more useful."

"More useful? More useful for what?"

Dr. Silva was already pulling over the hose, wetting down the grass in front of the sunroom. "How much did you need?"

"I don't really know. It soaked into the ground. I guess I ran it for a couple minutes."

A puddle formed at Dr. Silva's feet.

"You pulled it from the ground?"

He nodded.

"That's a very powerful gift, Jacob. Think about the implications. I wonder if you even need this," she said, waving the hose. She turned the water off.

"Show me. Jump to the roof of the sunroom."

He took his place in the middle of the puddle. The hum of the water surrounded him, whispered to him. He concentrated on the roof. Nothing happened.

"It's not working," he admitted.

"What was different last night?"

"Well, I was trying to get to my friend … wait, I think I remember now." He pretended Malini was on the roof. To protect her, he needed to get to her. The panicky feeling came again, the urgency. All at once, he was flying through the air. He bent his knees to absorb the impact of landing on the slate shingles.

Dr. Silva cheered from below. "Wonderful! What was different that time?"

"I remembered that I had to pretend I was protecting her to make it work. It was the same in the parking lot and the school. When I felt like I had to protect her, that's when it would listen to me."

"Her who?" Dr. Silva pursed her lips.

"My girlfriend, Malini."

"Malini Gupta? The insurance agent's daughter?"

"Yep."

"That must be the trigger then—the desire to protect. You must be a Horseman. I suspected it from the beginning but this confirms it. The trigger makes sense if you think about it. For as long as I've known you, I've known you were loyal to the people you care about. The desire to protect is an urge to act on that loyalty. First it was your mother and now Malini."

Horseman. The label sounded ancient. Jacob wasn't sure how much of her story he was willing to believe, but being called a Horseman didn't bother him. It was as close to an explanation for what he could do as he was going to get.

"What now?"

"Come on down and we'll try something else."

Jacob prepared himself mentally and jumped. The water rose to meet his feet and carried him gently to the earth, like a falling geyser.

Dr. Silva was in front of him in an instant. One second her hands were empty and the next a staff appeared in a flash of blue light.

"Ask the water for a weapon," she barked.

All at once, her eyes turned vicious and her lips pulled back from her teeth like an animal. She wielded the staff in her hands, her feet set wide. Dr. Silva could be scary when she wanted to be.

He searched the hum of the water and pretended Malini was standing behind him. The staff was the threat. He concentrated, searching the hum for the best weapon, something to defend her from the staff.

The water sprayed into his hand in a steady stream that filled his grip. As he tightened his fist, he was surprised to feel resistance. Never taking his eyes off Dr. Silva, he lifted the water from the ground; only it was no longer water but a broadsword of solid ice. The double-sided blade glinted in the afternoon light, as hard and sharp as steel. It was three feet long and perfectly balanced in his hand.

How was it possible that the ice wasn't freezing his palm or melting in the sun? There wasn't time to think about it much. Dr.

Silva's staff came around toward his head. Jacob circled the ice sword and made contact, gouging the wood. She spun and thrust the staff under her arm toward his gut. He swept the sword downward, blocking the staff.

The movement was much faster than humanly possible. It was as if the sword was anticipating his direction. Each time the blade made contact with the staff, he instinctively knew how to counter the attack. She parried, and he advanced. The battle went on until Jacob was covered in sweat and thankful for the cold hilt of his weapon.

Then, with lightning speed, Dr. Silva slashed the staff down toward the top of his head. Jacob's sword responded, flying upward in an arc. Only this time the water melted and reformed around the wood. He completed the circle, allowing gravity to help drive the blade around, and wrenched the staff from Dr. Silva's hands.

She stared at her empty fingers, surprise brightening her eyes.

"Congratulations, Horseman," she said. "You have won your first battle."

She bowed formally. Her hands spread to the sides in a gesture as ancient and out of place as a medieval knight jousting on a city street. Jacob was as sure as he'd ever been that she was not human. But he'd given up on asking her what she was. The truth was, it didn't matter; she was the only hope he had of getting his life back.

Chapter 20
Birthday

"Did you ever think we would make it through this year?" Malini asked.

Jacob followed her through the double doors of Paris High School, exhausted from a full week of final exams. "No, not really," he said. Between Dane, Dr. Silva, and Katrina, he was happy to survive most days. The year seemed a lot to ask for.

"I guess it could've been worse."

"How exactly?"

Malini stopped walking and looked at him.

"Flesh-eating spiders. There could've been spiders." Malini always did know just what to say. "So, how do you think you did?"

"You first," he deflected.

"Unless I absolutely bombed that one, straight As." She grinned. "Second year in a row. How about you?"

"I didn't do as well as you, but I passed everything," he said, embarrassed. He hadn't felt much like studying with everything else going on, and eked by with three Bs and two Cs.

"Oh, come on. Tell me," Malini said, as they walked toward the Laudners' shop.

"Not a chance."

He kissed her lightly on the cheek. Grades aside, nothing made him happier than knowing they had three months free from Dane Michaels and his posse. Even better, the graduation party last weekend for Katrina was a happy reminder that she would be gone at the end of August.

"Admit it, you actually miss school during the summer, don't you?" he asked Malini.

"Sometimes. But you know what I won't miss?" She beamed at him.

"What?"

"Walking. You turn sixteen in a week don't you?"

"Yes, I do. And, I suppose once I can drive you'll want to mooch rides off of me."

"When you can drive? How about now?" She leapt onto his back.

He carried her piggyback style halfway to McNaulty's.

* * * * *

With his sixteenth birthday just around the corner, Jacob practiced driving every spare minute. John came along on trips into town, but since the Laudners lived in the country he also practiced alone on the back roads where there wasn't any traffic. By the time June 9th rolled around, Jacob was sure he was ready.

He arrived ten minutes before The Department of Motor Vehicles opened and shifted restlessly in front of the door until a squirrely looking man with greasy red hair let him in. Since he was first in line, the man sat him down in front of a fat computer terminal. Jacob worked through each question slowly, relieved when he passed with only two incorrect. Then another man with a potbelly and a gray mustache called his name for the driving portion. He tested Jacob in a small hatchback, far more maneuverable than his uncle's truck. The gray mustache wrinkled with the man's smile when he told Jacob he'd passed with a perfect score.

"Let's see it, boy!" John said, pulling the driver's license from his fingers.

"Finally! You won't have to drive me around anymore," he said.

"Well, I didn't really mind, Jacob, but I can see why you'd be excited to have some freedom. You've worked hard these last couple months to pay off your debt and to learn to drive. I'm proud of you, not just for earning this but for adjusting as well as you have."

Jacob smiled and picked the license from John's fingers. Of course, he hadn't really adjusted. He'd just decided to be patient. He planned to go back home to Oahu as soon as Dr. Silva could find his mom. But John didn't need to know about that until it happened. The sad part was that he actually liked his uncle. Jacob wasn't sure when exactly it had happened but he'd started to care about him. He would miss John and the closeness that he felt to his dad when he was around.

"So, I don't think it's too early for your birthday present, do you?" An ear-to-ear grin lit up John's pale face.

"You didn't have to get me anything," Jacob replied.

"No I didn't—but I did anyway."

He followed John out into the parking lot where his uncle stood in front of the big blue truck looking like his head could explode with joy at any moment.

"Happy birthday, Jacob!" he said, slapping Big Blue.

"Thanks," he replied, wondering what his gift would be.

"This is it," John said, "I'm giving you Big Blue!"

"No way!"

"Your aunt has been on me for years to get a new truck and now I have an excuse to do it. She's all yours."

"John, this is awesome! Thank you, thank you so much." Jacob was so excited he allowed John to hug him and actually hugged him back a little. He caught the keys that John threw his way and crawled behind the wheel. John climbed in on the passenger's side.

"Guess what?" John said, as they pulled out and headed for home.

"What?"

"I've got something else for you. One more surprise."

"You've got to be kidding. What else could there be?"

"When you first got here, Jacob, I promised you that we would fix up that room for you. I think it's time."

Jacob swerved, and John reached over to correct the wheel.

"Easy now, you don't want to lose that thing on your first day driving. Drop me off at home and then go pick out some paint and things downtown at Johnson's Hardware. Doug and Judy will charge it to my account. Heck, take your girlfriend with you. I'm sure she'll be as excited as you are that you're driving. Anyway, I'll get started painting tomorrow while you're working with Abigail. That way it'll have overnight to air out."

"John, this is the best. I don't know what to say. This is more than I ever expected."

"You're more than I ever expected. I wish things were different with your ma, but I'm happy we've had this chance to get to know each other. That's the blessing in it."

Jacob said nothing, but the words were a two-fisted punch to the gut. He didn't believe in blessings and he wasn't happy to be in Paris. But he didn't want to hurt John's feelings by saying so, because he was happy he'd gotten to know John, too. So he kept his mouth shut and his eyes on the road.

* * * * *

Malini couldn't wait to help Jacob shop. She babbled endlessly about how much fun they'd have this summer, now that he had a car, and how cool his room was going to be. But the initial excitement he'd felt about the car and his new room gave way to anxious contemplation about the future. Tomorrow, he would meet the medicine woman.

Every day here, every moment, he grew more attached to John and Malini. If the medicine woman knew where his mother was, what would happen then? How would he leave them? And, what about when he found his mom? The apartment belonged to someone else now. Where would they live?

"What color are you thinking?" Malini said, handing him an assortment of cardboard paint swatches. They stood before a rack of thousands of two-inch color cards competing for their attention. He'd never known there were so many colors to choose from.

"I'm not sure. Not pink. How about black?"

"Too dark. It would look like a cave."

"What do you think then?"

Malini shifted the swatches between her fingers: deep burgundy, rich mahogany, dark greens and blues. "Don't get angry at me because I know you don't like to talk about it but ever since that day with Dane and the water ... I just think blue." She held up a dark grayish blue color called "stormy sea."

He took the swatch from her hand. The color was not something he'd have picked for himself but it gave him a calm feeling.

"It's perfect," he said, in a voice barely above a whisper. He moved closer to her. "I had no idea what I wanted until just now. This is exactly it. You know me better than I do."

He was inches from her now, taking in the sweet genuineness that was only Malini's. His words were true and not just about the paint. It was at that moment that he decided he wouldn't leave her behind. One way or another he would find a way to keep her with him.

"What do we do next? Does the paint come in this color?"

"No, they have to mix it."

"How do they do that?"

"Just trust me," she said, lifting the card from his fingers. "I'll get it."

"You're amazing, Malini," Jacob said.

"Don't you forget it," she replied. She cast a sassy grin over her shoulder as she moved toward the paint counter.

Chapter 21
Red Stones for Manioc

With all of the preparations made, Jacob jogged across the street to Dr. Silva's house the afternoon of June 10th. He'd barely slept the night before thinking about the journey. Tonight he would finally know for sure what happened to his mom.

In his heart, he was sure she was still alive. He didn't have the sort of peace or finality he did with his dad's death. But as he crossed through the gate into Dr. Silva's backyard, he wondered if that was because there hadn't been a funeral or a body to see. There was no proof. If she were alive, what he learned in Peru would be the key to saving her. But he also knew that it was equally likely his greatest fear might be revealed. If his instincts were nothing more than wishful thinking, he might find out she was dead.

As planned, Dr. Silva met him at the mouth of the maple orchard.

"Are you ready to go?" she asked with a quirky half smile, as if he couldn't possibly be ready.

"As ready as I'll ever be," he replied.

Dr. Silva handed him a safari helmet with mosquito netting and then coated him in a thick fog of bug repellant. From her shoulder, she removed a canteen on a long leather strap.

"Put it around your neck and shoulder so that it travels with you."

"What is it?"

"Tea. Just in case."

"In case of what? Early Peruvian tea time?" he laughed.

"It has medicinal properties," she said.

The pieces clicked together within Jacob's mind just as they approached the privet. Dr. Silva had told him her specialty was horticulture, and John had said that her plants were used to make drugs. Now she was admitting that the tea had "medicinal properties."

"The first day I was here … that's why I told you all of those things. You drugged me!"

"Now, now, I merely gave you something to help you relax," she said. "Anyway, it was for the best. I had to know enough about you to make sure you were ready."

Jacob wondered what other means she'd used without his permission to attain her goals. He crossed his arms over his chest as they entered the back garden. As he covered his nose to pass the corpse plants, he couldn't help but think that Dr. Silva had been pulling his strings from the very beginning. She wasn't human, that was for sure, and she'd never been honest with him about who or what she was. He'd trusted her because he'd had no choice.

While he trotted over the stone path and walked the sandy meadow trail, he realized trusting Dr. Silva might not be an alltogether wise thing to do. In fact, by the time he reached Oswald, Jacob was jumpy with suspicion about Dr. Silva's motives and sure this trip was a bad idea. But there was no turning back now, not with the hope of finding his mother so near at hand.

"Hey, where's Gideon?" Jacob asked, noticing for the first time that the cat wasn't in his usual place by Dr. Silva's side.

"Oh, he's in the house. He doesn't like to travel through the tree unless it's absolutely necessary," she replied. "Now, it's important we hold hands as we do this so that we aren't separated during the journey. We wouldn't want to end up on different ends of Peru."

Jacob hadn't thought of that scenario and wasn't happy to have something else to worry about.

Dr. Silva interlaced the fingers of her right hand with his. She looked him in the eye.

"It's time," she said.

Jacob nodded once, too nervous to speak.

She touched the branch.

Because he was not the person directly in contact with the tree, the experience was slightly different this time. Jacob could see the bark creep up Dr. Silva's left arm, shingling her skin. It layered itself across her chest before covering her face and swallowing her whole. It spread down her right arm before reaching his fingertips. Then the familiar slowing happened; however, Dr. Silva remained the same. It was as if they were in a bubble together as they floated up to the sky and then became the sky. They rolled down a tube, the bubble blown down a straw. As they reached the bottom, he felt himself pop out of the ground and land clumsily at the roots of a massive tree. He was still holding Dr. Silva's hand when his knees buckled. The sickness was evident but not as bad as the first time.

"Welcome to Peru," she said, opening his canteen and lifting it to his lips. "If I've calculated correctly, we should be near the border of Ecuador, deep in the Amazonian rainforest. I must warn you, this isn't a schoolyard. Quite a few creatures exist in this forest that would view you as lunch."

"So, where do we go next?" he asked.

"We don't. We wait for a guide." Dr. Silva removed a long, hollow piece of wood from her bag and raised it to her lips like a flute. She blew three long, deep notes. When the last tone ended, she raised her finger to her lips. He held very still and listened.

The jungle was loud. Birds called from the canopy and monkeys leapt from tree to tree above him. There was a constant ruffling of leaves from things he was glad he couldn't see.

After several minutes, he turned to Dr. Silva to ask if she should call again. He didn't say the words though, because standing between them was a small, mostly naked man with spikes through his nose and an intricate pattern of red tattoos on his face. He had arrived silently and Jacob got the impression that he'd been standing there longer than either Dr. Silva or he had noticed.

Dr. Silva said something to the man in a language Jacob didn't understand, then reached into her bag and produced two polished ruby red stones. She handed them to the man, who nodded in response and then pointed to his left.

"This way, Jacob," Dr. Silva said. "This is Pandu. He will be our guide to the village where the Healer lives. Why don't you go first?"

He lifted himself from his seat on the tree root and followed after the man.

"Watch your step," Dr. Silva said.

"What was that you gave him?"

"The red stones? They were payment. The Achuar believe any red stone is a link to their Earth mother. What I gave him was simply red quartz but here it is very valuable."

"Interesting."

Pandu carried blow darts that hung in a quiver from his shoulder. His dark hair and leathery skin blended well into the rainforest. Jacob lengthened his stride to keep up, fearful that he could lose the man in the jungle at the slightest lapse of attention. The man navigated the terrain as if it were a paved trail.

In the thick foliage, Jacob concentrated on the placement of Pandu's feet, hoping to avoid a twisted ankle. He was concentrating so hard he almost walked right into the guide's outstretched hand. Pandu had stopped abruptly and was watching a patch of jungle to his right. From his back he pulled the blowgun and inserted a dart without making a sound. A forceful huff sent the dart toward a group of leaves up ahead. Pandu smiled. He motioned for Jacob to stay where he was and walked to the place he'd blown the dart. Reaching behind the leaves, he pulled the scaly body of a snake from the foliage.

The reptile was easily eight feet long, which meant Jacob was enlisted to carry a portion of it, a task he wasn't thrilled about performing. He'd never touched a snake before and the cool, muscular body was unsettling.

Dr. Silva and Pandu spoke excitedly in the strange language. "We are fortunate today, Jacob! Our guide has caught dinner. He says we have good spirits with us!"

"What luck," he replied in a deadpan voice, as he readjusted the slippery weight of the snake in his arms.

Pandu led them to where the rainforest opened into a clearing bordered by woven huts bustling with natives. Some women came and took the giant snake from his hands and began to skin it. They smiled and said some words he didn't understand but supposed meant something like thank you. Hoping to appear polite, he smiled back and nodded. It was a smile-fest, a sea of awkward toothy grins and nods in lieu of actual communication.

"I'll be right back. I'm going to talk with the Healer," Dr. Silva said. She drifted off to a hut on the northeast side of the village.

She left him in the center of a group of naked children. They were pointing at him and talking to each other. Once again, he was set apart, different from the others. He wondered if this was his fate. Would he always be the stranger?

Chapter 22
The Healer

Jacob tried not to mind when the Achuar children poked at him experimentally. Not wanting to provoke any additional attention, he looked away, toward the painted brown skin of the Achuar women as they worked over a pot nearby. They mashed and chewed a root and then spit it into a large caldron. Near them, men with painted faces worked to bind the snake meat to a stake. Others stoked a massive pit fire. Soon, the stake was over the flames and the cooking snake meat filled the village with an aroma he could only compare to grilled fish.

Dr. Silva emerged from the hut and motioned for him to join her. She eyed the children, who were, by this time, swinging from Jacob's nonparticipating arms. "Jacob, stop playing around. The medicine woman is ready to see you now."

"Let go," Jacob said, jerking his hands away from his giggling tormentors. He stepped to Dr. Silva's side.

"It's because you're tall," she whispered in his ear. "We are the tallest here plus our skin is different, of course. They think we are a novelty. It's entertaining to them." She put her arm around his shoulders and guided him into the dimly lit hut.

He didn't respond to Dr. Silva's comment because he was too busy mentally digesting the scene within the hut. An old woman sat cross-legged on the dirt floor, drinking from a carved cup. Dr. Silva motioned for him to sit on the floor in front of her. Jacob slid down to his knees then positioned himself to mirror the woman's cross-legged form. She handed him a hollowed-out gourd containing a thick yellowish liquid.

"It's fermented manioc root. It's perfectly safe. Please drink it," Dr. Silva whispered from the corner of the hut.

He did. The thick, sour substance found its way down his throat with some effort. His head swam a little by the time he finished and he couldn't tell if he was slightly intoxicated by the stuff or just had indigestion.

From a clay pot at her side, the medicine woman pulled a thick piece of braided rope. She lit the end and a swirl of blue smoke wafted up to a hole in the roof. Around his body, she circled the smoke, the heady perfume filling the hut. The smell was sweet and musty, not unlike oak leaves burning. After three times outlining him in fire and smoke, she stopped and placed the burning rope in the pot.

With a tip of her head, she motioned for Jacob to lie down on a mat of woven palms. He hadn't noticed it before but it was just to his left. When he was positioned flat on his back, she placed a rolled-up animal skin beneath his head. Her hands hovered above him, moving in a random series of quick bursts and achingly slow pulls through the air. In a dance of ancient movements, she surrounded him until, after some time, she brought her hands down within an inch of his face. The calloused brown skin of her palms reminded him of dirt. Those earth hands passed over him, close to his skin, once and again, never touching him but skimming every inch of his body. They hovered over his shoulders, his stomach, and down each leg. Finally, her fingertips settled over his heart.

Through the smoke within the dimly lit hut, the lines in the old woman's face were a map of time. Her entire history and the history of her people were carved into her skin. Her dark eyes shone like stars from within leather folds: landmarks on the topography of her life.

Her fingers pulled air over his chest. While there was nothing in her hands, she pretended to scoop some invisible substance, cupping it in her palm before throwing it in the smoking pot near her knees. After she had done this several times, the strangest thing happened. A rising started in his body. It came from his toes, flowed through his fingertips, and emerged through his chest. She was pulling something out of him, something he didn't want or need. He felt lighter than before, as if his body might follow the smoke and float up from the mat toward the hole in the roof.

When the medicine woman had finished, she circled her hand over the bucket and dumped its contents out the back door of the hut. She sat Jacob up, supporting his shoulders, and said something to him in her strange language.

"She says you are ready," Dr. Silva translated. She took his hand and helped him up from the mat. When he emerged from the hut, he was surprised to find night had settled over the village and all the Achuar people were gathered for the meal. He sat at the edge of a grand circle to the sound of monkeys chattering and dogs barking. He had to remind himself he wasn't dreaming as a woman brought him a carved bowl of snake meat and something that looked like mashed potatoes.

"How long was I in there?" Jacob asked.

"A couple of hours," Dr. Silva responded.

"Hours? It felt like minutes."

"She had to purify you for the ceremony. Tonight you are Achuar. Notice how the children aren't bothering you anymore. It's because they know what she's done. She has blessed you as their own."

Jacob shivered. "This is easily the weirdest thing that's ever happened to me."

"Hmph. Well, I suppose you're young."

Jacob cast a dark look in her direction.

"Did you like the manioc beer?" Dr. Silva asked, digging into her bowl.

"Not really," he replied honestly.

"The women chew the manioc root and spit it into a cauldron. It ferments for several days before they serve it. The people here drink gallons of it a day." Dr. Silva smiled.

"That's completely disgusting ... and probably alcoholic. I'm a minor, you know."

"Relax. It was boiled down. Perfectly harmless to you or any other child."

Jacob's stomach twisted as he remembered the drink. "Do me a favor and don't tell me what this is," he said, pursing his lips and pointing at the pile of mush on the side of his plate.

Dr. Silva laughed.

When the meal was complete, the medicine woman positioned herself at the center of the circle. All of the villagers, Dr. Silva, and Jacob stood in a ring around her. She drank from a brightly painted gourd and began to dance and spin. A man played an instrument that sounded like a cross between a harp and a tambourine. The other villagers joined in the dance, as did Dr. Silva. Jacob followed along as best he could. The rhythm of the music carried him, faster and faster, circling around the Healer's form. Abruptly, the dance stopped and Jacob plowed into Dr. Silva's back.

The medicine woman collapsed, twitching in the dirt.

The urge to run to her was overwhelming; it looked like she was having a seizure or something. Jacob didn't know how to help her but he took a step forward anyway. Before he could break the circle, Dr. Silva grabbed his shoulder and pushed him back into position. He shot her a dirty look. When he turned back toward the center of the circle, the shaking had stopped. The medicine woman sat bolt upright, her eyes forward, unseeing. Her arm shot out and pointed at Jacob.

"This is it, Jacob," Dr. Silva whispered. She moved toward the medicine woman.

Jacob wasn't sure if he should follow or not. At her held-up hand, he stayed where he was.

She crossed to the center of the circle and squatted next to the old woman. Lowering her arm, the medicine woman began to jabber words in the Achuar language. Dr. Silva's expression warped. Her skin became an even whiter shade of ghostly pale and she frowned at Jacob through a curtain of her white-blonde hair. The flow of words ended abruptly and the medicine woman's body fell limp to the dirt. Dr. Silva stood and returned to her spot in the circle. Another Achuar woman ran to the Healer's side with a glass of manioc beer.

"What did she say?" Jacob asked, pulling at Dr. Silva's arm.

Her eyes bore into him, that winter sky stare colder than usual. Something about her face hardened, became statuesque. "She said it is best that you consider your mother dead."

"What does that mean? Is she dead?"

"No. She is not dead, Jacob. But where she is we cannot go."

"But that's great. She's not dead! Let's go find her."

"It's hard to explain, Jacob. Your mother is where the Achuar say the 'frightened ones' are. It's a place that is everywhere and nowhere. It's a spiritual destination not a physical one."

"Then she is dead."

"That's not what she said either."

"This doesn't make any sense! Is this some kind of a joke? You brought me all the way out here for this?" Jacob shoved her shoulder, not thinking or caring that whatever she was, she could hurt him if she wanted to. Her hand shot up and gripped his wrist with bone-crunching pressure.

"I'm sorry, Jacob. I'm sorry you didn't get the answer you were looking for. This is what she said. This is what she dreamed for you."

He wanted to hit her. He raised his free hand, clenched it into a fist, his knuckles white with rage. But Dr. Silva's face was ice, and the malice seeping off of her was enough of a warning. Instinctively he knew if he were to hit her, he might as well be punching stone. Instead he clutched the sides of his hair, moaning softly as she released him.

Doubling over, he rubbed his wrist. This was worse than any scenario he'd anticipated. He could've accepted his mother was dead. But this, this half answer, was torture. Knowing she was alive but not being able to do anything about it was worse than awful.

Dr. Silva just walked away, leaving him standing in the middle of the Achuar village, a writhing mass of emotions. He turned in circles looking for some outlet, aware that the people were staring again, aware that dark thoughts were bounding through his skull. For a moment he thought his skin might tear; it was too small for this thing inside him, this rage that wanted to shred the village, to burn down everything, including Dr. Silva. Jacob was a protector and tonight he needed desperately to protect himself, from the barrage of pain, the hollow emptiness that Dr. Silva had caused.

Unable to let it out any other way, Jacob turned his face toward the moon and released a primeval howl, a deep empty cry like a wounded animal. The emotion poured out of him, the release of his power happening almost without his knowledge. A series of popping sounds thundered around him and he was showered in water and clay. Every gourd of water the Achuar people kept in front of their huts had burst. There was no question he'd caused it.

At the sight of the destruction, the Achuar families huddled together. They stared at him with wide, fearful eyes. Ashamed, tears welled in Jacob's eyes, then flowed down his face until he completely fell apart and sobbed openly in the middle of the village.

When at last the tears ebbed and Jacob was quiet again, a young man about his age crept forward with a gourd of bitter tea. The boy rested a hand on his shoulder and offered the drink. Jacob sipped it, grateful for the merciful gift. Whatever was in the drink relaxed him and soon he was following the boy into a hut and lying on a hammock by a fire. To the lullaby of the jungle, his mind cleared of anything but thoughts of the crackling flame. Physically and emotionally drained, he slept.

Chapter 23
Earth Mother

*T*he medicine woman beckons him into the village center, to the place he was during the ceremony. Only it isn't a circle of dancing people this time, but a ring of spiky plants that surround her. Red stones lay between each of the plants and the medicine woman waters each one from a large gourd.

"Where's my mom?" Jacob yells. "Where is this place that is no place? Tell me, so that I can help her."

The medicine woman holds a finger to her lips. "Chuh, chuh," she says.

Under the starlight, the earth around the stones begins to move: to pull together into an increasingly large pile. The earth twists upward, building itself into two legs, an abdomen, chest and arms. When it stops its dusty ascent, an old dwarf woman stands before him, hunched and barely as tall as his waist. The dwarf woman holds out her hand *like she is the queen of England rather than the corporeal formation of a swell of dirt. The medicine woman motions for Jacob to kiss the dwarf woman's hand.*

"Yumi aishmag-jangke," she demands. Jacob has no idea what the words mean.

The dwarf woman is ugly and dirty but he understands that it would be an insult not to obey. He lifts the small hand in his, running his thumb along the gritty backside. Closing his eyes, he brings the shriveled brown offering to his mouth. Rough skin rubs his lips. And then, her fingers melt out of his. The dwarf woman comes apart. As he watches, earth sifts through his knuckles and the red stones scatter to the edges of the circle, back to the places where they'd been before the medicine woman had watered them. All but one. In his hand, under the spot where the dwarf woman's hand had been when he'd kissed it, one flat red stone shines in the moonlight.

The medicine woman grabs him by the collar and shakes. She points to the stone and says a word in the language he does not know but by some miracle he suddenly understands.

"Window," she says. She folds his fingers over the stone and grips his fist in both of her hands. "For you." Then she shoves him soundly in the chest with both hands.

* * * * *

He woke in the hammock and saw the Achuar boy standing over him. The boy's hand was on his shoulder, a look of concern on his features. Light cascaded through the window. Jacob could hear the village coming alive outside.

Suddenly, he was aware of a burning in his fist, his fingernails cutting into his palm. Opening his fingers, he saw the red stone. He'd been holding the flat disc so tightly that the edges had cut into his palm and blood ran over its smooth, surface.

The Achuar boy's eyes grew wide. A jumble of words spilled from his lips in the rhythm of a prayer or incantation. He was speaking Achuar but somehow, just like in his dream, Jacob knew exactly what his words meant. The prayer was for protection from the Earth Mother's wrath for allowing his guest to steal one of her precious red stones. He rubbed his eyes and blinked at Jacob.

"It's okay," Jacob said. "She gave it to me." The words sounded strange to his ears and he was surprised when the boy seemed to understand. Either he'd just spoken perfect Achuar or he was hallucinating again.

The boy turned to the corner of the hut. From inside a woven basket, he pulled out a black cord that looked as if it was originally some kind of animal tendon. He handed it to Jacob and motioned toward his neck. The stone fit perfectly in the loop at the base and Jacob tied the cord around his neck. He gave a nod of thanks to the boy.

He left the hut with the surreal feeling of walking straight out of a dream. Tucking the stone inside his shirt, he decided he did not trust Dr. Silva enough to tell her about it. After last night, he wasn't sure he could trust her at all.

Chapter 24
The Small Print

"There's something you should know about Oswald," Dr. Silva said as she approached the wrought-iron gate that led from the back garden to the maple orchard. She and Jacob had just returned from their visit to the Achuar medicine woman.

"What do you mean?" Jacob snapped.

"There are some rules, some cautions, I feel I must share with you," she said, holding open the gate for him to walk through.

"Like what?"

"Well, you must always keep this gate locked. This is very important. And, you must never, ever, travel through the tree without me."

Dr. Silva locked the gate behind them and sat down on the little hill at the base of the orchard. "There's something I haven't told you about the tree, Jacob. You know that Oswald's blood is a portal. That means we can travel places using it, but it also means that others can travel here. See, we put down tracks, more like vibrations. How do I explain this? It's like we unravel string. We are in the string, wrapping around time and space, and when we travel, others can slide down our string. Things can follow us back. We must be very certain that doesn't happen."

Jacob's vision went red. "Rules! Cautions! Don't you think you should have told me these things before I went through the tree?" He paced in front of her. He was sick of her releasing information little by little on her own terms. "Is there anything else I should know? Will I come down with the bends in an hour? Oh wait," he said, throwing up his hands. "If I do get the bends, it will be for my own good, right? You won't know or care what it feels like because whatever you are, you don't feel!"

Dr. Silva didn't acknowledge Jacob's tirade. She continued as if he'd said nothing. "The gate is a failsafe. It's enchanted. It keeps people here from finding out about Oswald and keeps them," she said, nodding toward the tree, "if there should be any, from gaining access to our world. I cannot stress enough how important this is."

He stared at her, waiting for more, waiting for her to show him some shred of understanding and decency. He needed answers. The silence was deafening, so he nodded, not so much because he agreed with her but because he was sick of standing there in the expectant stillness. She stood up and brushed off her seat. But Jacob decided he wasn't finished. Nothing made sense anymore and it was her fault. It all started with her.

"What are you?" He dug in his heels, determined to get an answer this time. "You said the gate was enchanted but before you said you weren't a witch?"

"I'm not a witch, but I can perform sorcery," she said toward the house.

"Show me."

She turned around to face him. All of the casual energy she usually displayed was gone and her face took on the icy hard look of sculpted marble, the same as the night before when she'd grabbed his wrist. Looking taller and straighter than ever, her presence knocked into him as if her aura were a living, physical thing. It was so unsettling Jacob took a step backward.

Exposing her right palm, she circled her left over it and a ball of blue fire appeared. It crackled as it burned, more than a flame. She threw the ball into the air and caught it in her left. Again she tossed it above her head, but while it sailed through the air she circled her palm and another fireball appeared. She repeated the trick until she was juggling three balls of glowing-hot energy.

This was no illusion. Jacob could feel the heat against his face as the fireballs sailed by, several feet away. He could only imagine how hot they must be in her bare palms. Then, as he watched, awestruck, she tossed them all in the air, tilted her head back and caught them one after another in her mouth. Jacob heard a sizzling sound as they hit her tongue. She swallowed them down in one gulp and then blew a ring of smoke over his right shoulder.

The whole scene reminded him of the fire-eater at the circus, only oddly disturbing, like watching her cut herself. His mouth was hanging open. He closed it. It fell open again. He closed it again.

Jacob swallowed hard. "So, you're a sorcerer?"

"Not really." She shook her head.

"Then, what are you? Tell me."

She whispered something under her breath and looked toward the horizon. "Why does everyone need a label?"

Jacob didn't know what to say. He just waited for an answer. None came. But he watched the humanity infuse into Dr. Silva's body, a tangible, warm thing that seemed to wash away the cold stiffness her magic had brought with it from the inside out. The hard, marble quality of her features softened and the unapproachable aura seemed to pull back within her. The next time she spoke, her voice and appearance were as normal as anyone Jacob had ever met before.

"Listen, Jacob, I have to go away in a few weeks—the first week of July. I'm visiting a group of ethnobotanists in St. Louis about these plants." Dr. Silva held up her leather bag. "We think there may be a cure for some types of cancer in these leaves. The government of Peru won't allow us to remove these by conventional travel but my colleagues will be very excited I got my hands on some samples. Now I just need to find a way to avoid the question of how."

She smiled at him but Jacob was barely paying attention. His mind was in another world, processing what he'd just seen.

"Would you mind caring for the garden and feeding Gideon while I'm gone? There will be extra wages for it."

He ignored her. "If you can do sorcery, why can't you help me reach my mom? What aren't you telling me? Where is she?"

"I told you. She's nowhere. She's in a place between places. Nobody can reach her. Not even I," Dr. Silva said, an empty sadness in her voice.

"I don't believe you." Jacob's hands balled into fists.

"I'm sorry it wasn't the answer you were looking for. I understand more than you know. I had a terrible time dealing with Oswald's death but I did deal with it and moved on. If you want to talk about your mother and moving on, I am here for you."

"But she's not dead!" he snapped. "Why are you talking about moving on? If she's alive, then she's someplace, and I am going to search until I find her."

Jacob stormed through the yard and threw open the heavy gate. Before he crossed the street, he turned back toward Dr. Silva, who was standing with her hands on her bag, looking disappointed.

"She's nowhere. You won't find her. She's no longer of this Earth," Dr. Silva said.

"I'm going to find her. I will find her, with or without you. You didn't hold up your end of the bargain, Dr. Silva. Don't think I'm going to forget that any time soon."

Jacob turned his back on her and trudged across Rural Route One.

He entered the Laudners' house and slammed the door behind him. He was relieved that no one was home. It was late morning on Sunday and he assumed they were still at church. The one highlight of this weekend was he wouldn't have to sit through another hour of Mass.

Up the stairs, down the hall, and to the pink room, he bolted. The shock of what he saw left him standing in the doorway. The pink room wasn't pink. The walls were the dark gray blue that Malini had picked out. The bedspread had been replaced with a light brown comforter and the floral wingback was now an orange chair. The antique furniture was gone, replaced with walnut, brushed nickel, and glass. On the desk was a laptop computer.

Leaning against the doorframe, he tried to shift gears from anger and disappointment to the emotion that overwhelmed him now, gratitude. Jacob could not process the generosity or the time and effort the room represented. He stared into the space, trying to sort it out, long enough for his shoulder to ache from the leaning.

"Do you like it?" Uncle John asked from the hall behind him.

Jacob hadn't even heard him come in.

"It's fantastic. How did you...?"

"Malini helped. She picked out most of this stuff. I just did the painting. She should be here any minute. Said she was coming by with a late birthday gift for you."

"It's amazing. It's really ... more than you should have."

"Don't mention it."

He felt like there was something else he should say but Jacob couldn't find the words. The most he could manage was a nod in John's direction.

"Well," John said, "you must be tired. Abigail said she would have you up all night running tests and by those bags under your eyes she wasn't kidding. Why don't you try out that new bed of yours? I'll wake you up when Malini gets here." He smiled before wandering toward the stairs.

Jacob crawled under the comforter, hoping for dreamless sleep. But the gratitude he felt about the room was not strong enough to hold back his worry for his mother. He closed his eyes. Why hadn't Dr. Silva told him the whole truth about what the medicine woman had said? He was positive she was holding something back. What was it she had said? *It is best that you consider your mother dead. She's in a spiritual destination, not a physical one.* Well, if that wasn't a load of crap, he didn't know what was. Just the thought that his mother might be some maniac's prisoner, suffering somewhere that was so bad she might as well be dead, was enough to make every muscle in his body tighten to the point of nausea.

As he rolled over to try to avoid getting sick, the stone that hung around his neck caught under his body and the cord dug into his skin. He adjusted himself, pulling the red stone off over his head. Turning it between his fingers, the light from the window exposed facets deep beneath the smooth exterior. There was something in there: something black, something shifting. Warm in his hand, the disc seemed to grow larger. He could feel himself being pulled forward into the redness.

"How'd it go last night?" Malini's head poked through the door. Jacob snapped out of it.

"Fine." Reluctantly, he set the stone on the nightstand.

"That's beautiful. Where did you get it?" she asked, moving toward the table.

"Don't touch it!" he snapped and snatched it back up. Immediately, he felt embarrassed about yelling at her. "I'm sorry, Malini. I'm really tired. That came out wrong. The edges are sharp. See I cut my hand." He held up his cut palm. "I made it from a stone I found in Dr. Silva's garden."

He hated lying to Malini.

"Oh," Malini said, a note of concern in her voice.

Jacob slid the stone under his pillow.

"I brought you something," she said, handing him a package.

"You didn't have to do that. This place is amazing. John told me you helped him do this."

"You're welcome, but I wanted you to have this, too."

When he yanked the wrapping paper off, a heavy book fell into his lap.

"I know for a fact you don't already have one," she added.

It was a Bible. He ran his hand over the black leather cover and frowned.

"What's wrong?" she asked.

"I don't believe in God," he said plainly. "God is something people made up to control other people."

"Why would you think that?"

"Malini, no offense, I know this is what you believe, but I just feel that more wars are fought over religion than anything else. If it wasn't for religion, we would have a more peaceful world." He looked away from her, out the window. "For one, my dad would be alive."

"What?"

"He died in Afghanistan. It started as a religious thing you know … Muslim Jihad."

"I'm so sorry, Jacob." She crawled onto the bed behind him and circled his shoulders with her arms. Her cheek rested against his ear. "It still hurts." It was a statement not a question.

"No. Not really. It's been years. I miss him but it's not as raw as it used to be."

"And your mom? Any word on what happened to her?"

"No one knows for sure, still."

"That's horrible. It must be so difficult for you."

"It is," Jacob whispered.

"I can't disagree with you on the war thing, but I will tell you that what people have done with religion hasn't always been what they should have done. People are corrupt; they make bad choices. They bend the truth for their own gain. But before you reject God, the entire concept of God, I think you should know what you are rejecting for yourself."

"No thanks."

"Well, for Dr. Silva's research then." She edged the book onto his nightstand.

"Okay," he mumbled.

Jacob stared blankly out the window. The last thing he needed right now was to have religion shoved down his throat. It was all voodoo, no better than the dancing of the Achuar tribe. There were different words, different objects, but it was all a false comfort. People needed a story to tell themselves and religion made a nice one.

"I won't bother you anymore about this." It was as if Malini could tell she was pushing him too far. "You don't need talk, you need hope."

She ran her hand over the black cover, as if to say that hope was right under her fingertips, just inches away.

Jacob turned his head to look at her. She had good intentions, but he knew better. He'd make his own hope. Jacob had a plan and, although Malini didn't know it yet, she was already a part of it.

Chapter 25
The Skeleton Is Thrown from the Closet

The next Saturday morning, Jacob woke to the front door slamming. He looked out of his window to see Carolyn and Uncle John backing out of the driveway.

"Whitaker Wedding," Katrina said from his doorway.

He jumped at the sound of her voice. He'd assumed she'd gone with them. Before he could tell her to take a hike, she helped herself to a seat at his new desk.

"So, how's it feel to be the family charity case?" she said. "My God, look at this place."

"Excuse me?" he said. "If you have nothing nice to say, just leave. Get out of my room."

"Well, I just thought we should get to know each other, I mean if you're staying and I'm leaving."

"Katrina, you haven't said more than a sentence to me in months. You've treated me like crap since I walked in that door. Why in the world would we get to know each other now?" He glared at her and pulled a T-shirt over his head.

"Do you want to know why I hate you, Jacob?" she said.

He did not dignify the question with an answer.

She seemed to be considering something. She tapped her fingers on the desk for so long Jacob was tempted to reach out and slap her hand. "Has anyone told you why we'd never met before you came here?"

"No. I never got a straight answer on that one."

She looked at the floor. "Paris is a small town, an all-American town. Do you know that almost every man in the Laudner family has served in the military?"

"No. I didn't know that."

"They did. See our grandfather served in the Navy during World War II." She motioned for him to follow her out into the hall and pointed at a yellowed picture of a man on an old battleship. "In 1944, he was on the USS Essex when a Kamikaze pilot hit it. You know what Kamikazi were, right?"

"Of course, I grew up near Pearl Harbor. They were Japanese suicide pilots. So what?"

"Grandpa's ship was hit by one," she repeated. "He lived but he never fully recovered. He had nightmares about that last day on the Essex for decades. And, as you can understand, he hated the Japanese until the day he died. It was just two years ago, you know?"

Jacob's face twisted. If Grandpa Laudner died just two years ago, he was alive at the time of his father's death. Why hadn't he ever met the man?

"Here's a picture of our great Uncle Jerry, Grandpa's younger brother." She pointed her finger at one of three uniformed men standing in front of the Laudner oak tree. Jacob recognized the man on Uncle Jerry's right to be a young Uncle John and on the left was the same man from the picture with the USS Essex. It was Grandpa Laudner but older.

"Grandpa must have been so proud when his brother left for Korea. I never met Uncle Jerry though. He was killed in 1952 in the war."

The picture of Uncle Jerry was yellowing but the man looked young, too young to die in a faraway war.

"My dad fought in Vietnam. Barely made it out alive."

"Katrina, I'm really sorry about your uncle and grandfather, but what has this got to do with me?"

"It has everything to do with you, Jacob. *It is you!*" she hissed. "Don't you get it? Your father, my Uncle Charlie, after all the pain these Orientals caused this family, brought one home to marry!"

Jacob's breath caught in his throat. "What?"

"You heard me."

He couldn't believe what he was hearing. Sure, there was bigotry in Paris, but Uncle John had treated him pretty well since coming here. Katrina must be exaggerating. There was no way marrying his mother was reason enough for John to cut off his own brother.

"Grandma was beside herself. Grandpa told Uncle Charlie it was your mother or the family. Uncle Charlie chose your mother."

"That doesn't even make sense. My mother was Chinese. She wasn't Japanese or Vietnamese, and she wasn't a soldier."

"So, there's a difference?"

Jacob stepped back as if her words had knuckles. It was all he could do not to punch the smirk right off her face. She was lucky he wasn't near water or she might be a Popsicle. Katrina was a liar and for all he knew this was a ploy to crack him. She would love it if he blew up again.

"That's why you've never met us. Uncle Charlie was estranged from our family since I was three years old. My mother told me he even changed his name as a last strike of defiance against our grandpa. That's why your last name is Lau, not Laudner. Apparently being married to one wasn't enough."

What she said was horrible, but was it true? He scanned the images lining the hall. Every one of them was white. It would explain some things. Was this what Uncle John was talking about when he mentioned the worst thing he'd ever done? Jacob had to admit the pieces of the past fit within this frame. Uncle John and the rest of the Laudner family had disowned his father for marrying his mother.

But something didn't make sense about Katrina's story. Something was missing. The way she paraded the family skeletons made Jacob believe there was more. He didn't trust her, but still, he needed to know the truth.

"So, you're telling me that your family is a bunch of bigots." His voice sounded louder than he'd intended. "If that were true, then why did Uncle John bring me here?"

"First of all, there's a difference between bigotry and good common sense." She sneered at him and he resisted the urge to slap her. Through her teeth, she said, "My father brought you here because I'm a girl. My parents can't have any more children. That means that you, as hopeless as you are, are the last male Laudner heir. Apparently, meeting the terms of our great-great-grandfather's one hundred fifty-year-old last will and testament is so important that it is worth associating with you."

"That doesn't make any sense."

"The shop, the Laudner livelihood, is held in trust based on a vision our great-great-grandfather had one hundred fifty years ago. The shop must be handed down to a male heir or the property will be donated to the city. No, it doesn't make sense. But it's the truth. So excuse me for not being overjoyed at your presence here. I've worked in that shop for my entire life and they pick you. I'll be gone soon enough and you can swoop in and seal the deal. My inheritance is all but yours. Obviously, my father hasn't had any problem casting me aside for you."

Katrina turned on her heel and stormed into her room, slamming the door.

"I don't even want it. You can have it," he yelled after her. He could hear the click of her door locking behind her.

Jacob rubbed his eyes with the heels of his palms. It made sense. This was why he'd never in his life heard of the Laudners. In a numb fog, he dropped his hands and backed down the hall, never taking his eyes off of Katrina's door until he was inside his own room. He collapsed onto his new comforter, bringing his knees to his chest. It wasn't his choice to come here; it certainly wasn't his choice to stay. At this point, he had very few choices.

Jacob had allowed himself to grow close to Uncle John these last couple of months. But now, now that he knew how twisted this family was, now that the evil of it was poured out at his feet, he knew for sure what he must do. He had to leave this place. He had to find his real family, the only real family he'd ever had. And, he had to do it soon. Because now that he knew how his uncle really felt about his mother, every minute here felt like a betrayal.

Chapter 26
Master Lee

The knuckles on Jacob's right hand were pale from gripping his phone so tightly. He'd been in this position a couple of times, chickening out before he dialed the numbers. What would he say? He didn't even know if he had the right place. But he wanted to try. He wanted to know why his mother had a box of knives among her things, and why she had so carefully kept it a secret.

Jacob took a deep breath and dialed. The sound of the phone ringing made him nervous and he was tempted to hang up again, but the call was answered before he could.

"Red Door Martial Arts," a young female voice said into his ear.

"Hi … I mean, hello. I have a question about something that I think was purchased there?"

"Okay, what's your question?"

"Well, I have this wood box that has knives in it and I was wondering if you sell many of those?"

"Not too many. Why?"

"Well, the key is missing and I was wondering if you can replace it. Your number was on the bottom of the box."

"Sure, we should be able to do that. Is it the black one?"

"No, it's a natural wood. Koa, I think."

"Koa, really? And you're sure you got it here?"

"Well, your number was on the bottom of the box. It has an engraving of a phoenix on the lid, if that helps."

"A phoenix?" The girl paused. "What did you say your name was?"

"I didn't, but it's Jacob."

"Hold on, I need to check something with the owner."

Jacob heard the girl's footsteps and then abrupt silence as if she'd muted the phone. A minute or two later the deep voice he'd heard on the answering machine came on the line.

"Hello, this is Master Lee. Who is this?"

"Um, my name's Jacob."

"Hi, Jacob. So, where did you find that box?"

"It was my mom's."

"And, where is your mom now?" The voice was calming, older, like a grandpa's voice should sound.

He hesitated. "Did you know my mom?"

"Where is Lilly now, Jacob?" Master Lee said more firmly.

"How did you know my mom?"

"Jacob, that question isn't easy to answer. If you bring the box to me, we can talk more. Can you come here?"

"I'm living on the mainland now. I don't know when I'll be back," he said.

"Can you tell me, where is Lilly? Is she with you?"

"No. I don't know where she is," Jacob admitted. "Nobody knows."

Master Lee made a sound like a sob. "We'd heard, but still we hoped. Jacob, this call isn't about a key, is it?"

"No. The box is open. I know what's inside. But I don't understand why my mom had these. And, how did you know her?"

"I'm sorry, Jacob, but I can't help you."

Jacob heard a click and then a dial tone. He'd hung up. Still, he'd learned what he wanted to learn. His mother had known Master Lee. The box did come from the Red Door. And, when Jacob made it back to Oahu, he knew just whom he'd visit first. He'd find a way to visit Master Lee—in person. Then he would find his mom.

Chapter 27
The Search

"What the hell?" Jacob said, pulling the plate from the refrigerator. He'd eventually agreed to care for Gideon while Dr. Silva made her trip to St. Louis and was following the directions she'd left for him. The note on the plate said *for Gideon* in Dr. Silva's tight scrawl but the food looked nothing like cat food. There was no meat. It was fresh peaches, cottage cheese, and a variety of fresh vegetables. Could a cat live on this? He placed the plate next to Gideon's water. The big red cat came running and buried his face in the dish. Not the weirdest thing he'd seen since coming to Paris, but a vegetarian cat definitely made the top ten.

With Gideon distracted, Jacob wasted no time. The relationship between Dr. Silva and her cat was something he hadn't figured out yet, but he had a gut feeling it was better if Gideon didn't know what he was about to do. Quietly, he walked toward the door and then veered left to the staircase.

Even with Gideon occupied, everywhere Jacob moved in the house, thousands of eyes followed him. Dr. Silva had a penchant for Victorian decorating and every conceivable type of angel could be found in her furnishings. There were statues and paintings; even the newel post was carved into the image of an angel. *Creepy.*

Jacob climbed the stairs two at a time. Instructions for navigating through Oswald were written in years and years of charts Dr. Silva had kept on her travels. She'd mentioned them to Jacob when he'd first asked her how she knew where the tree would take them. These notes were the key to going home and starting the search for his mom. He planned to return to the spot where she was last seen, Manoa Falls. It seemed like the best place to start, not to mention on Oahu where the Red Door was located. They might not give him answers over the phone but they wouldn't deny him in person. If Dr. Silva wouldn't help him, he would help himself.

The landing at the top of the stairs was a library. Shelves of books stretched from floor to ceiling in a three-sided square around several leather recliners and a large empty table. Against a window overlooking the backyard a huge book rested on a wooden stand. He walked over to it but was disappointed to find it was the Oxford International Dictionary. Of course it wasn't going to be that easy.

He perused the books on the shelves. There was a complete wall of volumes on exotic plants. Another shelf housed information on herbs, gardens, and landscaping. There was a shelf of botany textbooks that appeared to be written by Dr. Silva herself, and a row of organic gardening magazines.

Once it was obvious that the library didn't contain what he was looking for, he headed down the hall, opening doors as he went. There were six bedrooms filled with furniture covered in white sheets. Of course, none of these rooms would get any use; Dr. Silva lived alone and as far as Jacob knew had never had a guest. There were two bathrooms, as empty and unused as any of the other rooms.

At the very end of the hall, he opened the door to the master bedroom. This room looked lived in, or maybe a better description would be died in. Dr. Silva's bedroom was black—black walls, a black comforter, and wrought-iron fixtures. The only color in the room came from red candles whose wax had dripped in various patterns on the lacquer and the large stained glass window Jacob realized was the repaired version of the one he'd broken.

Malini was right about the black. It did look like a cave. He entered the room and was swallowed by the darkness. He wondered how it must feel at night, devoid of even the light that streamed through the stained glass window. Like everything else in her house, the image in the window was of angels, two reaching for each other. The background looked like the Garden of Eden, complete with snake and apple tree. The first angel, a glorious vision of blue and white, was depicted reaching down from the heavens above the tree in the garden. From the roots of the tree, the second angel was reaching up, the hand emerging from the slate depths. The wings were leathery black like a bat's, the body humanoid but with serpent skin and vertical slit yellow pupils. This was a dark angel, crawling from the depths of hell. What had Dr. Silva called it? A Watcher.

"Creepy. Who the hell would want that in their house?" Jacob said. He turned his attention back to his quest. "Where is it?" he whispered to himself. Opening drawers and digging through shelves, he searched for the notebooks without success, careful to replace everything exactly the way he'd found it.

When he was sure the notebooks weren't in her bedroom, he descended the stairs and opened the front door to leave. Taking one last look up toward the landing, he thought about places he could search the next day. Gideon was looking down at him, tail twitching.

"How long have you been there?" Jacob wondered out loud.

The cat answered with a menacing growl.

Chapter 28
Independence Day

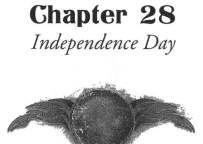

On the fourth of July, Jacob rushed through his chores at Dr. Silva's in order to join Malini and her family to celebrate. Although he'd searched every part of the Victorian, he hadn't found any clues to where the notebooks were hidden. He decided taking the day off to have some fun with Malini wasn't a bad idea.

The Guptas had a cottage on Lake Stelton, a relatively small natural body of water just under an hour from Paris. Homey vacation cottages lined the shore. The Guptas' place was one of the largest: a cedar two-story nestled in the pine trees with a gigantic wrap-around porch and a slip where Jim Gupta docked his ski boat during the summer. Jacob had never skied before but Malini swore it was a blast, so he promised to give it a try.

"I'll go first, so you can watch how it's done, right?" Malini said with a wink. She pulled her white cover-up off. Jacob pretended not to notice how unbelievably beautiful she was in her aqua-blue bikini. Her parents seemed completely oblivious to their daughter's level of attractiveness and he didn't want to be the one to draw their attention to it.

She donned a life jacket and climbed into the water. Mrs. Gupta handed her a ski and Malini leaned back in the gentle waves to get her foot into the boot. Once she was positioned, Jacob tossed her the rope. The boat idled against her weight.

"Hit it!" she yelled, and Jim Gupta threw the throttle forward. Malini popped out of the water and swung out to the side of the boat before the wake could meet her ski. She stayed out there for a while, getting comfortable, and then cut deep on her left edge, stretching her body out almost parallel to the surface of the water. Cutting in, she jumped the wake, catching air before landing on the other side and leaning on her right edge. After a few more passes and a lap around the lake, she let go of the rope and sank gracefully into the water.

"So that's how it's done, huh?" Jacob said, helping her up the ladder. "Something tells me you've done this before."

"Oh just about four hundred times," she laughed.

He donned a larger life vest that Mrs. Gupta handed him and climbed into the water. The sensation was remarkable. He'd grown up near the ocean and had always been at home in the water. But this was the first time he'd been submerged since he'd discovered his gift. This wasn't like the rain or a shower; he was surrounded by it. Like before, the individual molecules of water hummed to him but now they also buzzed against his skin. Over the last few weeks, as he'd continued to train with Dr. Silva, the power had grown stronger and more predictable. Maybe it was experience or that he had learned to listen more intently for the hum. But whatever the reason, today the whole lake felt like an extension of himself.

"Earth to Jacob?" Malini was holding out a pair of skis to him.

"Why two? You only used one." Jacob willed the sensation away and the hum stopped. He'd try this the old-fashioned way. A normal boy, who just happened to be a Soulkeeper, out skiing with his girlfriend.

"It's easier to learn with two."

"I think I'd like to give one a try," he said.

"Really, Jake, it's nearly impossible your first time. I've had loads of practice. You should start with two."

"One," he insisted, taking the one with the toe strap on the back from her hand. She pulled the other back into the boat.

"Suit yourself," she laughed, raising her eyebrows.

Jacob leaned back and put the ski on his right foot, sliding his other toe through the strap in the rear. He could do this. How hard could it be? The rope plopped down in the water in front of him and the boat trolled away. He bent his knees like Malini had and gripped the handle firmly, feeling the gentle tug. When he felt himself balanced over the ski, he yelled, "Hit it."

The boat lurched. Jacob overcompensated by bending at the middle. Big mistake. His bodyweight spilled frontward, the ski slid back and he skipped across the water like a stone, face first, before letting go of the rope and sinking into the lake.

"Owww," he said as the sound of the boat and Malini's laughter approached.

"Are you okay?" she yelled.

Mrs. Gupta tugged at Malini's elbow, looking concerned.

"Fine. I'm fine, Mrs. Gupta. I'm good. Let's try again."

"Are you sure you don't want the other ski?" Malini said.

"Positive." He readjusted in the water and grabbed the rope again.

"Just remember to lean back, bend your knees, and tighten your abs," she called.

The boat dragged him along in the water and he shifted his weight so he was almost sitting on the back of the ski. "Hit it!" he called.

When the lurching came, he was ready. He leaned back against the rope, arms straight, abs tight. The water flowed over his body as he straightened his knees to get above it. But then the wake of the boat knocked into him, the ski slipped forward and Jacob went rolling across the water again, the ski popping off his foot and clipping him in the shoulder before he sank. He grabbed it before it could float away.

"Jacob, stop being stubborn and just try the second ski. That was a really good try, but trust me you are not getting up on this ski today." Malini smiled but there was a note of frustration in her voice. Mrs. Gupta frowned over the side of the boat.

He was testing their patience but, for reasons he didn't fully understand, proving to Malini he could do this was important to him. He wanted to show her he was strong, she could trust him, and he could protect her. Maybe it was a childish thing to do, but he couldn't stop himself. He wanted to impress her.

"One more time. I'm fine, really!" Jacob said and then closed his eyes and called the water. The hum started again and the feeling of vibration on his skin. Malini threw the rope and he snatched it out of the air with one hand. His ski back on, he willed the water steady beneath him. Once the rope was taut, it was less like being dragged than standing on an underwater conveyor belt that was moving at the same speed as the boat. Everything became clear. He could feel the water and everything in it. He was the water.

"Hit it!" he yelled, and couldn't help remembering the day in Dr. Silva's garden when he'd thrown the bowl of water on the dirt. *If I'm a Soulkeeper, shouldn't I be able to walk on this stuff,* he'd said. Today, he was about to find out.

The boat lurched forward and he concentrated on keeping his body straight. Only now it was not only his muscles that did the work but also the water around him. One thousand hands lifted him to standing. When the wake hit, it didn't knock him down like the last time. It flowed around a patch of smooth water the exact size of his ski that carried him forward as if he were coasting across glass.

Jacob decided to push his luck and swing out to the side of the boat. There was a moment of panic as he jumped the wake and lost contact with the water, but when he landed the water adjusted, steadying the ski. He stole a glance toward Malini. She was facing him in the spotter's position, her mouth hanging open. One more lap around the lake and he felt like he'd proved his point. He let go of the rope and willed himself to sink.

The boat circled to him and the Guptas gave him a round of applause before helping him up the ladder.

"That was amazing!" Malini said. Her eyes twinkled, flecks of gold and red breaking up the chocolate brown in the light reflected off the water.

"I had a good teacher," he replied, placing an arm around her waist.

"Have you kids had enough?" Mr. Gupta asked, reaching for the rope in such a way as to wedge his body between them.

"Yeah, I'm through," Jacob said.

Malini nodded.

Once everything was safely stowed, Mr. Gupta sped toward the cedar cottage. He was talking about dinner, something about hamburgers on the grill, but Jacob was hardly listening. He was watching the way Malini's hair flew back from her face in the speed-driven wind. The sun was a red ball of fire surrounded by streaks of pinks and purples behind her. She smiled and, in that moment, there was not a thing that he wanted or needed in the world. He had everything.

Chapter 29
Fire and Ice

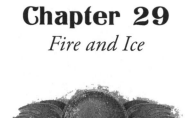

The sand in front of the Guptas' cottage was dark and coarse, littered with clamshells and stones. It wasn't the type of beach Jacob was used to, not an ocean beach, but as he lit the pile of driftwood under the starry sky and saw the gold in Malini's eyes spark in the glow of the fire, he could think of nowhere he would rather be. She spread a blanket a few feet from the blaze. Sparks floated into the night sky.

Mr. and Mrs. Gupta sat on the balcony of the cottage having an after-dinner cup of coffee. The path from the beach to the cedar steps of the balcony was sufficiently wooded to give Jacob the privacy he wanted to tell Malini what he needed to tell her. He'd been thinking about it for a long time, rolling it around in his brain. If his plan had any chance of working, she had to understand what she meant to him.

He took Malini's hand and sat down with her on the blanket. His arm wrapped around her back in a way that was instinctual for him now. She was a puzzle piece, fitting into his side where there had always been an empty space.

"You did really well today, Jake. I can't believe this was your first time skiing," she said.

"You too. You're amazing. Is there anything you can't do?"

"Lots of things. But none that I'll admit." She smiled at him and he couldn't resist leaning in for a gentle kiss. He pulled back a fraction of an inch.

"How long have we known each other, Malini?"

"About six months."

"You're my best friend."

"You're mine, too. I don't know what I'd do without you."

"I feel the same way. I just … I want you to know." Jacob reached his toe forward until it touched the edge of the water. "I feel like I can trust you. I want to show you something. Something you've been asking me about for a while now. But don't freak out, okay?"

"This is about that day at the grocery store with Dane, isn't it? Something else has happened."

He nodded.

"Anything. You can tell me anything," she said.

"You'll keep it a secret."

"Yes. Of course."

Jacob asked the water to climb his leg to the hand that rested on his knee. Once it flowed into his palm, he willed it into a chain, freezing each link as it formed. Instead of the last link, he made a solid heart. The crystals formed facets within its center, flickering in the firelight like a gemstone. He wrapped the bracelet around her wrist. He didn't need a clasp; the water melted and refroze in exactly the right size.

Malini's face was a mask of astonishment, her mouth slightly open, her eyes wide.

"What is this, Jake? This thing with you, is it getting stronger? You can control it now. When did that start?"

"Malini, can't you just relax and enjoy this?"

"No, I want to know. I'm worried about you. Do you understand this at all? I want to help you."

"For tonight, just for tonight, can you just enjoy it? Can we decide to talk about it tomorrow? I have something I want to tell you."

Malini's mouth twisted into a disappointed scowl but he could see how much she wanted the night to continue. She was in as deep as he was, and she didn't want to get out. As much as she was dying to understand the how of it, he was sure she was more interested in knowing what he had to say.

"It's cold," she finally said, smiling again. Her shoulders relaxed as she admired the ice in the firelight.

"That's one of the problems. The other is, if I let go, it will melt. But I'll get you a real one someday."

"I love it," she said.

"There's something I want to tell you."

"What?" she asked. He watched the fire dance inside the heart.

"I think I love you, Malini. I feel like I've known you forever and I will know you forever. I love you. I know we're young but I want us to stay together."

Malini looked up from the heart, into his eyes. "I love you, too." And, then she was kissing him. She lifted her wrist from his hand, the bracelet melting down her arm, and placed her palm on his face.

Jacob hardly noticed the cold water that dripped down his chest. His whole world was her mouth, her face. Even when the fireworks began, sending showers of twinkling light over Lake Stelton, they had nothing on her. In front of the water, stretched out on the blanket, something told him nothing ever would.

Chapter 30
The Hardware Stone

*S*nakes are everywhere. They drip from the branches of the tree, falling like strands of spaghetti to the sand and surrounding his feet.

"Help, Jacob! Help me," a voice calls from behind him. He turns to see Malini, her eyes wide with terror. The snakes close in. Jacob leaps into the air, flipping over the serpents and landing directly in front of her. He reaches for the canteen around his neck and pours the water into his hand. He wills it into a scythe of ice and slices at the snakes writhing at Malini's feet. Scaly skin flies, rubbery flesh piling in the sand. They die, but more come.

They talk to her in hisses, all of them at once.

"Come with us." They ignore the slashing scythe. "We will give you the world. Think of all the good you will do when you control it."

Jacob glances back, expecting to see fear on Malini's face, but she is serene. She is resolved, calm as a stone. She lifts her hand to Jacob's shoulder and, as she makes contact, everything becomes clear.

Jacob knows exactly what to do. He drops the scythe, circles his arms, and delivers a two-handed push. Not a human push, a push from somewhere greater, with power beyond his own. The sky opens and the rain pours down. The serpents don't stand a chance.

* * * * *

God, he hated his dreams. Jacob rolled over and looked at the clock—five-thirty. What he wouldn't give for a full night's sleep. He reached under the pillow to try to get comfortable. His fingers tangled in a cord. Rolling onto his back, he pulled his hand out and the red stone came with it, twinkling in the early morning light.

Between his thumb and forefinger, he examined the stone again, the light picking up the network of facets under the smooth surface. When he would orient it in just the right way, a black square was visible, as if the stone had formed around an imperfection. He brought the stone closer to get a better look and the redness seemed to grow larger with his shift in perspective. A weightless shift, like free falling, overcame him. He reached out to grab the bed but it was gone. His room was gone. He fell into the black square at the center of the red and stood up in the oddest place he could have imagined. It was blank, an empty page.

"Where am I?" he asked. His body felt funny, disconnected somehow.

"In between," a voice said.

In the blink of an eye, he was standing in a hardware store. Behind the counter, an old man in overalls and a cap drummed his fingers.

"Who are you?" Jacob asked.

"You don't remember me? Well, I guess I looked different when I gave you the stone." Abruptly, the man shrank into the hunched dwarf woman, and then grew back into himself. "I thought this form would be easier for you," he said.

"What are you? What is this place?"

"A gift from the Achuar. The Healer felt sorry for you, for the loss of your mama. She wanted to give you something. I am a window."

"A window?"

"I am part of the Healer's medicine, her gift of sight. I am a shadow of her mind. Ask me and I will answer."

"So I can ask you anything?"

"You can. But I can only answer questions about the future, as it stands today. The future is always changing. Every decision is a fork in the road. I can tell you only where the road leads, today. But mind yourself, Horseman; knowledge of the future is a dangerous thing. Are you prepared?"

"Yes," he said, too quickly.

"Then ask what you will."

"Where is my mother?"

"That is a question about the present, not the future. I cannot answer."

"Then, will I find my mother?"

The man pulled out a hubcap from behind the counter. He selected a variety of nuts and bolts from various bowls, and folded them into his greasy palm. Shaking them vigorously, he threw them like dice into the hubcap. They crashed and clanged. When they'd settled at the center the man leaned over them, reading their position against the metal. "Yes," he said.

"Is she alive?"

"I can't answer that question."

Jacob was beginning to understand. He tried again.

"Will she be dead or alive when I find her?"

The nuts and bolts made a sound like a cymbal as they hit the pan.

"Neither."

"Neither. That doesn't make any sense. Explain?"

The man shook his head. Frustrated, he tried again.

"Will I use the tree to find her?"

Clang

"Yes."

Jacob thought hard about how to phrase his next question.

"How will I find the notebooks about the tree?"

Crash

The man studied the pattern of nuts and bolts. "Gideon," he said.

The white walls of the store bled to pink, then red.

"Looks like it's time for you to go. Y'all come back now, real soon," said the man, waving his meaty hand. Backward Jacob flew, as if the stone was spitting him out. He fell onto his bed, into the square of light streaming through the window. Someone was banging on his door.

"Time for church, moron," yelled Katrina.

"I'll be right there." He slid the stone back under his pillow and bounded out of bed, bracing himself for another long morning.

Chapter 31
Gideon's Passage

As soon as his obligatory Sunday brunch was eaten, Jacob crossed the street to Dr. Silva's. He didn't need an excuse, it was his job to feed the cat and weed the garden. In fact, he would do those things, but he would do something else as well. He would find Dr. Silva's notebooks and learn how to navigate Oswald.

The mosquitoes were becoming a nuisance after dark, so he decided to work in the garden first. He finished up by late afternoon, and then let himself in through the sunroom to feed Gideon. The big red cat was waiting, pacing the tabletop. Jacob pulled the next plate from the refrigerator and placed it on the floor.

"You must be hungry, huh, boy," Jacob said.

Gideon didn't move. The tip of his tail twitched.

"You can eat now." He tapped the edge of the dish and made a kissing sound with his lips. Gideon blinked in his general direction.

"Okay. Whatever," Jacob said. According to the stone, Gideon would somehow be the key to finding the notebooks but he didn't understand how. Maybe it wasn't the cat but rather something about the cat. He decided to search the library again. Maybe a book on cats or a picture of Gideon would be the clue he needed.

He walked toward the front of the house. When he reached the bottom of the grand staircase, Gideon leapt in front of him, teeth bared. The cat growled a low warning, the hair on his back standing straight up.

"Gideon, get out of the way," Jacob said and tried to step around him. The cat struck, shredding his shin with his claws.

"Owww. Son of a ... damn it, Gideon! What the hell?" He reached down and pulled up his pant leg. Three rips in his skin dripped blood onto his sock. He limped back to the kitchen, not wanting the blood to stain the white marble floor. With a wet paper towel, he dabbed at the cuts. They stung fiercely. He had to sit down and put the scratched leg up in a chair to get a good look at it.

Gideon followed him into the kitchen and sat too close for comfort, glaring in his direction. The stare was knowing, almost ... human. An idea clicked into place as fast as his brain could process it. Dr. Silva was not human, and her cat was probably not a normal cat. What exactly the cat was, he didn't know for sure, but what he did know was that if he wanted Gideon's help he would have to take a more direct approach.

"Gideon, I need to go upstairs." Jacob looked the cat full on like he was talking to a person.

The cat shook his head from side to side. He *did* understand.

"I have to find Dr. Silva's notebooks. The ones that say how to use Oswald. It's important."

Again, the cat shook his head vigorously.

"It's the only way. I have to find my mom. I can't just forget about her. She's the only real family I have left." He rubbed his eyes. "It's not that I don't like the people I've met in Paris. My friend Malini, my Uncle John, Dr. Silva, they've all become important to me. But the thing is, my mom is all I have left of my history. She's my roots, my only link to who I really am. If she's alive, the thought that she could be somewhere and need my help…" He shook his head. "I have to find her. I have to help."

The cat continued to stare but his eyes softened. Jacob was getting through.

"Gideon, how do I make you understand?" He rested his head in his hands. "After my dad died, when I was, I think, eleven, my mom took me to the beach. It was a Sunday afternoon and our first time back since we lost him. I was boogie boarding. It was a great day for it because the water was rough and the waves were big. I'm not sure when exactly I knew I was in trouble. The water swept me from shore but I thought I could swim through it. I lost my board in the waves but I was a strong swimmer, always have been. But the harder I swam, the harder the water pushed. I swam until my muscles ached but went nowhere.

"I think I realized I was caught in a riptide when I saw my mom wade into the water. She dove straight into it and let the water carry her out to me. While I struggled and panicked, she just went with the current. I was so tired by then that I stopped swimming. The ocean swallowed me and I saw the sun grow smaller through the surface as I sank. Frickin' hilarious now, don't you think, to know I almost drowned when my body was just waiting to give me the ability to control water?

"My mom got there just in time. She put her arm under my chin and pulled my head to the surface. I caught my breath again and struggled against her grip. I thought we were going to die. She told me to relax, to let the riptide take us out to sea. Somehow, I calmed down enough to listen to her. Sure enough the surge of water eventually spat us out. Once outside of the riptide's hold, she floated on her back, my head in her arm, and kicked us back to shore. It wasn't until we reached the beach that she started to cry. She said, 'You've got to be more careful, Jacob. We are all we have now. It's just us. We've got to take care of each other.' Don't you get it, Gideon? She's lost, somewhere, in her own riptide. No one is coming for her. I. Am. All. She. Has."

Gideon looked down at his paws. Jacob sensed that if the cat could shed tears he would.

"Gideon, have you ever lost something, something so important to you that you felt like it didn't matter if you lived or died to find it? What mattered is that you tried."

The red cat blinked slowly, and nodded. His green eyes expressed sheer agony. Jacob was surprised at the depth of it and out of pity reached out to scratch him behind the ear. Gideon jerked his head away, annoyed.

"What matters to me is that I can look in the mirror tomorrow and know that I tried everything in my power to get her back. So what do you say? Will you help me?" he asked.

Gideon's whiskers pulled back from his teeth. At first Jacob thought he'd offended the cat. Then he realized Gideon was smiling. The cat leapt from the table and ran for the stairs. Jacob stood on his bloody leg and followed at a limp. The scratches must have been deeper than they looked because they oozed blood and burned like his leg was on fire. Hobbling up the stairs proved to be pure agony and took much longer than it should have. When he finally reached the library, Gideon looked irritated.

"Don't look at me like that, Gideon. You did this to me," Jacob said. "My leg is shredded." He held up his pant leg to show off the swollen red wound.

Gideon twitched his whiskers. With a coughing fit that sounded like he had a hairball caught in his throat, he ejected an enormous wad of spit onto Jacob's hurt leg.

"Ewww," he said and was about to rip into the cat for adding insult to injury, when to his amazement the pain started to ebb. As the saliva dripped down his shin, the scratches visibly healed.

"I wasn't expecting that," he said.

Gideon made a sound between a laugh and a growl. Jacob followed him to the wall farthest from the bedrooms. A tapestry of *the Four Horsemen of the Apocalypse* hung from a dowel, its length spanning floor to ceiling over the silver paint. Gideon looked back at Jacob and then walked into the tapestry. He disappeared.

Mouth open, Jacob approached the wall that had just swallowed the cat. The cloth of the tapestry was rough against his fingers. Once, when he was younger, he'd seen a magic show where the magician had used layered mirrors to disappear. He ran his hand behind the tapestry, looking for an explanation for the illusion.

The cat popped up beside him again, shaking his head. He closed his eyes in a deliberate way, and leaped through again. What was he trying to say? Jacob closed his eyes. The first time Gideon had gone through with his eyes open. Why would he want him to close his eyes? What happened when he closed his eyes? He couldn't see the wall. Gideon didn't want Jacob to see the wall. What else had he done differently? He had jumped. Why would it be important to not see the wall and to jump? Maybe because seeing was believing. Maybe, Gideon was trying to tell him to not believe in the wall. Maybe, the wall was an illusion.

With this in mind, Jacob kept his eyes closed and leapt forward. His feet left carpet but landed on hard floor. He opened his eyes at the base of a winding iron staircase on the other side of the wall. Gideon's white teeth stood out from his silhouette, framed in light from above. Jacob followed as the cat led him higher and higher up the spiral. The stairs ended in a round room with hardwood floors and walls made almost entirely of windows. He was in the tower!

The witch's hat tower loomed over the west side of the house. It was what gave the gothic Victorian its characteristic dark mood. Jacob hadn't noticed before that there didn't seem to be any way up to it from the inside of the house. Without Gideon, he might never have found it at all. The view was stunning. Dr. Silva protected this place for good reason. He could see Oswald from up here, as well as the entire enchanted garden.

He took a look around the room. A sophisticated telescope stood near the east window. In the center of the room, a gigantic mahogany desk with a marble top was covered in papers. Behind the desk, every square inch of a standalone bookcase was covered with books and papers. There was no lamp or overhead light. Instead, candelabras circled the room. With enough natural light still streaming through the windows, he didn't feel the need to light them.

Jacob walked over to the desk and started riffling through the mass of papers, mostly drawings of roots and leaves. Several experiments used chemical formulas that he didn't understand. On the bookshelf, no less than twenty versions of the Bible took up an entire shelf along with books on Buddhism, Judaism, and Taoism.

He rolled the wooden chair aside and squatted down to look at the pile of papers on the lowest shelf. A corner of a picture frame poked out from under a bowl of bark samples. He moved the bowl aside and picked up the picture. The portrait was painted, oil on canvas, in the style you see in museums. The man in the picture had slicked-back hair, a three-piece suit, and a perfect smile. But it was the woman in the photo that gave away his identity. Dr. Silva stared back at him from behind Oswald's shoulder, looking exactly the same as she did today except for her dress, which reminded him of something out of the Wild West.

So, she didn't age? He wasn't surprised.

Under the frame was a stack of leather-bound journals. *Jackpot!* He thumbed through them and saw hundreds of entries, dates, times, places. And then he noticed a poster-sized roll of paper stuck between the corner of the shelf and the books. He pulled it out, slid the outer band off, and unrolled it on the desk. It was a map of the world, covered in a web of dated lines, all of them leading back to one place: the tree in the garden. Oswald.

Chapter 32
The Wrong Direction

The map and Dr. Silva's notebooks looked complicated, but Jacob forced himself to sit down and go through each page. After an hour or so, he checked his watch. He would have to hurry. If he wasn't back by dinner, John might come looking for him. Fortunately, he found the concept quite simple, once he saw the pattern.

The tree accessed power connected to the longitude and latitude of the Earth, like a spider on a web. The web connected the tree in Paris to the place the spider crawled. The spider moved around the globe at an angle, reaching every other tree in the world over the course of a year. Over twenty-four hours it moved along the longitude of the Earth. At the same time, the months of the year caused it to climb the lines of latitude. The power reached the equator halfway through the year, which was why, he realized, they had visited Peru in June.

The calculation of longitude was fairly straightforward, mapping exactly against the time zones and International Date Line. Latitude was much trickier. The rise from South to North happened more quickly at the poles and slowed as the force reached the equator. He thought of it like this: the spider's web was stretched more tightly across the middle of the Earth and the spider had longer to crawl to complete the circle to reach its next thread.

He smoothed the map out on the desk and searched for the North Pacific just beneath the Tropic of Cancer. When he'd found Oahu, he traced it with his finger. The island was small in the vast blue ink that represented the Pacific Ocean. If he didn't know exactly what he was doing, he could easily drown in its depths, emerging in a mass of seaweed, miles from dry land. Of course, he could control water now. If he missed, he could ride a wave to shore—he hoped. A date near the island read August 15th, 1992. It was logical that August 15th would be the date he tried to get home to find his mother.

He thought he understood the basics, but there were things he couldn't explain, anomalies that didn't follow the rules, like a rogue date in Munich, Germany in January 1945, and Hong Kong in December of 2000. Dr. Silva said it had taken her decades to learn to use the tree. Jacob only had a few minutes more. As luck would have it, he found the answer in her journal.

Dr. Silva could use sorcery to build a string between Oswald and any other tree, regardless of the date. Her power acted as the tree's power; she stood in for the spider. But following the string backward from a normal tree was only possible while the string was still open, twenty-four to forty-eight hours. According to Dr.

Silva's earliest entries, climbing back up the spider's web always took magic. She could follow someone or something else, if their string was still open. But once the string was gone, a normal tree wasn't enough to amplify her magic.

No wonder she had been so adamant about Jacob not using the tree alone. Without her, there was no way he could get back. It also explained why their trip to Peru had to be short. She needed to help him return before the string dissolved.

Jacob slapped his hand on the desk when he realized Dr. Silva could've used her magic to take him to visit the Medicine woman much earlier. What she'd told him had been a half-truth. Yes, if he were traveling alone, June 10th was the day of connection. Dr. Silva could've built a string from Oswald. He suspected she hadn't offered because she knew the trip wouldn't help. She wanted to dangle the carrot long enough to fill his head with her story about being a Soulkeeper. He'd been such a fool.

The trip to Oahu would be risky. He wouldn't have Dr. Silva to help him back. If he went through with this, it would be permanent. But after everything he'd learned this week about Dr. Silva's half-truths and the Laudner family history, he didn't care. He had to go.

He rolled the map and tucked it back into the corner of the shelf. With the help of some notes he'd made, he replaced the notebooks exactly how they'd been. Dr. Silva was returning the day after tomorrow and it was imperative that she not know what he was planning. He folded his page of notes and slid it into his back pocket.

Making his way toward the stairs, the ruddy cat seemed to pop up out of the floor at Jacob's feet, and he stumbled trying not to kick him. Gideon was statuesque, staring out the window. On a whim, Jacob decided to throw him off the trail, just in case he changed his mind about being helpful.

"Thanks, Gideon. I guess my plan won't work after all. Not without Dr. Silva anyway. I wouldn't be able to get back. But thanks for giving me a chance. Now I feel like I've done what I can."

The cat's eyes wrinkled at the corners and he wondered if Gideon knew he was lying. He walked down from the tower side by side with the cat. Before he left, he saw Gideon eating. That was all the assurance he needed.

Chapter 33
The Dishonest Mistake

"**M**alini, I want to show you something," Jacob said.

He placed his hand on the small of her back. It was August 15th. After a month of waiting, he'd packed the phoenix box, a small bag of provisions, and as much money as he could get his hands on into a backpack. There was only one thing left to do and that was to convince Malini to come, too. The promise he'd made to her that night in his room was only part of the reason. He knew, in his heart, she wanted to go. She hated it here.

"What's going on?" she asked. She was sitting on her front porch, enjoying the last hours of the morning before the August heat became oppressive.

"Look, I can't tell you; I have to show you. But it's important."

"What is it?"

"Just trust me, okay? It's a surprise."

"Of course." Malini leaned forward and kissed him lightly on the lips.

"Good, come on." He took her hand and led her to his truck.

They drove in silence. Malini was abnormally quiet, as if she could sense the tension in the air. Jacob was nervous about what he'd have to do. When he was within a mile of Dr. Silva's, he parked Big Blue on the side of the road. Instead of going up the front yard toward the house, he walked Malini directly into the maple orchard.

"What are we doing at Dr. Silva's?"

"This is where it is, what I have to show you."

"Does she know I'm here?"

"No. But it's okay."

In fact, he knew what he was about to do was far from okay with Dr. Silva. At this very moment, she was inside the house. She would be furious when she found out, but by that time he would be long gone.

Once Jacob was deep inside the orchard, he relaxed a little. With Malini by his side, he hiked down the sloping hill to the wrought-iron gate. The key was in the lock as always and he gave it a quick turn before opening the gate for Malini. It wasn't long before she noticed the magic of the garden.

"Oh, it's hot back here," she said. She was wearing shorts and T-shirts but the weather was notably more humid as they walked through the gate. "It's so weird. This is unbelievable."

"Unbelievable, yes, but this is not what I have to show you." Jacob flashed an unfamiliar sideways grin. The power was intoxicating. He was about to take her someplace she'd never been. In all of his life, he'd never been the taker. He was always the taken. It was a nice change of pace. He intended to be an excellent guide.

Reaching for her hand, he led her down the path. When they passed the corpse plants, he motioned for her to cover her nose. He helped her gingerly over each of the rocks in the blood dragon patch and through the meadow.

Although she said very little, Malini's eyes were filled with wonder at her surroundings. She followed closely behind him, squeezing his hand in hers. Jacob was filled with her need for him. It surprised him how much he enjoyed it. Her utter dependence made him feel strong, protective. It filled a hole he'd never known he had.

Jacob was so distracted with impressing her that he ignored the feeling that someone was watching him from behind the trees. The whisper of his name on the wind in the meadow was likewise not acknowledged. And when a ripple danced across the sand of the dune, he shrugged it off. This was the magic of the garden. It was trying to scare him off, just like the first time.

He led her through the maze and emerged near the gnarled tree that he knew as Oswald.

"Jacob, this place is amazing but I'm getting a funny feeling. Should we be back here?"

"Malini, it's fine. Trust me. I want to tell you about this tree."

"It's really unusual. I've never seen anything like it, not even in India."

"No, it's one of a kind." Jacob laughed. "If you touch this tree right now with me, it will take us to Oahu. It will take me home and you can come with me."

She looked at him blankly for a moment, and then laughed through her nose.

"What is this all about, Jacob? Why are you teasing me?"

"I'm serious. Hold my hand and I will touch the tree. I promise you in two minutes we will be in Hawaii. I'll show you where I grew up."

Malini searched his face.

"You're insane!" She backed toward the entrance to the maze but the prickly twists and turns thwarted her. She had not paid enough attention to find her way out on her own.

"What if I'm not? Don't you want to try? Don't you want to get out of this town, Malini?" Jacob held out his hand. His other hand hovered over the bark of the tree.

Malini's face held a mix of agony and fear. She approached him slowly. At the last second, she snatched her fingers back before Jacob could take them. Something in her features changed, the fear replaced with resolve.

"If this is true, I don't want to go. I don't want to try this, Jacob."

"But why? Ever since I met you, you've said you hated Paris."

"Don't you see, Jacob? This isn't normal. Is it even safe? How does it work? What will it do to me? What will it do to my soul? I know nothing about it. How can I trust myself with it? How can you? And what if we do make it there, how will we survive? What if something happened to me during the trip? How would my parents know?"

Jacob listened to her words and knew what she said was true. For a moment, he regretted not thinking about these things when he'd gone through with Dr. Silva. But the truth was he didn't want to be careful with himself or his soul. She had more to lose than he did. All he had to lose was her.

It isn't worth it without her, came the voice.

"Did you hear that?" Jacob asked Malini.

"What? There's no one here but us."

Take her. You'll have to. She'll never go on her own.

Jacob grabbed Malini's wrist.

"What are you doing?" she gasped.

"It's for the best, Malini. You'll thank me once we get there." He dragged her toward the tree. "I have to go and I need you to come with me."

Malini dug her heels in the sand and pulled against his hand. Jacob squeezed tighter and reached toward the tree.

"No. NO! Stop it, Jake. Let me go. LET ME GO!" Her free hand beat against his arm.

"Just calm down. It will all work out. Just go along. It will be fine, Malini, you'll see." He succeeded in dragging her two more inches in the sand and touched the tree.

The bark climbed up his arm and he felt the familiar slowing. From this perspective, Malini's struggle appeared in fast-forward. She was crying now, her eyes wide with terror, her hands and feet thrashing against him. He was hurting her. She struggled like he was killing her.

Jacob lost his nerve and pulled his hand away from the tree. He let go of her wrist and she fell to the sand, sobbing.

"Why did you do that?" he yelled. "Why can't you trust me?"

"I told you, I don't want to," her voice cracked.

"Malini, you don't understand. I have to. I need to go back. I need to find my mom."

"I'm not going. Jacob, please don't do this. At least walk me out. I can't find my way out without you." Tears cascaded down her cheeks. Jacob had no choice. She wouldn't make it back on her own and if she refused to go, he couldn't leave her here alone in the deadly garden.

He led her back to the gate in silence. The tension was a noose around his neck, growing tighter with every step. This wouldn't be right, not for a long time. Once they were through the gate, Malini collapsed on the mound at the base of the orchard and let all of the air out of her lungs.

"Why did you try to force me?" she whimpered.

"I just wanted you with me when I go. I wouldn't hurt you. It's perfectly safe."

"Safe! Jacob, that tree is not safe. Did you see the bark climb up your arm like it was going to eat you? Why would you believe it was safe?"

"I've done it before and I'm fine," he said, touching his chest.

"You've done it before?" Malini held her stomach like she was trying to hold herself together. "This has something to do with your gift. You've been hiding it from me. All of those times I've asked you if you knew anything more…"

Jacob did not deny it.

"You lied to me."

"It was more like I omitted the details."

"Same thing, Jacob. I have always been there for you. I knew about this thing with you, with the water. How could you keep this from me and then try to force me to be part of it against my will?"

"I didn't want to force you."

"You didn't? I told you, no." Her face was red with anger and wet with tears. "You didn't tell me ahead of time because you didn't want to give me the option of saying no."

"I'm sorry, Malini. It never occurred to me that you wouldn't want to go."

"No, I'm sorry. Because I don't trust you anymore. I don't want to be near you anymore. You've broken my heart, Jake. You are not the person I thought you were."

"Malini, please, don't cry."

"Why shouldn't I cry? I lost my best friend today."

"You didn't, okay. I won't go. I won't leave you."

"You don't get it, Jake. I'm leaving you. I never want to see you again."

She buried her face in her hands and cried, shaking with the effort. Jacob reached for her shoulder.

"Don't touch me!" she screamed. "Just go away!"

He took a step back, stung by her words. He waited, standing in front of her as she cried into her hands, but she was serious. The crushing realization of what he'd done almost brought him to his knees. Why had he gone so far? Why had he hurt her?

Jacob thought about returning to the tree and going through on his own. But he'd promised he wouldn't leave Malini. If he broke that promise, he would lose her forever. Maybe he already had. As long as he was near her, there was a possibility she would forgive him someday. But if he left, it was hopeless.

And for what? His mom wasn't on Oahu. It was as good of a place as any to start looking for her, but was it any more home than here without her? Without Malini, would it be worth it?

"I'm sorry, Malini. I made a terrible mistake," Jacob said.

Malini's sobs were heart-wrenching.

Defeated, he checked to make sure the gate was locked and walked away without looking back at her. He would wait in his truck to drive her home, but for now she needed to be alone. The orchard seemed darker than before. A gray cloud gathered in the summer sky and thunder rumbled in the distance. A storm was coming and, by the looks of it, a bad one.

Chapter 34
Fired

"You worthless human. What did you do?" Dr. Silva spat in his face. She said the word human like it was something vile.

Jacob dangled from her grip. The fingers around his neck contracted like talons, crushing his windpipe and pinning him up against the house. He struggled with everything he had, but Dr. Silva's arm was as unflinching as iron. Utter disgust twisted her expression and, as beautiful as he'd once thought she was, at this moment she was equally terrifying.

"Do you know what you're dealing with? Do you understand the kind of evil you might have unleashed? Do you have any idea the cost of your stupidity?"

Jacob tried to speak but the crushing force on his neck stopped any air from coming through. She narrowed her eyes and threw him to the ground like he weighed nothing.

"Wha … what did I do?" he gasped, staying on all fours and rubbing his neck.

"You broke the rules. You went through the tree without me." She paced in front of his crumpled form. "Just tell me one thing, how the hell did you make it back? It would have served you right to get stuck somewhere—painful." She kicked him in the ribs as if to prove her point. The kick hurt but he knew she was holding back. His ribs weren't broken.

"I … didn't go through. I touched the tree but I stopped. I pulled my hand away."

"Why?"

"I wanted to go home. I wanted to find my mom."

"Not why did you want to go. Why did you pull your hand away?"

"I changed my mind," Jacob started, but decided to keep what happened with Malini to himself. Something told him that he was in real trouble. Dr. Silva looked like she might kill him at any moment. He wanted none of that fury to fall on Malini.

"You changed your puny, arrogant, mind, huh? Well, you left the gate open!"

"I didn't. I locked it!"

"I found it open and guess what, Jacob? The key is enchanted; only you or I can turn it. Unless you did something stupid and invited someone else into the garden, it was you."

"I must have forgotten."

"You will want to forget if something came through. You will be begging to forget your pitiful life."

The dark expression on her face was not at all human. It was the face of a killer, and so close he could feel her breath. He tried his best not to pee his pants and hugged himself to stop from shaking.

"You know, never mind, this is a stupid waste of time. You're not ready. You're not ready for the responsibility of who you are and I'm done trying to help you. Go back to your stupid, meaningless, shallow life and forget who you are."

With that she picked him up by the scruff of his neck and dragged him around the front of the house. When they were within eyesight of the Laudners, she put him on his feet and gave him a shove forward. She followed as he walked across the street to the front door of the cheery yellow house but, when he reached for the doorknob to let himself in, she slapped his hand away. Instead, she rang the doorbell.

After a moment's pause the door swung open. "Oh ... Hello." Uncle John's voice sounded surprised. His eyes darted to Dr. Silva and then to Jacob.

"Hello, John," Dr. Silva began, her voice honey sweet. The striking, crooked smile had replaced the terrifying scowl. "I just wanted to let you know that Jacob has completely worked off his debt for my window. I will not be in need of his services anymore."

John nodded. There was a look of confusion on his face but he said nothing. Dr. Silva turned to Jacob, her eyes conveying a warning although her face stayed soft.

"Jacob, thank you for your help these last few months. You are free to go about your business. I won't be seeing you near my house again, will I?"

It wasn't really a question; it was a threat.

"No," he replied.

"Good." And with that she gave a little wave to John and crossed the street.

Chapter 35
Apology

Days and then weeks went by without any word from Malini. Jacob tried to call but she refused to talk with him. He decided to send her an email, apologizing for the way he'd treated her. He sat down at the glass desk, which she'd picked out, and booted up the computer, that she'd also picked out. Everything in this room reminded him of her.

Malini,

I know there's nothing I can say that can make up for what I did. I tried to force you to do something you didn't want to do. I have no excuses. But I am sorry.

I'm not sure how to live in Paris without you. I decided to stay because of you but here I am without you anyway. It feels like I've lost everything. When I think about starting school again, everything hurts. Please forgive me. Hit me, scream at me, anything, but please talk to me.

If you ever talk to me again, I swear I'll tell you everything; everything I know about the water, the tree, and me. I am still Jacob. You do know the real me. But I'll tell you the rest, if you just talk to me again.

Love,
Jake

As hopeful as he was when he hit the send button, the last days of August faded away and school rolled in with no response. The first day of his junior year at Paris High School was spent in silence, moving from classroom to classroom in zombie-like indifference. He didn't have to see Malini in trigonometry or foreign language because she'd passed into college-level Spanish, French, and calculus. For once, he was happy that she surpassed him academically.

But English was the great equalizer. He saw her take a seat at the front of the room. Thinking he didn't want to feel her stare in the back of his head all period, he sat in the back. Unfortunately, the strategy backfired. He spent the entire period watching her and didn't hear a word Mr. Brown said.

Lunch was an endurance exercise. He sat on the opposite end of the only empty table in the cafeteria. She seemed completely engrossed in her pulled pork sandwich, never even looking in his direction. Jacob, on the other hand, didn't touch his lunch. He spent the period feeling like his heart was being dragged out of his body through his throat.

Chemistry was even more of a problem. There was no getting around being lab partners. Everyone else in the class paired up immediately, leaving the last table empty. Jacob sat down first. She eventually followed, taking the stool diagonally from him with a huff and never making eye contact. Luckily, they didn't have to talk with each other. Mrs. Casey covered the requirements of the class and then ran a movie on taking accurate measurements. Jacob couldn't stop looking at Malini, but she never turned her head. When the lights came back on and the bell rang, he leaned across the table and put his hand on her arm.

"Meet me at McNaulty's?" he pleaded.

She didn't look up but yanked her arm away. Grabbing her books, she was out the door before he could close his mouth.

After school, Jacob walked alone to McNaulty's anyway and waited. He left alone.

By early September, Jacob was ready to chew his own arm off. With no place to go and nothing to do, he spent entire days staring at walls. He hated to admit it, but he missed working for Dr. Silva. Even a fight with Katrina would've been a welcome distraction, but she'd moved out at the end of August to attend college. So, when he saw the cross-country team gathering after school on the football field with Coach Schroeder, he found himself joining them for no other reason than an absence of nothing better to do.

"Coach Schroeder?" Jacob said.

"Yeah. What's up, Jacob?"

"I know I missed the informational session but I was wondering if I could run on the team."

Coach Schroeder stared at him blankly for a second, as if he was trying to tell if Jacob was joking. Then he looked at the group of four girls and two boys stretching in the grass. Most of them were freshman and all of them looked like this was their first year running. "Sometimes I forget you're not from here, Jake," he said. "This is Paris. If you want to run on the cross-country team, you just show up."

Jacob showed up. Not only was he the fastest on the team but the rhythmic fall of his feet allowed him welcome respite from the guilt and regret that controlled most of his thoughts. When he was running he felt nothing. He'd always lived by two very important rules: don't feel anything and don't expect anything from anybody. Oh how he wished he could close himself off again and go back to the person he was before. But he'd changed. He felt something now and while he still didn't expect anything from anyone, it hurt worse than ever when people lived up to his expectations.

Every day after practice, he waited outside of McNaulty's, but Malini never even passed by. He remembered her birthday. He found a stainless steel bracelet with a heart that looked similar to the one he'd made her on the beach at Lake Stelton. He wrapped it in a section of a map he found of New Zealand from an old National Geographic that the Laudners had around the house. On September 21st, the night before she turned sixteen, he left it on the balcony outside her window with a note.

Malini,

Even if you never forgive me, I want you to be happy. Here is the heart I promised you. I'm so sorry I ruined us. It was the worst mistake I ever made. But someone once told me, a person isn't the worst thing they've ever done. I can't take away what I did but I can promise you that I've learned my lesson. The offer still stands. I'll tell you everything. The absolute truth, if you just give me a second chance. Happy Birthday.

Love,
Jake

Two days later he noticed she drove a new red Miata to school. Uncle John told Jacob it was a gift from her father. He never saw the bracelet on her wrist.

The weather in Paris turned disagreeable in October. It rained almost constantly. Jacob ran for the cross-country team anyway. Coach Schroeder was ecstatic to have a runner who ran faster in the rain. In fact, Jacob could hear the hum of each drop as it fell around him. When his muscles began to fatigue, he would simply ask the water to lift his legs for him. The only reason he ever slowed was because he finished the race.

Near the end of the season, however, the storm was so severe that Coach Schroeder had to cancel. It was just too dangerous for the team to run in the lightning. Jacob walked to McNaulty's in the sheeting rain without an umbrella. He could've asked the water to part. It was possible for him to walk through the rain and remain completely dry. But the cold sting of it felt good. It was an echo of what he was feeling inside, and for some reason it gave him peace.

Jacob entered the little restaurant dripping wet and took a seat at a booth by the window. Mrs. McNaulty handed him a dry towel and a Coke before he even ordered. He reached for his wallet but she shook her head. A sad smile crept across her face. Without a word Jacob understood she knew more about lost loves than she was willing to talk about. She returned to the kitchen and left Jacob staring absently out the window.

"Excuse me, may I join you?" a girl's voice said. He assumed she was talking to someone else. A hand on his shoulder caused him to turn. "Is anyone sitting here? May I join you?"

"Yes, um, sure," he replied clumsily. The girl was breathtaking, tall and thin like a runway model. She was wearing a St. Mary's uniform—a plaid skirt and white button-down blouse. St. Mary's was a small Catholic High School, the only other school in town and connected to the church the Laudners attended. The red plaid hit high on her thigh and he caught himself watching its hem move dangerously higher as she sat down. Her wavy blonde hair was swept up behind her head with pieces falling loosely on her shoulders. The effect was that his eye was drawn to her neck and then down the vee of her blouse, open a button lower than it should have been for a town like Paris. As she smiled, he tried to remember his name to introduce himself. No one on Earth could be this beautiful.

"My name is Auriel," she said, holding out perfectly manicured fingers.

"I'm Jacob," he replied, taking her hand. Zaps of electricity coursed up his arm and his skin suddenly felt warm. He held her hand for a moment too long before nervously letting it go. "Do you go to St. Mary's?"

"Yes, I'm a junior … and you?"

"PHS. I'm a junior also. I haven't seen you around here before."

"I'm new. Just moved here. Does it always rain like this?"

"No. But the weather is constantly changing. They get every kind here." He noticed for the first time that she was completely dry. She must have hung a raincoat by the door.

"They? You sound like you're not from here."

"Actually, I'm not." Jacob described how he'd come to Paris. She was easy to talk to and he went on and on about himself.

"It sounds like you've been through a lot," she purred. She was leaning across the table toward him. A whiff of her perfume reached his nose and he closed his eyes.

"You smell nice," he said.

"Thanks." She tilted her heart shaped face toward him and his stomach went topsy-turvy. He swallowed hard and forced himself to blink.

Jacob checked his phone. "Crap, Auriel, I've got to go. I can't believe how late it is."

"Time flies when you're having fun."

As he got up to leave, his cheeks warmed when he realized he'd spent the entire time talking about himself and knew almost nothing about her. "I'm sorry. I've been talking the whole time. I'm usually not this rude."

"That's fine, Jacob. I know better than anyone how hard it is to make friends here. It's only natural. You needed to talk. Anyway, I enjoyed hearing your stories."

"Can I see you again?"

"Sure."

"Tomorrow? Same time and place?"

"I wouldn't miss it for the world," she whispered and his heart raced as she stood up from the booth and the hem of her skirt fluttered against her thigh. A half-smile crossed her lips. "I'm glad we met, Jacob. You're a rare breed."

"You too, um, I mean, well, see you later." He watched her walk past him, out of McNaulty's, and then slapped his forehead. He replayed the conversation in his head. She was so sophisticated and beautiful. He would seriously have to get better at this if he were going to keep her around.

With Malini gone, she was his only chance at a friend in Paris.

Chapter 36
The Gift

Malini climbed through her bedroom window with a flat of mums in her hands. The balcony outside her room was small but it was also her most prized space. It was hers, just hers. No one else ever came out here, which was good because it was just big enough for one.

The flower boxes served as her garden. The petunias she had planted in the spring were dying off. Today, she would replace them with burgundy mums that would withstand the cold October nights. Her mother purchased them for her from the Laudners' shop. Malini wouldn't go in there anymore. Just walking by the window broke her heart all over again.

She set the tray of flowers down and picked up her spade. As she turned toward the first box, ready to dig out the petunias, she noticed some garbage in the corner of her balcony. It looked like a wad of wet newspaper. How rude of someone to toss their junk up here, into *her* space. She bent over to pick it up with every intention of throwing it away.

The paper turned to mush in her hand. Still wet, it came apart in soggy sections. There was a box wrapped in it. By the looks of it, the box had been out there a long time.

She opened the lid.

When she saw the silver bracelet, she knew exactly whom it was from. But she pulled out the note and read it twice anyway.

She agreed with him on one thing: what happened was the worst thing he'd ever done. However, the note made her wonder if one event defined her opinion of him.

Was Jacob the worst thing he'd ever done? Could she forgive his trying to force her through the tree? Or did what happened mean that he was and always would be someone who tried to manipulate her?

Jacob had lived a hard life, losing his parents and being forced to leave his home. Of course it had affected him. After what happened that Saturday afternoon with Dane, he had probably given up any hope of a normal life. Malini wondered what that could do to a person, what she might do in that situation. What risks might she take, if she had nothing left to lose?

The truth was that Malini hadn't been completely honest with Jacob either. Technically, he'd never asked her why she was so interested in his gift. He'd never wondered aloud, why she felt they were brought together for a purpose. And she had never offered the information.

A lie of omission.

She crawled back through her window and walked to her closet. On her tippy toes she felt around on the top shelf for another box, this one covered in red velvet with gold embroidery. As her fingers found the soft edges, she remembered the day the man had given it to her.

Malini was six years old and still living in India when her father took her on a journey to Ladakh. She didn't remember much about the travel itself, although with how remote the region was they must have driven for hours to get there. What stood out in her memory was the Buddha. The gigantic gold man seemed to be watching her from his seat, his hand raised, as if he was waving hello to her. In the background, the snap of the prayer flags created a soothing hum.

Her father was taking pictures. The job he wanted in England had come through and they would be moving in just a couple of months. This was his last chance to capture the beauty of the region. His right eye saw the Buddha through the camera lens. His left eye was closed to the world, which explained why he didn't see the man approach his little girl, an event that would have surely caught his attention at any other time.

"Hello, sister," the soft voice had said to her.

She looked up into the smiling face of a man with very short hair and a bright red robe.

"Hello," she said. "But I am not your sister. I am the only child in my family."

"Not that kind," the man said. "Sister in faith. You are visiting our Buddha, yes?"

"Yes," she said.

"I have something for you."

"Because I'm a visitor?"

"No, because you are you and being you, there is a need for it."

Malini did not understand what the man was talking about and looked back up at the statue, hoping he would go away. Instead, the man handed her the box. She opened the lid. Written in calligraphy on parchment, there was a word in Sanskrit.

"What does it say?" she asked.

"It is the name of your destiny, given to me in meditation."

"What is my destiny? What does it say?"

"It is pronounced *apas*, translated *water*."

"Water is my destiny?" she giggled.

The man giggled too, as if he found it as silly as she did. "Well, little girl, for now maybe it is just a pretty box that you should keep to remind you of your visit here."

"Okay," she said, looking at the word. When she looked back up, the man was gone.

Ten years later, Malini found herself looking at the word in a new light. She opened the blue box from Jacob and removed the bracelet. She remembered the way he had brought its predecessor from the water and froze it around her wrist. The metal felt just as cold on her skin as she worked the clasp.

It was time for her to forgive Jacob and to learn the whole truth. It was time for her to face her destiny.

Chapter 37
Reconciliation

*J*acob *squirms in the uncomfortable chair. Auriel stands in front of him, smiling, what looks like an apple pie in her left hand, a fork in her right. The smell is delicious, spicy and sweet. The air is warm like she's just pulled the dish from the oven.*

Her bare knees brush his, her little plaid skirt just inches away from him, her blouse stretched tight over her chest. He tries to reach forward, to touch her, but his hands won't move; they are tied to the chair behind his back.

Auriel places one high-heeled black boot on the seat between his legs.

"Where do you think you're going, Jacob? You can't leave now. I've got something for you." She scoops up a bite of the pie.

He opens his mouth and she spoons it in. At first it tastes sweet, sweeter than pie should taste, but he hardly notices. Her closeness demands his full attention.

Then the bite in his mouth moves. He spits it onto the floor and looks at the pie in Auriel's hand. Under the crust, it isn't apple at all. In the hole where she has pulled up the first bite, the pie is alive. Maggots bubble up and crawl across the fork. Maggots move in his mouth, tasting sickeningly sweet.

He spits again and yells for her to stop. She laughs and scoops up another bite.

* * * * *

Jacob woke spitting into his pillow, relieved that the knocking on his door had interrupted the nightmare.

"Everything okay in there?" John asked.

"Bad dream. Everything's fine."

"Time to get going, Jacob. You're going to be late for school."

"Okay," he yelled back. In fifteen minutes, he was dressed in a long-sleeve black waffle-knit shirt and jeans. He tossed his backpack over his shoulder and headed for the door.

"No breakfast, Jacob?" Aunt Carolyn asked as he walked past the pine table.

"I'm not hungry." Dream or not, he could still taste the maggots in his mouth.

"Okay. Don't forget, this weekend is the Pumpkin Chuck. We want to take you, so don't make any other plans."

"Sure," he replied and walked out the door into the fall wind. Aunt Carolyn was nicer to him since Katrina moved away. Katrina never called from school and he was sure the change of heart had everything to do with Aunt Carolyn having an empty nest. He didn't mind. It was nice having one less person hate him in Paris.

He jumped into Big Blue and headed toward town. The road was lined with deciduous trees celebrating their last waking days with leaves of red, gold, and chestnut. Fall in Paris was beautiful. It was the first time he'd seen trees change like this, and it was almost worth the cold.

Pulling into the school parking lot, he was surprised to see Malini standing in front of his usual spot. It looked like she was waiting for him.

"Malini?" he said hopefully as he got out of his truck.

She held up her hand and the stainless steel heart glinted in the sun.

"You know, I don't go out there every day, Jacob." She grinned.

"Wait … You are talking to me and wearing my bracelet. Does this mean you forgive me?"

She paused, her face serious. "This means I will forgive you as soon as you uphold your end of the bargain and tell me everything."

"Deal. After school today." He reached out and caught the silver heart between his fingers. "It looks beautiful on you. Happy birthday."

"Thanks." She smiled a genuine Malini smile that made him feel like the weight of the world was finally off of his shoulders. It was the kind of smile that made everything good again and, as they walked toward the school, life felt normal for the first time in a long time.

She sat next to him in English and ate lunch directly across from him at their usual table. It was just like old times, except something about it was more fragile.

"Why can't you tell me now?" she asked.

Jacob glanced in both directions. When it was clear there was no one listening, he leaned forward and whispered, "I can start but I'm warning you, it's complex."

"Try me."

"Well, Dr. Silva says I'm a Soulkeeper."

"A Soulkeeper?"

"She says that God allowed water to flow out of the Garden of Eden, to reach the descendants of Adam and Eve. Only the ones who were pure of heart, who genuinely wanted to rid the world of evil, could see and drink the water. Those people who drank it experienced changes. It altered their DNA. I am a descendant of one of those children. Actually, more like two or more. See, the gifts were lost—like recessive genes—as the sons and daughters married normal people. But every once in a while, two people with a recessive gene get together and their child—"

"—shows traits of the recessive gene. Jacob, are you telling me you have a *heavenly gene*?"

"Yeah I know it's crazy but I guess you could call it that."

"But how did she know?"

"She said there are records. I don't think Dr. Silva is … normal. Anyway, when I found the tree, she said it was a clue. She said only a spiritual being could have found it on their own."

"What does the tree have to do with any of this?"

"It doesn't have anything to do with me. It has more to do with Dr. Silva. She buried her husband in her garden and it grew out of his body."

"Eww. Creepy. And you didn't think that thing was dangerous?"

"Malini, I've been through it twice, safely. But again, I'm really sorry."

"So, what does being a Soulkeeper give you? I mean besides being able to control water."

"I don't really know. Dr. Silva was supposed to be my Helper. She was helping me discover my gifts. She said that every Horseman has different abilities and you have to exercise them to know what they are."

"Horseman?"

"Oh, that's what she says I am. I guess there are three types of Soulkeepers. There are Horsemen like me who are supposed to battle evil, like soldiers who protect humans. There are Healers that fix things, cure people and situations. And then there are Helpers, who serve the other two by getting them what they need. My gift, as far as I know, is that I can control water. I guess that's a Horseman thing, a weapon."

"You said Dr. Silva was supposed to be your Helper. What happened? Isn't she helping you now?"

"No. She found out about my taking you to the tree. I must have left the gate open. That's against the rules. She freaked out and said she wouldn't help me anymore."

"Wha—what happens if you leave the gate open?" Malini's face had gone white. He supposed this was a lot to take in at one sitting.

"Evil things can get to our side. This is the part that I never really bought into. She says there are fallen angels among us. She calls them Watchers. Says they come to steal people's souls from God. That's why I'm a Horseman, to protect people's souls. I don't really believe it though. Sounds pretty crazy."

"So does moving water with your mind, but you can do it."

"Point taken," Jacob said. The bell rang. "We'll have to finish this later."

"Yes. I want to know everything. McNaulty's after school," Malini said. It was not a question but a demand.

Jacob nodded. "Oh, Malini, my aunt and uncle want to take me to something called a Pumpkin Chuck this weekend. Do you want to come?"

"Yeah! I went last year—very cool. I heard it's supposed to be better than ever this year."

"That makes one of us. I haven't heard anything. How is it you always know what's going on?" Jacob asked.

"Because I listen," she answered, giggling.

The rest of the day crawled on as Malini and Jacob tried not to talk about his secret. During chemistry, Malini knocked over a beaker of water and it was all he could do to allow the liquid to spread across the table. The afternoon was heavy with knowing glances and words left unspoken. Finally, the last bell rang and they headed out toward the parking lot chatting about Malini's new car. She promised to give him a ride to McNaulty's so he could check it out. He was almost to the cherry-red door when the weight of someone's eyes boring into the back of his skull distracted him.

"Jacob," a voice said from behind him. Auriel was leaning against his truck. She smiled but it didn't reach her eyes.

"Oh hi, Auriel," Jacob said. He tried to ignore the butterflies that charged his throat from his stomach. With Malini right there, it was more embarrassing than ever.

"I thought we were going to talk today. I came to meet you."

He cursed under his breath. He'd forgotten that he'd invited Auriel to meet him today at McNaulty's, too.

"Auriel, this is my friend, Malini. Malini, this is Auriel. She's new here. She goes to St. Mary's."

Auriel held out her hand toward Malini. "Nice to meet you."

Malini didn't move. She was covering her nose with the back of her hand. Her face turned a pale, greenish color and she ran to the nearest garbage can to vomit.

"Oh my God, are you all right?" Jacob ran to Malini's side and placed a hand on her shoulder.

"Yeah, I think so," she said. Then she looked up at him and grabbed his wrist. "Jake, I can't explain why, but something tells me that she's not right. Stay away from her."

"What do you mean? I just met her yesterday."

"I know. I can't explain it. It feels like when you're a kid and something in you just knows that a spider is more dangerous than a butterfly. No one has to tell me that she's a spider. I just know. Please…" There was a familiar look on her face as if she'd decided something. The same one Jacob remembered from his snake dream and when she'd refused to go through the tree.

"Hmm." He thought about how his dreams had a way of coming true lately, even if things didn't happen in exactly the same way. There was something unusual about Auriel, unnatural. "I think you're right," he told Malini.

"Good, because I'm going home. I've obviously got the flu or something. Sorry we couldn't hang out but we are still going on Saturday, right? To the Pumpkin Chuck?"

"Definitely. We'll pick you up." Jacob walked her to her car and helped her in, backing toward Auriel as Malini pulled out of the now almost empty parking lot.

"So are you still up for McNaulty's?" Auriel asked. She closed the gap between them and said the words into his ear. With her body this close, he could smell her scent, spicy and sweet, like fresh-baked pumpkin pie. The scent was irresistible. Even with the memory of his nightmare and the warning from Malini, he found himself drawn to her. As he turned and saw the bend of her neck above the clingy white blouse, he felt helpless to resist. It was as if he were seeing fire for the first time. He knew it could burn but every cell in his body wanted to play with it, craved to see how close he could get.

"I think I should go," Jacob forced himself to say. His voice sounded weak, the hesitation of uncertainty lengthening the vowels. She moved in closer and her presence wrapped around him, an intoxicating and tangible thing that flowed through his body like electricity. Everything felt warm. His fingers and toes tingled. Oh, how he wanted to kiss her. Just. One. Kiss.

"What are you doing here?" Dane Michaels descended the last steps to the parking lot, attitude rolling off of him like bad cologne. He looked at Auriel and then at Jacob with blatant jealousy in his eyes.

"Dane," Jacob said, taking a step back from Auriel, whose expression morphed into rage. "Have you met Auriel?"

Dane didn't acknowledge him. "Do you have some of that stuff you gave me before?" he said to Auriel, sliding up to her and taking her waist. Apparently, she smelled just as good to Dane because Jacob saw him breathe deeply and lean in closer to her. "It was great but I'm all out."

"Leave or die," she said through her teeth.

Dane backed off a half of an inch and gave a shrug like he was just goofing around. "What's with you? I told you Lau has a girlfriend. I've been trying to get him to come meet you since last year. He's not interested. Why don't you come hang out with me like before?"

Jacob backed up another step. The wind picked up and the coolness of it brought him to his senses. The smell of pie was replaced with a hint of burning leaves and all of that fresh air brought clarity. Dane had met Auriel. He said he'd been trying to get Jacob to meet her since last year. That meant Auriel was lying when she said she was new in town. Jacob thought about the day at the grocery store and the afternoon in the hall at the school. Dane had insisted there was someone he'd wanted to introduce him to. Auriel had been trying to reach him for a long time. But why hadn't she introduced herself before? Why was she so interested now?

"He's right. Dane is much better company than I am. And, I'm not really feeling well. Maybe another time." Jacob moved around Auriel to get to his truck.

"Problem solved," Dane said. Auriel looked confused, like she couldn't decide what to do next. She bit her lip in frustration and then, as Jacob opened the truck door to slip behind the wheel, she cracked.

Her arm shot out and grabbed Dane behind the neck. At first she looked like she was going to kiss him. She brought his face within an inch of her own and said in a voice he could barely hear, "You should've left when you had the chance."

Dane's body folded in half over her knee. She flung him onto the pavement with one arm, his body limp like a rag doll. His head hit the concrete with a sickening crack and blood splattered the hood of the truck. Jacob didn't want to think about how hard someone had to bust a head to get blood to spray like that. He couldn't see if Dane was moving because his body had fallen too close to the front of the truck but he could hear a high-pitched wheeze. Dane was trying to suck air back into his lungs.

Auriel didn't let up. Her lips were pulled back from her teeth like an animal. Her upper body flinched as she kicked Dane again and again. The rage in her eyes, it didn't seem human.

Leaving now, just driving away, would be the smart thing, the simplest thing. He didn't owe Dane anything. But Jacob couldn't do it. It just seemed cowardly, what with him having the power he did and Dane as helpless as he was. Jacob decided to take the high road. In the cup holder of his truck was exactly what he needed.

"Auriel, stop," he commanded as he opened the car door and stepped toward her, a half-empty bottle of water in his hand.

She stepped back from Dane, who Jacob could now see was trying desperately to crawl away from her, his head bleeding profusely and his face a swollen mass of bruises. One arm hung oddly against his body, probably broken. He stepped in front of Dane and faced Auriel.

"I was just protecting myself, Jacob," she said, her hand going to her neck. "You saw how he practically attacked me."

"Sure," Jacob replied, thinking hard. One wrong word and he could be next. "But maybe you should let me take him home now. I think you've made your point. I'm afraid someone might see and blame this on you."

"You're right." She looked down at Dane and said, "If you know what's good for you, you'll keep your mouth shut about this." Then she turned back toward Jacob. "Will I see you later?" she breathed. The warmth, the scent, folded around him again, only this time Jacob held his breath. He could feel the water sloshing against the side of the bottle, pointing at Auriel.

"Of course. I wouldn't miss it." He forced himself to smile.

"When?" she demanded, and then smiled to cover her harsh tone.

"Tomorrow? McNaulty's. We can pick up where we left off." Jacob watched her consider this as she gave the situation a calculated perusal.

"See you then." She turned to leave looking like any gorgeous teenage girl might, except for the blood that covered her legs and boots from the knee down. She climbed into a red Jeep in the corner of the lot and took off.

As soon as she was gone, Jacob knelt down beside Dane. He wasn't moving. There was blood everywhere. With shaky hands, he placed his fingers against Dane's neck, relieved to feel a pulse, even though it felt too fast to be normal. He tried to lift him but he was too heavy, easily two hundred pounds of muscle. Jacob poured the water over the sleeves of his sweatshirt and willed it to help. He scooped Dane up, taking care to place him in the passenger's side as gently as possible. After wiping Dane's blood from the front of his truck with some paper towels John had in the glove compartment, he climbed in behind the wheel and sped for help.

St. Mary's hospital was barely the size of a large clinic. He pulled into the emergency entrance and tried to think up a story that would explain Dane's condition. He decided to stick with a version of the truth.

"I need help!" he called through the door and a group of people in scrubs came running. They carefully transferred Dane to a stretcher. As they rolled him toward the double glass doors, Dane's good hand shot out and grabbed Jacob's elbow.

"Thank you," he wheezed.

The staff had Dane inside before Jacob could respond.

A nurse returned through the doors and asked him the question he knew was coming.

"How did this happen?"

"I don't know," Jacob said. His voice sounded authentically shaken. "I came out of school and found him like that in the parking lot." It was a good lie, a necessary lie.

"You found him like that after school?"

"Well, not right after. I left but had to go back into the school because I needed something out of my locker. When I came back out, the parking lot was empty except for Dane. He was like that when I found him."

"That must have been horrible thing for you to see, honey," she said empathetically.

This time, Jacob could be entirely honest. "Yes, it was."

Chapter 38
Taken

P *foosh.*

The pumpkin rocketed from the giant metal pipe, an orange blur against the graying fall sky. It arced across the horizon before plummeting to its inevitable doom well past the point that he could discern it from the rural landscape. Morton's Pumpkin Chuckin' festival was just beginning.

Jacob stood behind a row of giant cannons and catapults, watching teams of adults make last-minute adjustments to the machines with the sole purpose of projecting a pumpkin farther than any other. He smiled to himself and pulled his coat tighter around his chest. When you didn't have the ocean or mountain to keep you busy, he supposed you hurled pumpkins.

"That was amazing." Malini stared as the next pumpkin disappeared behind the horizon. The bowl of pumpkin ice cream in her hand was disappearing rapidly. She offered a spoonful to Jacob.

"Thanks." The thick creamy texture was accentuated by the flavors of nutmeg and cinnamon with a subtle pumpkin pie finish. "It's really good," he said honestly, "but I can't believe we're eating ice cream at nine in the morning."

"It's always sold out by lunch." She scooped in another bite. "So, have you heard if Dane's going to be all right?"

"Yes. His dad called my uncle and said he had a concussion, two broken ribs, a punctured lung, and a broken arm. But they've patched him up and he's in stable condition."

"And, you didn't see who did it? You have no idea?"

Jacob lowered his voice. "Malini, that's what I told the hospital. That's not what happened." It was the first time he'd been alone with her since the incident and the last thing he wanted to do was text her the entire story. There was no way he was putting it in writing.

"What did happen?"

"It was Auriel."

The bowl fell from Malini's hand, the sickly pallor returning to her face. He took her waist to hold her up.

"What's wrong? Are you sick again?"

"No. I just knew. I knew there was something … evil about her. There's something I need to tell you, Jake."

A loud bellow interrupted them. "What did you think of that one, Jacob?" Uncle John was waving his hat about ten feet away, a bottle of pumpkin beer in his hand. Linda and Mark stood in front of him with the twins. Next to him, Dr. Silva smiled up at the flying pumpkins. She did not spare so much as a glance toward Jacob.

"Why don't you go get some more ice cream?" he said to Malini. Jacob tilted his head toward Dr. Silva. Whatever Auriel was, if there was one person who would know what to do about her, it was Dr. Silva.

Malini nodded.

Jacob made his way over and stood between John and Dr. Silva. "That was really great, how far do you think it went, Uncle John?"

"Oh, easily a mile," he said.

Jacob turned to Dr. Silva. "It's good to see you again, Dr. Silva." He tried hard to sound casual. "I was wondering if I could ask you a question about your garden?"

"Her garden's why she's here, Jacob. She donates the pumpkins from her patch."

Dr. Silva briefly glanced down her nose at Jacob, her eyes icy daggers. "Oh, Jacob, you've proven yourself capable of figuring out all of your questions on your own. You don't need me." She smiled up at John. "It was nice to see you again, neighbor. I've got to get back. Enjoy the show."

"See you later, Abigail," John called with a wave of his hand, never taking his eyes off the flying pumpkins.

Dr. Silva rushed off toward a weathered red barn that stood on the property. Jacob followed. He had to practically sprint to keep up. As he watched her black cloak flutter through the open barn door, he saw Auriel.

She was leaning against a tree near the side of the barn, her hands in the pockets of her jeans jacket and one booted foot propped against the gnarled trunk. When she saw Jacob, she began to walk toward him, a brilliant smile lighting up her eyes. She smoothed her blonde curls back from her face.

"Hi, Jacob! Did you forget you were supposed to meet me today?"

"No."

"Then why didn't you come? Don't you like me anymore?"

"What are you?" he blurted, backing up as she advanced toward him. She abandoned the facade of sweet teenage girl, her smile melting into an expression that could only be described as deadly.

"I'm the girl you want to kiss." Her arm shot out and grabbed the nape of his neck, so fast it reminded him of the strike of a snake. She crushed his body to hers as if he weighed nothing and her lips covered his before he could even scream.

And then he was surrounded by her spicy, sweet smell and the too-sweet taste of her breath in his mouth, both intoxicating and nauseating. While his body was drawn to her, his mind and soul were screaming to break free. He remembered too well the maggots in his dream and how she had maimed Dane.

But Jacob was powerless. He felt dizzy, the field spinning. Auriel stopped kissing him and numbness crept over his body like a poison. She pushed him toward her red Jeep in the parking lot. By the time he reached it, his body would barely respond at all. Auriel had to lift him into the passenger seat. He was so disoriented he could hardly feel the Jeep accelerate, even when the speedometer reached ninety miles per hour.

"Stop," he managed to say. "I want to go back." His voice sounded weak, unsure, even to his own ears.

"You don't mean that, Jacob. We are going to go someplace special. I'm taking you home to meet my dad. He is going to love you."

"Why?" His mouth felt dry. The word was all he could force out of his lungs.

"Because it's time for you to go where you belong. You chose this!"

"Chose?" he mumbled. His tongue was swelling.

Auriel recklessly weaved in and out of traffic, sliding around the corners, tires screeching.

"Don't play innocent with me. You've made choice after choice that led me to you. You broke the dolls, you trespassed in the garden, you lied to John about your trip to Peru, you stole Abigail's notes about the tree, and you traveled using the blood of Oswald Silva without permission. You even tried to force an innocent." She turned to look at him, taking her eyes off the road for a dangerously long time for how fast she was driving. "That's right, Jacob. I know every sin you've ever committed. You are quite the offender. I don't think there's one in the book that you haven't done and I am going to see you get what you deserve." She was nodding her head self-righteously. "Now I don't want to hear another word about it."

As she said these last words, his tongue pushed to the back of his throat and his head slammed against the seat like an invisible hand was gagging him. The harder he tried to speak the more frustrated he became as he could produce nothing but choking sounds. He searched out the window for any sign of water but if they passed any, he was traveling too fast to connect with it. What was she? What gave her this power she had over him? What she accused him of … only half of it was true. But how did she know that much?

"Whaa, whaa, whaa. Is wittle Jacob sad because he finally has to pay for all the bad stuff he's done?" Her blonde head shook with the loud toothy laugh and she stuck her tongue out at him in an expression both immature and cruel. Jacob turned away to face the window.

After watching the rural landscape fly by, he recognized landmarks that made him certain she was taking him back to Paris. It was only minutes before Auriel was pulling into Dr. Silva's driveway, leaping from the driver's side and practically tearing the door off its hinges to yank Jacob out.

Auriel dragged him from the car by his collar. Mysteriously, his leg muscles began to work again, as if whatever venom she'd stung him with was wearing off. Like a dog, she led him forward by the neck, her fingers clawing into his flesh. She half dragged, half pushed him through the orchard and up to the wrought-iron gate.

She turned the key and popped the lock.

"But—" Jacob muttered.

"You thought I couldn't open the gate? Once you invite a Watcher in, Jacob, it renders the enchantment powerless against them. Abigail should have taught you better." She cast him a wicked smile that sent a chill up Jacob's spine.

Jacob didn't understand. Even if he had accidentally left the gate unlocked, he certainly never invited Auriel through it. Asking didn't seem wise. She moved him down the trail and through the cactus maze quickly, with one single goal: to bring him to the tree. Each time he struggled to get away, she buried her nails deeper into his neck and lifted him from the ground like a puppy. Her strength was boundless.

Standing before Oswald, Auriel's hand moved to his wrist and she dragged him the last few feet toward the tree. "What's good for the goose is good for the gander," she laughed.

Jacob remembered saying those words the night he visited Malini in her room. What he saw in his mind, however, was what he'd done to Malini at the tree—from her perspective. He felt her terror as Auriel dragged him toward the tree. Worse, Jacob realized he'd been in Auriel's position, the tyrant, the coercer. Whatever Auriel was, she knew his past. She knew everything he'd done wrong in his life and could pump it into his brain at will. He collapsed from the guilt and saw his own tears hit the sand. Auriel's demonic grip only strengthened on his wrist, as if she was drawing strength from his suffering.

Auriel touched the bark and Jacob watched it grow up her arm, shingling her shoulder before absorbing the rest of her body. The familiar slowing took over as the tree swallowed him, too. But this time, instead of rising and becoming the sky, he felt himself sink. The earth and every crawling creature that lived in it became one with his flesh. He slid down the roots of the tree, deeper and deeper until, at last, he emerged in a dark garden of twisting thorns.

From the spot on the ground where he lay recovering from the effects of the tree, he glanced back at Auriel. She was more beautiful than ever. But his eyes could not miss what had changed about her, even in the faintest of light. Behind her back, two feathery wings folded against her body. Fluffy and white, they arced over her shoulders and extended down her back. As she fanned them out, stretching like a bird first one than the other, each looked about eight feet long.

"Welcome to Nod, Jacob. Welcome to your new home." She yanked him to his feet and led him forward into the darkness.

Chapter 39
Malini's Confession

Malini picked up the bowl of ice cream she'd dropped and tossed it in the trash. By the tilt of Jacob's head and his deadly serious expression, she knew this was about Auriel.

"Why don't you go get some more ice cream?" He was going to ask Dr. Silva for help.

She moved toward the ice cream vendor but kept her eyes on Jacob. Dr. Silva walked away from him. After all this time, she still blamed Jacob. Maybe some of that blame was deserved but Malini knew that most of it wasn't.

As Jacob followed Dr. Silva across the field to the barn, Malini trailed close behind. She hid behind the closest cart and watched. Vomit filled her mouth when she saw Auriel. She hurled onto the grass. What was it about that girl that made her feel sick? Unless her illness was brought on by wanton jealousy? Definitely a possibility.

Without warning, Auriel snatched Jacob and kissed him, full on the lips. A toxic energy flooded Malini's body. It was a mixture of fury and envy with a splash of guilt. With nowhere else for the emotion to go, it came pouring out from her eyes in the form of tears. *No. Not that. Get your lips off of him,* she thought. The idea of that disgusting creature touching Jacob made her retch. The upside was there was nothing left in her stomach. When she saw Auriel leading Jacob to the red Jeep, she didn't waste another minute. She ran into the barn.

Dr. Silva was shoveling what looked like cow manure into the back of a truck. When Malini cleared her throat, she looked up from the pile.

"It's for my garden," Dr. Silva said. "Fertilizer."

The odor hit Malini and she covered her nose and mouth with her shirtsleeve. She walked forward, until she was just a foot away from Jacob's neighbor. "Dr. Silva," she said, "there's something I need to tell you."

"What would that be?"

"I know about the tree in your garden. The one in the back garden." Malini lowered her chin as she said this and watched Dr. Silva's eyes squint skeptically.

"What do you know? Tell me."

"I was the one who left the gate open. I was with Jacob that day and saw him lock it behind us. After he left, a little girl, maybe three or four years old, came to the gate from the inside. I thought she followed us in there. She was crying and begging me to let her out, so I did. I didn't know it was against the rules."

"Who are you?" Dr. Silva demanded.

"Malini Gupta. I'm Jim Gupta's daughter. We met in his office when your window was broken."

"Yes. I remember you. You say you were there the day Jacob went to the tree?"

"Yes."

"Why are you telling me this now?"

"Because Jacob's in trouble. The girl I let in through the gate. I think she, somehow … it's like she grew up. Jacob introduced me yesterday to a girl that looked exactly like her, but older. And I just saw her kiss him and then take him away."

Dr. Silva stared at Malini, her pale face expressionless. She might as well have been made of stone.

"Do you smell that?" Malini asked, pressing her shirt more tightly over her mouth. "God it's awful. Not the manure, it's a sweet, spicy smell, but more metallic … like arsenic."

Dr. Silva took a step back and then her eyes darted toward the barn door.

"Please, Dr. Silva. You are the only one that can help. I know it."

"How much do you know, girl?"

"Not much, but you can fill me in on the way. We have to catch them. She's not right. I know she's evil. You can't let her take him."

"Well to be clear, I *can* let him go, but it seems you, Malini, cannot. He's important to you?"

"Yes."

"And you think he is worth getting back?"

"Of course!"

"Then I believe you. But we must make haste if we are to have any hope of reaching him before it's too late." She looked at the truck. "This won't do." She grabbed Malini's wrist and ran for the door.

In the parking lot, Malini had to sprint to keep up with Dr. Silva, who was scanning the rows of cars until she saw one that seemed to have promise. She waved her hand over the lock and helped Malini into the passenger side of a silver BMW roadster. She crawled behind the wheel. With another pass of her hand, the engine started and she peeled out of the parking lot.

"Seatbelt, Malini," she said.

Malini reached over her shoulder for the belt. Her shirt fell from her nose. She clicked the belt into place, gagging.

"There it is again. That smell. What is that?"

"Do you believe in God, Malini?"

"Yes, of course I do."

"Do you know the story of how Lucifer fell from grace?"

"Lucifer? Like, the devil? Yes, I've heard it."

"Where do you think the fallen went?"

"Obviously, the story isn't true. The Bible says they were cast to Earth, but if fallen angels were here I think someone would have noticed by now."

"We are talking about the Lord of Illusions. They are deceivers, tellers of lies. I could be one of them right now and you would never know."

"It's not meant to be taken literally. It's a myth to teach a lesson."

"So, in this myth then, where does the Bible say that Eve encountered Lucifer disguised as the serpent?"

"In the garden of Eden."

"Yes, and how did he get there? They were in Eden, after all, the most perfect place created by God. How could evil walk right in?"

"I don't know. It's never explained."

"Well, I wasn't there personally, but I knew," Dr. Silva said. "We all did."

"What do you mean? How could you know?"

Dr. Silva did not answer.

She was flying down Rural Route One now, in control but speeding as fast as she could safely drive on the long stretch of road. "All angels exist to serve God. Lucifer and his followers rebelled and were cast out of the presence of God. They still have powers, although they are limited compared to the power of God. They are no longer considered angels but Watchers, fallen ones."

"Then the story is true?"

"Yes."

Malini's throat felt dry. Her hands trembled. "What powers do they have?"

"They are sorcerers, illusionists, and herbalists."

"Herbalists?"

"Think drugs. An easy way to control people's minds and Watchers are all about easy." Dr. Silva pulled into her driveway in the shadow of the dark Victorian. She turned and looked Malini directly in the eye.

"The odor is so strong here," Malini said, trying to breathe through her mouth.

"Tell me, Malini, have you smelled that smell before?"

Malini thought about it. Of course she had.

"Auriel. But why am I smelling it now?"

"And is there anything about me that reminds you of Auriel?"

Malini stared in horror at her perfect features. Dr. Silva's hair was straight, Auriel's curly, but both were platinum blond. They were both tall and thin although Auriel was slightly shorter than Dr. Silva. And they both had the type of eyes that cut right through a person. They weren't twins but there was something, a likeness, that couldn't be denied.

"Yes," Malini said, suddenly terrified.

"Do you know what we are?"

"I think so."

"Then say it. Call it out so that we can put it behind us."

Malini swallowed hard. "You're a Watcher—a fallen angel."

"Very good," she said, nodding. "I'm proud of you. Now can you answer one more question for me?"

"I can try."

"What are you, Malini?"

"What do you mean? I'm a human being."

"Normal humans can't smell Watchers. There are some occasions when we use our smell to lure a human being to us. We are lazy creatures after all. That's why we are called Watchers: we watch, we wait, and we use what opportunity is presented to us to our advantage. But you … I wasn't trying to lure you. You smelled what I was, not what I wanted you to smell. So, what are you?"

"I don't know." Malini's hands shook. She reached behind her back for the door handle.

"And therein lies the problem. You see, where we are going, where we must go to save Jacob, will be very dangerous. I could be captured but you could be killed. And if you are something else, something more than just human, it might give us away. The good news is that I couldn't see you. All the time you were spending with Jacob, I never suspected you were anything other than a normal, everyday girl."

"I don't understand. Why would you be captured? I thought you were one of them?"

She laughed mockingly. "Malini, if I was like them, you would already be dead or taken. It's true I fell from grace. But I changed.

I want to be a Helper, a Soulkeeper. I regretted following Lucifer from the very beginning. I've been living among humans ever since."

"But how do I know you're not deceiving me right now? If you're a Watcher, that's your strongest power." Malini pressed her back against the door.

Dr. Silva didn't answer but got out and started walking toward the house. Malini sat in the car for a moment and then sprinted after her. If Dr. Silva wasn't telling the truth, there was no way she would have left her in the car alone.

When they reached the door, Dr. Silva stopped and met Malini's eyes. "The hardest thing you will ever do in life is to know for sure what is true. Where we are going is a place ruled by illusion. Saving Jacob will be difficult and terrifying. I don't recommend you come with me."

Malini had always done the right thing, the safe thing. But the thought of Jacob with Auriel ignited fervor deep within her. Whether it was a sense of possession, jealousy, or old-fashioned loyalty, Malini's jaw hardened. At that moment, she would have walked through fire for Jacob.

"I'm going. I'm not going to let that evil bitch steal my best friend!" Malini spat the words out like they tasted bad.

"All right then, come with me. We need to pack some things before we go."

They entered the house and Dr. Silva began filling an old leather bag with things from her cupboards. Malini was fascinated by the odd combination of items she grabbed.

"…salt, for clarity, flowers, for beauty, water, and finally, light." She grabbed a candle from a wooden box on the mantel. As she placed it in the bag, Malini glimpsed a name in its wax—Abigail Drake.

"What is that, Dr. Silva?"

"My baptism candle." She threw the pack over her shoulder.

"You were baptized?"

"Later. We have to go. Gideon!" Dr. Silva called. The largest red cat Malini had ever seen ran into the kitchen. "It's important, Gid. Will you come with us?"

Malini watched as the cat nodded. She tried not to let her mouth fall open.

They raced out the back door and into the orchard, through the gate and down to the meadow, up the hill, and finally through the cactus maze.

"You never finished telling me the truth," Malini said as they walked toward the tree. "How did the serpent get into the garden?"

"The fallen ones are not of this Earth, Malini. They are under it. They live in a land of illusions, a land that is not with God but is a spiritual realm bound forever to this Earth. They live in a land where God sent Cain when he cursed him to wander. They live in Nod. They are connected to all living things through their wrongdoings. Sin attracts them. Why was the serpent in the garden? The woman brought him there. She was already thinking about taking the fruit; angry with God for the rules he had given Adam. Her pride opened the portal in the tree. She invited the serpent."

In front of the tree, Dr. Silva's hand hovered inches above the gnarly bark. "Are you ready?"

Malini's remembered vividly the bark crawling up Jacob's arm. All of the same questions plagued her. What would this do to her body? What would it do to her soul? The difference was that this time Jacob was on the other side, the Jacob she loved, her best friend and the person who needed her. Regardless of the question, Jacob was the only answer that mattered.

"I'm ready." She held out her hand.

Chapter 40
Into the Dark

Darkness is a relative term. There is the darkness of an evening with a full moon, or of a candlelit room. Or the inky blackness of a bedroom at midnight, where the only light comes between shadows that dance in the space beneath the door. But the darkness that Jacob experienced as he followed his captor, hitched to her wings with sweaty palms, was not like that at all. It was a darkness that had perhaps never experienced real light, a black hole absorbing any flicker into its depths. It was the darkness of the bottom of the ocean, or the cold blackness of a grave. Jacob hoped it would not be *his* grave.

While the outline of the garden where he'd arrived had been visible, he could see nothing now. He followed Auriel by touch, holding on to the feathers of her wings as she walked. She seemed unaffected by the lack of light and moved quickly. Jacob didn't try to get away. Where would he go? He was helpless here, completely dependent on her.

"Where are you taking me?" His voice was shaking more than he wanted it to. He was trying to be brave, but truthfully he felt there was little hope. An hour ago he would not have believed that this place existed. No one would know where to look for him, if they looked for him at all. The others probably didn't even realize he was gone yet. When they did, what could they do? The only person who could follow through the tree was Dr. Silva and she would have to know where he was to get here. That was, if she even cared to save him.

"We are going to see my father. He'll be very interested in adding you to our collection. You're a rare breed, Jacob. Maybe, if you are lucky, he'll put you on display. Look, we are almost there."

Jacob could barely make out a bluish fluorescent glow ahead of him. A series of steel boxes of various heights appeared on the horizon, illuminated by humming artificial light. A skyline, but there was no artistry to it, no architecture of any kind, just the monotony of box after box. Simply stone and steel.

Auriel approached the gate and it opened before her. She escorted him into a bustling city both beautiful and disturbing. Creatures with wings walked up and down the streets, each one more beautiful than the next. They weren't angels; they were Watchers, fallen angels. They were thin, tall, and muscular with perfect hair and features that would put a supermodel to shame. But as he watched them, Jacob had the undeniable sense they were too perfect. It was like seeing a football field full of plastic surgery recipients. The eye knew it was unnatural, somehow wrong.

More disturbing still were the people. The city was filled with humans just like him, serving the Watchers in every capacity: chained to wagons like horses, on their hands and knees on the sidewalk polishing Watchers' shoes, picking up the trash that the Watchers arbitrarily flung into the street. Some were on leashes, dragged around by the neck. All of the humans were dirty, dressed in rags, and treated like dogs.

Jacob's scalp prickled. Wherever or whatever Nod was, it was not a place that valued human life. As he looked around, the people would not meet his eyes. They hung their heads with vacant expressions, empty shells responding only to the kicks and screams of their captors.

"In here." Auriel held open a door and pushed Jacob through it. As he stumbled over the threshold, it was like walking into the atrium of any office building. A Watcher sat behind a circular desk, her light blue wings in sharp contrast with the dark mahogany of the wood. Beyond the desk was a set of elevators.

"Depositing," Auriel said. The blue-winged Watcher did not look up from filing her nails but nodded her head in response.

"This way." Auriel shoved him toward the open elevator doors and pushed a button at the top of the panel. He was startled when he felt the elevator drop instead of rise. It descended to the thirty-sixth floor below the atrium. When the doors opened, Auriel led him down a sterile white hall to a room with a stainless steel examination table over an ominously large floor drain.

"Sit here." Auriel pointed at the cold steel table. Jacob walked toward it, noticing he had to peel his feet from the floor with every step, as if he were walking down the soda-drenched row of a movie theater. Looking at the pattern on the floor, he tried to think what might be sticking to his shoes. As he neared the table, he discovered to his horror that the floor was not patterned at all but peppered with drops of drying blood. The table was similarly filthy.

"No," he stated firmly, turning to face Auriel. "Take me home."

"It will not speak!" a male voice boomed from behind him. A huge Watcher with shiny black wings entered the room. He ran a hand through his wavy blonde hair, and flashed a set of perfect teeth. Spreading his monstrous black wings, he coasted across the room in one powerful motion. His eyes were solid black, as dark as coal, and not reflective as a human eye. Instead the dark irises were black holes absorbing all. Looking into them, Jacob felt like he was falling hopelessly into nothing.

The Watcher kissed Auriel.

"Hello, Father," she responded. "I've brought you a gift."

Jacob was confused because the male Watcher looked barely older than Auriel, but he was beginning to understand that things were not as they seemed in Nod.

"What breed is it, Auriel?"

"A rare breed, a Horseman of mixed blood. He is half blood from the east, Chinese, and half blood from the west, German. Does he not have fine features and so young?"

"Yes. I am pleased. Do you know what its gifts are?" he asked Auriel.

"No. He did not fight. I could find no one that had seen him train."

Jacob silently thanked Dane for being too proud to admit how he'd kicked his ass in Westcott's parking lot. The less Auriel knew the better.

Auriel's father pointed a manicured finger at him. "It will tell me what its gifts are."

"Gifts? I don't know what you're talking about." Jacob tried his best to lie convincingly. Keeping his abilities secret seemed like his only hope.

"Auriel, perhaps you took this one before he was told. Very good! One less to kill later."

The dark angel squinted at him. "It will undress now."

"Excuse me," he said, shivering in the cold room.

"Jacob, you must put this on." Auriel threw him a rag sack with holes for his head and arms.

"Why do you talk to it like that, Auriel? It will learn soon enough its place here. Why prolong the process?"

"Just avoiding any need to damage it before it reaches the display case," she answered.

"Very well. I must go. You will deal with it then?"

"Yes, Father."

The Watcher left the room in a movement so fast Jacob didn't see it. The woosh of air was the only way his senses could perceive the dark angel had flown away.

"Auriel, can I ask you something?"

"Quickly, human."

"I heard Dane say that you've been asking to meet me all year. Why didn't you come after me yourself, sooner?"

"You have no idea how difficult it is for us to stay above ground. It would have been so much easier if you had just gone with Dane. But you're too hardheaded for that. Without a portal, we must return through the same tree as we arrive. We are flesh eaters. If we stay above ground for too long, our powers fade and we lose our illusions ... until we eat flesh. Eating flesh usually means killing and if we kill, the Soulkeepers come. They always feel the kill. I couldn't risk leaving my tree, so I sent that idiot Dane after you. Of course, once I knew who you were, I thought I would capture you, using Oswald. That would've been the easiest way. You know, I almost had you. Twice."

"Twice?"

"Your first time through the tree, I was there, in the garden. You don't recognize my voice? If it weren't for Gideon keeping me away, I would have taken you then. Before that, I knew a Horseman had come to Paris, but I didn't know who it was. That day, when I saw you navigate the garden, I realized you were the one I was after."

So, it was her voice he'd heard in the garden. "I heard you again, when I brought Malini to the tree," Jacob said.

"Yes. I was there, hoping for a two-for-one deal, actually," Auriel snorted. "I was inside the tree, waiting. Had you manned up and forced Malini through, you two would have traveled straight to Nod. But then you had to go and do the self-sacrificing thing and help her back to the gate. There's nothing more repelling than self-sacrifice."

"So then why did you risk coming after me now?"

"After Malini let me through the gate, I had free access to the portal. The two of you had been fighting. The anger in the air was yummy. I thought it would be easy to prey on your loneliness, to lead you back here. It would have been so much easier if I could have posed as your girlfriend and convinced you to show me the garden. But then that girl had to go and forgive you. And Dane." She shook her head. "I came awfully close to alerting the Soulkeepers. I had to do things the hard way and take you."

The weight of despair that settled on his shoulders was intolerable. He'd brought this upon himself. This whole time he'd been playing with forces he didn't understand. Dr. Silva had tried, in her way, to warn him. This was his fault.

"Enough. Change now," Auriel demanded.

Jacob did as he was told. He took off his favorite Matsumoto's T-shirt, the black turtleneck, the blue jeans, and his hiking boots and donned the smelly rag. He was freezing now and crossed his arms over his chest, shivering.

"Let's go." Auriel grabbed his bare arm.

A rush of adrenaline coursed through his body and Jacob tried to twist away. The extension of her white wing swept him like a piece of dust to the floor. His hands caught his fall, landing in the tacky half-dried blood of the humans who had been there before him.

"Give me a break," she laughed. "Since it cannot take direction, it will follow Mordechai to its cage. Father!" she yelled.

To his horror, the black-winged Watcher returned, grabbed him by his upper arm, and yanked him from the room. Jacob chided himself. He would've been far better off with Auriel than Mordechai.

Mordechai forced Jacob down a long hall before exiting the building and boarding a train made entirely of glass. At first he wondered why the Watchers would want a train with clear walls but when he thought about it, it made absolute sense. They were all about appearances. This was a world of illusions. Even traveling, they lived to watch and be watched.

Everywhere he went other Watchers bowed to the one holding his arm and said, "All hail Mordechai!" or "The great and powerful Mordechai, your presence is an honor." Mordechai must have been someone important in this society but Jacob made no guesses as to his station. He was too busy glancing rapidly from wall to wall, looking for any way to escape.

When the train stopped, Mordechai pushed him down a dusty path and through a huge metal archway labeled *Zoo*. It wasn't until they came to the first cage that Jacob realized the full extent of his fate. The room was eight-foot square with bars on three sides and a full-size picture of a living room pasted to the far concrete wall.

There was a bed, a chair, a toilet, and a ball behind the bars. Sitting on the chair was an African man with ebony skin, a muscular frame, and a proud jaw. He looked sadly at Jacob. The sign above the cage read *African*.

The next cage was exactly the same except the woman was blonde with large blue eyes. The sign said Swedish. She looked vaguely familiar, but Jacob couldn't quite place her and her blank expression didn't help. Cage after cage went by, *Italian*, *Lebanese*, *Cambodian*, *Egyptian*. Every color and ethnicity was displayed like animals. Each clothed in rags. Each with the same bed, chair, toilet, and ball. The only thing that differed was the background picture, a twisted reminder of what the prisoner was missing.

Two Watchers walked up to a cage marked *Indian*. A gorgeous human girl, who painfully reminded Jacob of Malini, lay on the bed in rags. One of the Watchers, a redhead with fair skin and pink wings, peered at her through the bars, circled her hands above her head, and transformed into an Indian Watcher, an exact replica of the girl, but with parking cone orange wings. Her red hair turned black, her green eyes brown, and her pale freckled skin a light russet. The other Watcher giggled.

Jacob stared in astonishment. Was this what they used people for: a physical image to copy for their amusement?

"It will go there," Mordechai said, opening the door to a cage exactly the same as any other except for the back wall, painted to look a lot like the Laudners' living room. The door clanged shut behind him. Almost in a trance, he trudged to the chair and sat on the uncomfortable hard surface.

"What's this one, Mordechai?" a young male Watcher asked.

"Mixed breed—very rare. Another Horseman." And before Jacob's eyes the boy circled his hands and transformed into him, but with wings. It was surreal, watching his own image walk away from the cage.

He stared out the bars for what seemed like an eternity. In his mind, the same thoughts played over and over in an endless loop. This was his fault. He had brought this upon himself. He deserved this. The guilt was a straitjacket. Jacob knew he belonged here— after what he'd done to Malini, to Dr. Silva, and to John. Auriel was right. If he rotted in this cell for one thousand years, he would never feel like he'd paid his debt. The worthless feeling settled over him like a shroud. He would never forgive himself. He understood now why the people here acted like shells. The despair in this place was impenetrable. There was no hope, no escape.

The zoo was clearing out now, the last Watcher making his way out the archway. Jacob's eyes wandered down the row of cages, at his fellow prisoners. *Vietnamese, Korean, Japanese,* and finally, *Chinese.*

The Chinese cage enthralled him. Something about the person in the cage was familiar, more familiar than the Swedish woman or the Indian girl, more familiar than a casual resemblance. Her back was to him as she sat on the floor of her cage, rocking back and forth, her straight black hair sweeping her shoulders as she did. As she rose to move to her bed, she turned, giving Jacob a clear view of the outline of her profile.

Even at a distance, the soft brown eyes, the wide nose and the strong jaw Jacob shared were unmistakable. After all the time he'd tried to find her, after planning and scheming ways to go back to Oahu to look for her, Dr. Silva had been telling the truth all along. Here in this hell, in a place that was everywhere and nowhere, there she was.

Jacob was looking at his own mother.

Chapter 41
The Other Side

D r. Silva, Gideon, and Malini landed silently in the garden, the first two crouched ready to attack, the third in a heap in the sand gasping for breath. Dr. Silva pulled a bottle of something that looked like tea from her pack and brought it to Malini's lips.

"Drink," she whispered. "There's no time to rest."

Malini did as she was told. The tea burned through her veins like a shot of adrenaline. Her heart raced in her chest and she had a sudden urge to run. She leapt to her feet.

"Do I want to know what was in that?" Malini gasped.

"No."

"As long as we're clear." Malini blinked her eyes several times in the darkness. She could make out the outline of thorn bushes but there was no visible source of light. Even the night sky was empty of stars. There was a statue of an angel at the center of the garden that looked menacing in the darkness. Malini wondered if it was supposed to be a fountain because the figure stood in a concrete pool, but it was bone dry.

"There's no water in Nod," Dr. Silva said, as if in answer to her unasked question. "That's why it's so dangerous for Jacob here. He's powerless."

"Do you know where we're going?" Malini asked.

"Not exactly, but I know someone who will." Dr. Silva turned to the large red cat. "This is Gideon. You could say he has a nose for Nod. I could get us there, by magic, but I might accidentally hurt you in the process. Gideon, on the other hand, is much better at navigating in a way that's safe for you." She clipped a long black leash to his collar. "Sorry, Gid, I know this is humiliating, but without it she'll never keep track of you in the dark."

She placed the leash in Malini's hand.

"Gideon and I can see in the dark. He will be our guide and I will follow from behind. No matter what happens, stick with him. If you get lost on the way, you'll never find your way out."

"Wait! Aren't you going to light the candle so we can see where we are going?" Malini asked, desperately hoping for some break in the darkness. The blindness was terrifying.

"No. We can't risk it. Light is a powerful thing anywhere but especially here where its presence is so rare. Above all things, we need stealth if we are going to help Jacob. Just hold on to Gideon and follow along."

"You want me to trust your cat with my life?"

"Do as you wish, but he's more trustworthy than I am."

Malini couldn't argue with the logic. Gideon pulled gently on the leash and she followed him blindly. She tried not to dwell on the *what if* thoughts that teased her brain. *What if* the cat didn't know where he was going? *What if* they were somehow separated in the darkness? *What if* one of them was injured and couldn't get back to the real world? She decided to leave the *what ifs* behind and instead concentrated on the prayer that she repeated under her breath as she walked.

At first, Malini thought the blue glow that arose in the distance was a trick her brain was playing on her, like when you turned out the lights at night but could still see spots on the inside of your eyelids. But as they continued down the path, the blue grew brighter and taller on the horizon until she could make out her hand in front of her face. Closer still and she could see the outline of Gideon in front of her and Dr. Silva behind her.

The glow was not a warm natural light but the color of a cheap fluorescent bulb. It bounced off the steel gate and the bland silver buildings stacked like boxes against the desert landscape. The style of the gated city was almost surgical, with no gables or etchings or decorative architecture of any kind. The gates were not scrolled or weathered and had no more character than a concrete slab. The city's massive size did give the illusion of grandeur but anyone who had experienced the magically historic skyline of Chicago or the twinkling majesty of New York City would find it ugly and repulsive. Malini, who was a veteran traveler of three continents, was sure she was looking at a glorified dog kennel.

"Is this Hell?" Malini asked.

"No. Hell is for the dead. No one in Nod is dead, just lost. Hell is much worse. Much more permanent," Dr. Silva answered.

Malini looked out over the twisting thorns in the cold dark behind her and then at the ugly mass of steel and stone. It was hard to believe there was a place worse than this.

"Gideon," Dr. Silva whispered. "You'll have to wait here for us." She turned toward Malini. "There are no cats in Nod and even in disguise, they would recognize him."

The cat nodded and disappeared into the thorns.

"Now, how about something to help us blend in?" Dr. Silva faced Malini and pulled an orchid from her pouch. "It won't take much of a change for you," she said, pulling a tiny tube of water from the stem. She passed her hand over the flower and it melted into a blue ball of energy. She worked the ball between her fingers like clay and it grew. When it was about a foot in diameter, her head snapped up and, before Malini could protest, she hurled the energy at her chest.

A fifty-pound medicine ball hit Malini in the ribs and kept going. She doubled over in pain. The magic burned in her chest, producing a crushing sensation. Was she having a heart attack? Her upper back ached. A heavy weight formed between her shoulder blades and her bones popped as if she were on a stretching machine. Before her eyes, her arms grew longer, her nails painted themselves, and her clothes changed from jeans, a T-shirt, and sneakers to six-inch heeled boots, a mini-skirt, and a skintight sweater. It seemed like hours passed before the pain eased. She faced Dr. Silva, ready to tell her off.

"You could have warned me—" she started, but was distracted by the hot pink wing that reached around from her back and pointed at Dr. Silva. Malini's mouth fell open. Over her shoulder she could see her new pink feathers and with some concentration she flexed and stretched them. The effect was fascinating. She snapped her jaw closed and nodded in Dr. Silva's direction.

"It hurts more if you can see it coming, or so I am told. Now something a little less recognizable for me."

Two platinum wings unraveled from Dr. Silva's back. Malini raised her eyebrows, wondering how it was physically possible for her to retract her wings. Dr. Silva circled her hands above her head and a blue energy ring traveled down her body like a hula-hoop.

When it reached her feet, she was a tall redhead in a shimmering green dress with two silky red wings that matched her hair. She was just as gorgeous as before, but in a completely different way.

"Remember, your illusion will only last an hour within these walls. This is very dangerous for you," Dr. Silva said to Malini in a voice that was lower than it had been minutes ago. "These beings do not understand compassion. They do not know or follow any law, and they do not respect any boundaries. You must move quickly and not draw attention to yourself." With that she walked up to the gate and, with a flick of her hand, opened the door to Nod.

Immediately, the smell of the place overwhelmed Malini. The difference between the foul, poisonous odor from before and now was like the difference between smelling a dirty toilet and being submerged in raw sewage. She covered her nose with her arm.

"Sorry, forgot about your special ability." Dr. Silva directed a snowball of energy toward her face. "Is that better?" she whispered, as they walked through the gate.

Malini sniffed but couldn't smell anything. She nodded.

The chaos that was Nod struck Malini as soon as they entered the city. A mob of angels moved in every direction in the space between buildings. The street was in poor condition, the packed earth covered in garbage and dangerously uneven. Malini supposed roads weren't important if you had wings.

Malini was taken aback by the beauty of the glamorous Watchers that surrounded them and of the wretched treatment of the humans who seemed to serve as pets to the creatures. Scantily clad Watchers with full, feathery wings certainly looked angelic. However, every form of evil behavior was clearly visible on the street. Nearby a Watcher in a rickshaw whipped his human mule mercilessly, its face contorted into a grisly mask of rage. Two perfect-looking Watchers sat at a café table eating strips of flesh off of a man's arm. The man would shriek a bloodcurdling scream every time the knife sliced his skin, but as soon as the Watcher took a bite, the wound would regenerate itself. The man was being forced to endure the first cut, the most painful cut, again and again. Malini had to look away.

They turned a corner. A Watcher in front of them raged over his stolen bag. The leather backpack in his hand was full of merchandise and another Watcher accused *him* of stealing. While they argued, a third Watcher lifted a sparkling chain from the pack and disappeared into the crowd.

"Don't let it suck you in," Dr. Silva whispered to her. "Don't look."

"Where do you think Jacob is?"

"I don't really know. I haven't been here in several hundred years."

Malini looked at her, horrified.

"Don't worry, we'll figure it out." They found a corner of concrete that was fairly empty and distanced themselves from the others. "There are only three things that dark angels do with human souls. The first is they ingest them, but Jacob's not a good candidate for that."

"Why not?" Malini asked.

"Well, he doesn't scream when he's in pain. They like the ones who scream." Dr. Silva paused and shook Malini by the shoulder when it looked like she might vomit.

"What's the second thing?" Malini managed.

"They make slaves of them, a real possibility for someone as strong as Jacob. Although I doubt they chose that for him."

"I'm afraid to ask why."

"Because the third thing they do with humans is display them, in order to remember and copy the image of God."

"There is nothing here in the image of God," Malini blurted, still sick from the thought of Jacob being eaten alive.

"Yes, yes, you have to remember that Watchers do not understand good. They assume that since they know man was made in the image of God that it is his physical image they must emulate. It's like a spiritual cosmetic to them. There is nothing a Watcher loves more than power, so they emulate God's power. It's not real, of course, but they take pleasure in the shallow illusion."

Malini nodded.

"You may have noticed that Jacob is easy to look at?"

A blush crept across her face.

"Don't be embarrassed, girl. You'd have to be dead not to think so. That is why I believe we will find him on display."

Dr. Silva led Malini to an odd sort of train with glass walls. They boarded in a crowd of pushing and shoving Watchers. It was less of a conscious decision really and more of a necessity to board as the crowd had surrounded them and rudely forced them onto the train. Malini stuck close to Dr. Silva as fights broke out for the limited seats. After several minutes of violent pushing and angry yelling, Malini worried they'd be detected by their lack of obnoxious behavior. She was about to scream an obscenity just to fit in when the doors opened again and the crowd emptied into an ill-lit alleyway with red neon signs in a language unfamiliar to her. When the doors closed again, they were alone in the car.

"Tell me again, why are they called Watchers? Why not fallen angels?" Malini asked.

"They are called Watchers because their entire purpose is to observe human weakness and seize every opportunity to corrupt and enslave. They are voyeurs, doing and feeling nothing that isn't immediately gratifying to them. Instead they watch the unraveling of the universe, contributing only to its chaos."

"So, if they just watch, how do they have so much power?"

"Think of it this way. If you have a garden plot and plant nothing, what will grow?"

"Weeds."

"Yes. The evil is already there. And how do you hold back the weeds?"

"You plant things to crowd them out."

"Exactly. The good people of the world are the ones who hold the evil at bay. They crowd out the weeds. See, the Watchers wait for opportunity, a corrupt politician or a failing corporation, and they pounce. They push the weak ones over the edge. They lure them to do things they would normally never do. And after their evil has taken root and corrupted everything in its wake, they bring any guilty humans they desire here."

"So, Jacob?"

"Yes. It was his sin that allowed Auriel to take him. An innocent person cannot be taken unless they choose to come here of their own free will. But the reason Auriel chose Jacob was not because of his indiscretions. She chose him because he is a Horseman. Everyone is guilty, Malini, of something. The Watchers choose the important ones, the ones whose taking will leave a bigger space in the garden, so that more weeds can grow. They leave the weeds."

The train jerked to a halt and the doors opened. They exited the train, alone on a poorly lit dirt path. They could see a metal arch ahead of them. The path led toward it and was otherwise surrounded by desert and garbage that protruded randomly from the sand.

"Dr. Silva, I feel something here."

"What do you mean?"

"I feel a … tingling. There's something like butterflies in my stomach but in a good way. I don't know why but I think Jacob is in there."

"Good. You two are close. Perhaps the connection between you will work to our advantage."

They continued up to the arch and Malini stared at the strange language that was carved at its peak. "I wish I knew what it said."

"It says *zoo*," Dr. Silva whispered. "It's Aramaic."

They tried to blend into the Watchers, milling between the cages. In the first cage, a black man dressed in rags did not look at them. His eyes stared vacantly at a stone on the pathway.

"What does this say?" Malini whispered.

"African," Dr. Silva answered sadly. "Italian, Portuguese, French, Swedish…" she whispered the name on each cage as they walked by.

Malini's heart sank into her stomach. These people were completely dehumanized. But more than that, they weren't talking to each other or fighting to get out. Expressions vacant, their bodies were propped up like empty shells.

"Why don't they struggle?" Malini asked under her breath.

"They've lost hope," Dr. Silva said. "You would be surprised how easy it is to make a human feel worthless."

"But—" Malini grabbed Dr. Silva's upper arm. A group of Watchers gathered around one cage in particular. The occupant was pacing, agitated, yelling something not at the Watchers but at a person in another cage. Dr. Silva placed her hand on Malini's and they moved in, joining the outskirts of the crowd.

Even at a distance, the captive was definitely Jacob.

Chapter 42
The Emancipation of Jacob Lau

"Lilly!" Jacob yelled toward his mother. He was afraid to yell *Mom*, afraid the Watchers might use their relationship against them. "Lillian!" he called again but she would not turn, would not or could not stop rocking herself in the shabby bed. It was as if she couldn't even hear him.

A group of Watchers had formed around him, imitating him and laughing. They were taking turns changing their features to resemble his. Jacob watched as their skin became lighter or darker to match his own and their hair changed to his untamed cut. The female Watchers would keep their long locks but try on his skin tone or cheekbones.

Oddly, two Watchers at the back weren't participating in the game. They stared at him, a hint of something he might have interpreted as compassion in their eyes. One was a gorgeous Indian

Watcher, tall with iridescent brown skin and eyes the color of dark amber. Her friend had long red hair, piercing green eyes, and a low-cut emerald green dress. They looked familiar to Jacob. He glared in their direction, trying to sort his thoughts.

The green eyes sliced right through him, as if they could see into his soul. But it was the amber eyes that attracted him. The golden hue warmed him from head to toe. Where had he seen them before? He stared more intently and the Watcher did the oddest thing, she nodded and smiled.

That small tip of her head, that smile, Jacob's brain flooded with memories of Malini, the way the gold and red had danced in her eyes by the fire, the sweetness of her grin. One of these creatures might have copied her appearance, but they could never copy the genuineness of her smile. It had to be her. But how did she get here and why was she one of them?

Jacob turned away. To get her alone, he'd need to be less entertaining. With a stretch and a yawn, he walked to the bed and crawled under the pitifully dirty blanket. Peeking out from a tiny crack, he made his chest rise and fall rhythmically.

As expected, the crowd began to make disgruntled noises. After a few rocks thrown in his direction, the Watchers wandered off one by one. All except for Malini and the Watcher she was with. The redhead approached the cage door.

"Jacob," she called in a raspy whisper.

He pulled back the blanket.

"Jacob, it's me, Dr. Silva."

He approached cautiously. "Dr. Silva? What happened to you?"

"It's a long story. We've got to get you out of here. Malini's here as well."

"I saw her."

"She's keeping watch, in case we have company."

He looked down at Dr. Silva's fingers on the cage door. "It's locked."

"Yes, of course, Jacob."

"Dr. Silva, I'm so sorry about what I did. I know I don't deserve it but thank you for coming for me."

"I forgive you, and based on what Malini has been through to get this far, I think she has also."

"Yes, I have." Malini walked up behind Dr. Silva. "But Jacob already knew that."

Jacob's whole body tingled at the sight of her. "It's nice to hear it out loud," he said. In fact, the forgiveness seemed to heal some of the despair that hung in the air. His chest felt lighter.

"I have something for you, my friend," Dr. Silva said. She handed him a bottle of water. "I recommend using discretion. We are not entirely alone."

If there were a way for him to fit inside the bottle, he would have done it. As it was, the familiar hum of the water was soothing beyond belief. He took a small sip, strength seeping into his flesh with the liquid. Then he filled his palm. A disc of ice shot from his hand, slicing the lock in two before returning to its source. He willed every drop back into the bottle.

"Here," Dr. Silva said, handing him a mass of garbage she picked up from behind the cage, "to stuff under the blanket as a decoy. I could use magic for this but I have a feeling I'd better save my energy for later."

With his bed stuffed to look like he was sleeping, he exited his prison, relieved at his unexpected freedom. He hid under Dr. Silva's left wing. Watchers passed by but, luckily, they were so caught up in themselves they did not question why two others would be huddled next to the cage door of a sleeping human. Dr. Silva figured out that her wings were long enough to completely conceal all but Jacob's feet. He pressed up against her back and slowly they moved away from the empty cage.

"We can't leave without my mom," Jacob said.

"What? Your mother is here?" The words sounded surprised, but Jacob had a hunch that Dr. Silva had known about this place when they visited the medicine woman.

"She's in the cage marked Chinese."

Dr. Silva stopped in her tracks. "How do you know what her cage says?"

"It's on a sign above her head."

"Jacob, all of the signs here are in Aramaic."

He peeked between her feathers and looked at the sign again. As he focused on the letters, he could tell they were not English, but still he could clearly understand their meaning.

"I guess I can read Aramaic," he replied.

"Hmm. I guess you can," she said, rubbing her chin. "Now let's go get your mom."

The three of them made their way to the Chinese cage. Nearby, three male Watchers wrestled a female Watcher to the ground, tearing off her clothes as she screamed and clawed at their faces.

Malini gasped.

"Look away," Dr. Silva whispered. "If we help her, they will know we aren't Watchers."

The distraction worked in their favor, as all of the other Watchers circled the act of violence, watching and laughing. The three of them arrived at his mother's cage and Jacob used the water to break the lock.

"Hurry, Mom, it's me, Jacob. Come with me now." He held out his hand. His mom stared in his direction, her brown eyes vacant. She did not move.

"Mom, what's wrong? Come on, we've got to get out of here!"

"Jacob." Dr. Silva put her hand on his shoulder. "Your mom has been here a long time. This could be problematic. She doesn't remember herself, only her weakness."

"I don't understand. Why?" They needed to hurry, before the crowd broke up again.

"Oh for heaven's sake." Malini pushed Jacob out of the way and leaped into the cage. She shoved a wad of paper under the blankets and scooped his mom up. She was a small woman. Malini easily lifted her with her enhanced arms and was out the door in seconds. She wrapped her wing around the front of her body, shielding his mom from view. The position was noticeably awkward but, with Dr. Silva leading the way, they reached the entrance without notice.

"That was incredibly stupid," Dr. Silva said.

"Oh, come on. Damaged or not, we were not leaving Jacob's mother behind. Now change them to look like us so we can get out of here."

"I can't, Malini. I only brought one other flower—for Jacob. But if I use it on him now, the magic could draw attention to us. Plus, we'd have to wait for the pain to stop. There's no time; we have to keep moving. Anyway, what would we do with Lillian? If I made her look like a Watcher, she'd just be harder to carry. It's an illusion. It doesn't affect the mind."

They headed toward the train and luck was with them. The car was empty. Malini sat down and lowered her wing so Jacob could take his mother's hand.

"Mom, it's me, Jacob. Everything's going to be all right."

Her eyes focused on his face, squinting and blinking. He rubbed her hand between his own, but she didn't respond.

"Why is she like this?" he demanded.

"People don't end up in Nod unless they've done something to invite evil into their lives. In the beginning, it was Eve's pride that invited the snake to the garden. It was the blood of Abel that brought the Watchers to the sons and daughters of Cain. And it was your dishonesty, your lie to me, and your treatment of Malini that brought you here." Dr. Silva's eyes cut through him and Jacob stared at the floor. He knew exactly what she spoke of, and he wasn't proud of it.

"Your mother, too, invited evil. When people come here, at first they fight, but after a while the illusion of this place overruns their soul. They begin to believe that they are no better than their worst sin. Their guilt makes them think they belong here, and so they give up. Your mom has given up. She is empty because she has no hope."

"How do we bring her back?"

"It is not within our power to do so. Only she can decide to forgive herself. As we get her away from here, her thoughts will become clearer. After that, it's up to her."

The conversation ended as the train came to an abrupt and unexpected halt. Malini quickly covered Lilly with her wing and turned her body sideways. In this position, she appeared to be drunk or sleeping, holding her stomach. Jacob, however, was hopelessly exposed and met Dr. Silva's eyes with trepidation. Thinking fast, he fell to his knees in front of her and began polishing her shoe with the hem of his rag.

His back exploded with pain as the last to board, a huge Watcher in the image of the African man with bright purple wings, kicked him squarely in the back.

"Use your tongue, maggot," the Watcher screamed at the back of his head, "and when you're done there, you can start on mine."

Thankfully, the Watchers walked toward the large group at the center of the train and didn't stay to watch him. He'd lowered his mouth toward Dr. Silva's shoe out of sheer terror. As soon as the other passengers were distracted, she reached down and stopped him. Standing up, she grabbed a pole at the center of the train and Jacob slid beneath her wing.

The train screeched to a stop in the city and the doors opened to reveal the bustling streets of Nod.

"Where is that little maggot?" the Watcher screamed into Dr. Silva's face as he moved toward the door.

She didn't answer, just shrugged her shoulders and looked down her nose. He left the train disgruntled, looking up and down the street for another human to do his bidding. The three exited near the back of the crowd, trying their best to blend in.

Crossing town to reach the gate proved to be more difficult than they'd anticipated. Watchers packed the streets, each going their own way with no semblance of order. Halfway to the gate and beyond the most congested part of the city, Malini's feathers began to drop one by one. Her body contracted, shortening like gravity had quadrupled and was pulling her to the ground accordion style.

"Malini, your hour is up," Dr. Silva said. "Run!"

Yanking Jacob into her arms, Dr. Silva flew for the gate. Malini's wings disappeared completely and her arms could no longer support Lilly. Jacob yelled as Malini collapsed to the sand. The sound did nothing but call more attention to their plight. Every eye in Nod turned in their direction.

Dr. Silva tossed Jacob through the gate, where he hit the sand and rolled toward the thorny brush beyond. She returned, sweeping Lilly into one arm and Malini into the other. With one powerful thrust of her wings, she carried them outside of Nod.

Watchers pointed at them through the gates and then Jacob's worst nightmare came true. Mordechai emerged from the office building, his jet-black wings stretching in anger. He blazed toward them, his model perfect face contorting with fury, his black eyes burning.

"Mordechai!" Jacob screamed, pushing at the gate, but it would not budge.

"It will only move for a Watcher, Jacob," Dr. Silva said. With a flick of her wrist the gate slammed shut. A ring of blue energy flew from her hand and sealed the gate.

Dr. Silva transformed into the platinum blonde version of herself. She did not bother to tuck her wings away.

"So that's what you are. You're one of them?" he said, unable to disguise the note of disgust in his voice.

Dr. Silva ignored him. "It will not hold. Gideon, where are you?"

The large red cat leapt from the thorny darkness. Dr. Silva handed him the cat's leash, and placed Malini's hand into Jacob's. Then she lifted Lilly into her arms.

"Gideon, move!" she said as the pounding against the gate became more urgent. "I can't hold them for long." Gideon took off down the thorny path with Malini and Jacob following close behind and Dr. Silva, Lilly in tow, bringing up the rear.

The absolute darkness swallowed them all.

Chapter 43
Showdown

Jacob tried to run in the dark behind Gideon, but the narrow path was bordered with thorn bushes. In the blinding darkness, the barbs tore his skin and more than once the front of his foot stepped on the back of Gideon's. He could hear the brushing of wings and the stomping of feet in the distance behind them. Malini's hand was cold and clammy in his.

"Gideon, we won't make it to the garden. We need a place to do battle," Dr. Silva whispered, panic evident in her voice. The cat jerked to the left and Jacob followed, pulling Malini along with him. Abruptly, Gideon stopped, causing his feet to plow into the cat and Malini to slam into his back.

"Jacob, reach in front of you at waist level and push," Dr. Silva said from behind him.

Jacob did what she asked, finding a doorknob. The door was extremely heavy and he had to throw his shoulder into it to get it open. Once he did, Gideon pulled them inside.

Dr. Silva set Lilly down and rummaged through her backpack. The hiss and dim light of an igniting match broke the darkness. She lowered the flame down to a candle. He could see the wick catch and then a pale light washed over them.

"Hold this." She handed the candle to Jacob and returned to digging in her bag.

They were in some kind of a church. At least, it was shaped like a church with pews, stained glass, and an altar, but the similarities ended there. Unlike the one the Laudners attended, no crosses or statues of saints filled this church. The pictures in the stained glass were of Watchers. Instead of a crucifix, a statue of a Watcher stretched its wings above the altar. A day ago, none of this would have meant anything to him. But after experiencing Nod, Mordechai, and the zoo, Jacob realized the evil of this place. This was not like a human church, where people came to think about how they could be better people, tried to live up to a higher standard or help each other. In this place, the Watchers worshiped themselves. It was, sadly, a testament to their egos. This was a world where the only priority was the desire of each individual at any particular moment. There was no law, no rules, and absolutely no guilt about anything because the only thing that mattered was obtaining more of what each Watcher desired.

"Ah, here it is. Malini, you and Jacob push all of these pews to the side. Quickly! Clear as large a space in the middle of the room as possible," Dr. Silva said. She held a container of salt in one hand and pushed pews aside with the other. Jacob continued to hold the candle but pushed with his hip and free hand as well.

Lilly sat on a pew near the front, still motionless but looking more awake than before. There was a hint of awareness in her eyes.

When they'd cleared a large circle in the middle of the building, Dr. Silva set to work drawing lines of salt on the altar, a giant triangle, and then another inverted atop the first. When she was done she had formed a large six-pointed star inside of a giant circle.

"The star of David," Malini whispered next to him.

"Gideon, I'm going to need your help, darling," Dr. Silva said to her cat.

In response, Gideon moved into the space at the center of the room. Front feet forward, he stretched his hindquarters into the air. His waist grew longer and his red fur tightened on his body. A pillar of flesh erupted from the cat's mouth toward the floor. The flesh split into a pair of legs and the cat turned itself inside out, fur moving up the legs and then the body of a man. When the process was finished, nothing was left of the cat but green eyes and wild auburn hair.

Gideon was easily seven feet tall, with long, lean muscles and a twenty-foot wingspan. The pearly white wings were similar to Dr. Silva's, but Jacob couldn't say he was a Watcher. What set him apart from everyone in the room was not his height, or his frame, or his wings, but his glow. Looking directly at Gideon was like looking into the sun. It filled the room. In fact, with Gideon's light flooding over them, he wondered if he should blow out the candle.

"He's an angel—a real one," Malini said into Jacob's ear. "He has to be."

Jacob opened his mouth but nothing came out. He was awestruck.

"It really is you," Lilly said. She was not looking at Gideon but at Jacob. It was like the light from the angel had opened her eyes for the first time since he'd rescued her. "Jacob, how did you…? You shouldn't have come here."

He ran to her and threw his arms around her neck. She hugged him back.

"Mom, whatever happened, however you got here, I forgive you. Please stay with us. We need your help."

She looked around the building, at Gideon, and then at Dr. Silva. Jacob thought he would have to explain, but before he had a chance she was on her feet, more determined than he'd ever seen her.

"How long?" she demanded of Gideon.

"Minutes." Gideon's voice reverberated off the walls. It was deep and hollow, like a cross between a harp and a baritone.

"I need weapons." She looked at Dr. Silva, Gideon, and then Jacob.

"What?" Jacob asked.

She spoke directly to Gideon. "My name is Lillian Lau. I am a Horseman," she said. "I was captured in battle." She stood to her full height. "My gift is weapons. Help me find something to use before it's too late."

"Mom. How long have you known?" he asked.

"I'll explain everything later, Jacob. This must be very confusing for you but trust me."

With two beats of his wings, Gideon flew up to the rafters and stripped a steel girder from its place. He rolled it in his palms, which must have been hot because the metal took on a bright red glow. Throwing it down, he stomped on the last foot of metal with his heel, flattening it pancake thin. Then he jumped on the other end in the same way. When he was finished, he tossed Lillian a bladed staff. She caught it and twirled it around her body, as if she'd been born with it in her hands.

"The candle," Dr. Silva said to Jacob. The thick white wax in his hands had a name and date carved into the side in gold. He moved to hand it to her but she shook her head. "It's my baptism candle. When you step inside the star and place this candle within it, I must warn you not to be afraid of what you see. The star will reveal truth within itself. It dispels illusions. You may see things that you find disturbing. I beg you, stay within the circle. Your skills are not ready for battle." She handed him three bottles of water from her pack. "Just in case."

"Just in case? Who are you? How do you know my son?" Lillian crouched in fighting stance, looking suspiciously at Dr. Silva.

"Lillian, water is Jacob's gift. I'm his Helper," she said, as if she were talking to a two-year-old.

"Oh. Wow. Jacob! I didn't know." His mom beamed.

"He's not ready," Dr. Silva repeated.

The sound of flapping wings outside of the church made everyone's head turn toward the door.

"They're coming! Jacob, Malini, into the circle!"

Dr. Silva, Gideon, and Lilly positioned themselves at the center of the clearing. Jacob grabbed Malini's wrist and pulled her into the star. Placing the candle inside the triangle at the front, the salt around the outside of the circle ignited and the star burned an eerie, purple flame.

Gideon and his mom looked exactly the same through the purple glow, but Dr. Silva changed. Her already tall frame extended another foot and her muscles pulled against her clothes. Her skin became scaly black like a serpent and her wings, leathery like a bat. Her blue eyes turned yellow with cat-like vertical slits. Jacob understood now why the devil was often portrayed as a snake. Watchers, in their natural form, looked like serpents.

With a deafening crash, the window shattered above them and Jacob pulled Malini into his chest. He turned his back toward the storm of falling glass but nothing reached them. The purple flames licked upward and swallowed the shards as they fell.

Auriel stood in the broken frame of the window. From within the star, she looked like a snake, although slightly smaller than Dr. Silva. But Jacob could tell who she was from the murderous expression on her face, the same one she'd had when she attacked Dane. He fought back the memory of maggots on his tongue.

"Mordechai, they are here!" she yelled and then turned, seething, toward Dr. Silva. "You have something of mine, Abigail." Her eyes darted toward Jacob.

"He's not yours, Auriel. He's just a boy. He did not choose this place."

"He's a sinner, a cheat, and a liar. He has plenty of anger, too. I had every right to take him."

"He did not come willingly. You will not have him!"

Just then, the heavy door swung open. Mordechai stood in the doorway along with another Watcher. Through the purple flames, they looked nothing like their borrowed images, but Jacob would know Mordechai anywhere. He was easily the biggest Watcher he'd seen in Nod and the blackness of his eyes was unmistakable. That hadn't been an illusion. His friend was only slightly smaller but equally terrifying. Male Watchers, it seemed, had horns that grew from their forehead, giving them a more demonic look than Dr. Silva or Auriel.

When he spotted Jacob sitting in the center of the purple circle, Mordechai smiled a wry grin and rapped his taloned fingers against each other. He cocked his head to the side and laughed toward Dr. Silva.

"Abigail! To what do I owe the pleasure of a visit from my sister?"

Malini's sharp intake of breath was Jacob's cue to take her hand.

"I am yours no longer," Dr. Silva hissed.

"You've met my friend, Turel?" He motioned toward the Watcher who stood next to him.

Dr. Silva flinched and Jacob wondered how she knew Turel.

Mordechai swaggered toward the Horseman, the Helper, and the angel who crouched ready for the attack. "Hand over my prisoners and you may leave," he said to Dr. Silva.

She did not answer.

"Suit yourself," he said through clenched teeth. "But you do realize that I have no intention of losing two of my prized specimens." He glared at Lilly and then at Jacob, rubbing a pale scar on the scaly skin of his chest.

Jacob remembered! It was Mordechai in the center of the road. It was Mordechai he hit with the car, and it was Mordechai who'd taken his mom. The scar was the place his mom's knife had dug in. All this time he'd thought the memory was a hallucination. Now, he realized, it was painfully real.

"And you," Mordechai said, nodding at Gideon, "know very well that He won't help you here. You'll make the finest specimen of them all."

Gideon flexed his wings in response.

"Have it your way," Mordechai spat.

Jacob pulled Malini tighter against him as the dark angel raised his taloned hands.

Chapter 44
Battle

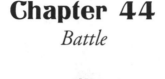

Mordechai rolled one hand over the other and formed a ball of orange flame. He hurled it toward Dr. Silva with a hissing sound that made the hair on Jacob's arms stand on end. Gideon crossed his forearms and a purple shield glowed to life in front of him, absorbing the impact of the flames inches from Dr. Silva's face. In response, Dr. Silva circled one hand over the other behind Gideon. She nodded to him to lower the shield and hurled the blue orb that formed between her hands at Mordechai. It hit him in the shoulder and howl escaped his mouth.

Lillian lunged at Turel, her blade sinking into his stomach. The Watcher grabbed the staff and yanked it from his gut, tossing it and her aside like she weighed nothing. She flipped gracefully to the top of a pew, spinning her staff back to fighting position. Gideon's shield just barely stopped Turel's fireball from taking off

Lillian's head. Black goop oozed from Turel's stomach but the wound didn't stop him from retaliating. Lillian spun through the air, dodging another ball of energy. She sliced into Turel's collarbone on the way down, landing and jumping again to deliver a tornado kick to his head as she yanked her staff from his flesh.

A red ball whizzed toward Dr. Silva, this one exploding into a swarm of locusts. Gideon blew them away with a gust of his breath.

Turel struck back. The fireball skimmed Lillian's calf and she screamed louder than Jacob had ever heard a human scream. He smelled burning flesh.

The magic the Watchers wielded was more than natural fire. Through the purple flames, he watched the smoky blackness eat the flesh off his mother's calf. This was dark magic.

Gideon held the shield in a dome over Dr. Silva and Lillian as they endured a storm of fire from Mordechai and Turel. The angel reached out and touched Lillian's calf. Her screaming stopped and the open wound healed.

As Jacob saw it, Gideon was the only one who could shield and heal, which left Dr. Silva and Lillian to fight. Only they were smaller and weaker than the Watchers that attacked them. The battle was unbalanced and not in their favor. Auriel was still watching lazily from her perch. In typical Watcher style, she was too self-serving to join the battle until she absolutely had to, but if she changed her mind they were all doomed.

Turel turned toward Jacob and aimed a ball of flame at his head. Jacob ducked but he didn't need to. The purple flames shot up and ate the fireball out of the air. Turel cursed and his yellow eyes searched the boundary of the salt star.

"Pray with me, Jacob," Malini whispered into his ear. Tears streamed down her face. "Please pray with me. I'm so scared."

"Why? What good would it do? We can't waste time, Malini. We have to think of a way to help."

"Please, Jacob, please pray with me."

"I don't … I can't, Malini. We need a plan. Help me figure out what to do."

"Jacob, listen to me." She grabbed his shoulders and shook. "Look around you. We are going to die unless we get a miracle. I am here, in this hell, because of you. I believe there is a God and I need that comfort right now. The least you can do is give it to me."

Jacob shook his head and grabbed a bottle of water. "The only one here to save us is me, Malini. Stay here. I'm going to try to help."

He stepped through the flames.

Pouring enough water into his hand to form a sharp, jagged star, he hurled the weapon into the side of Mordechai's head. Black ooze drained from the Watcher's temple. The beast turned on him, howling. He poured more water into his hand, willing it sharper and faster than the last.

"You want to play too, maggot?" Turel yelled. Now outside the circle, Jacob could tell Turel was the Watcher from the train.

He released a barrage of sharp discs toward Turel's neck. The distraction allowed Dr. Silva to come out from behind the shield. She hurled blue energy, a storm of electric light, at Mordechai. The Watcher drew a shield, a circle of fire, around himself, absorbing Dr. Silva's sorcery and turning Jacob's weapons to steam.

Jacob dove out of the way as a fireball from Auriel bulleted toward his head. The smell of his own hair burning filled his nostrils. Somersaulting across the floor, he motioned for Malini to throw him another bottle. She rolled it to him from within the circle.

"Who do we have here?" screeched Auriel, who had jumped down next to Mordechai to join the fight. It was as if she was noticing Malini for the very first time. "This one is hard to see. What are you, my dear?"

Malini didn't answer.

"Why, Nod is teeming with humans today, Mordechai." She sent a golden ring toward Malini, like a lasso, but the purple flames swallowed it before it could reach her.

Meanwhile, Lillian speared Turel, sinking the blade into his back. He struggled to reach it, to pull it out, buying Dr. Silva time to send a barrage of blue energy toward Mordechai and Auriel. With Turel's defeat eminent, Mordechai abandoned him where he fell and swallowed Auriel into his flaming safeguard. Jacob hurled knives of ice toward him. It was useless. The fire easily turned his weapons into puffs of steam.

Lillian and Dr. Silva took down Turel, ripping him apart and binding the pieces to the floor with glowing blue rope. Auriel and Gideon battled behind them. Lightning flowed from Auriel's fingers, through Mordechai's shield, but Gideon reflected the power back at her with a mirror of energy. The trick worked. Where Auriel's power rained down on the ring, the fire weakened.

There was no one left to battle Mordechai but Jacob. With everything he had, he attacked.

Mordechai reached through his dwindling shield and caught one of Jacob's razor-sharp icicles in his bare hand. He watched it melt in his snakeskin palm. The grin on his face was triumphant as water dripped through his fingers.

"Normal water?" he dropped the remaining shield. "You don't believe in God!" He laughed, sauntering closer to Jacob and swatting off his attack as if the razor sharp weapons were merely an annoyance. "Good choice, boy. You've never seen God after all.

But you've seen me. Why don't you just believe in me?" And, with that he hurled a fireball that plowed through Jacob's shield of ice and landed in his lower abdomen.

Jacob fell, screaming. The spot where Mordechai's power hit him burned like acid. He beat his body with his hands but succeeded only in splattering his own blood. This type of fire had no flames. Blood covered his hands and splashed his face. It pooled under him. There was something coming out of the hole in his gut, something his mind couldn't process through the pain, something that should've been under his skin.

Jacob looked toward Gideon for help. The angel was across the room, shielding his mom, whose weapon lay kicked aside. Dr. Silva was also behind the shield, staring at Jacob with pity and launching a barrage of power at Mordechai and Auriel in a last attempt to save him. She was losing. There was no way Gideon could reach Jacob in time to heal him. Tasting blood in his mouth, Jacob came to the icy realization he would die in Nod. His body shook uncontrollably and the light dimmed around the edges. He was falling. He was dying.

"Oh, Jacob, there's so much blood!" Malini was over him, pressing her hands against the open wound.

"Malini, you've got to hide. I'm dead anyway. Get out of here."

"No," she said through her teeth. "You've got to believe, Jacob. Miracles happen every day. I'm not letting you go. No way."

With his last ounce of strength, he lifted his hand and placed it over hers.

"Pressure. You're supposed to put pressure on an open wound to stop the bleeding." Malini's eyes were wild with panic.

Death came for Jacob for the second time in his short life. Again, he walked the obsidian tunnel beckoned forward by the light. This time he moved toward it without fear or anger. He'd let that stuff go the moment he saw his mother in the Watcher's cage. He'd forgiven himself, he'd forgiven her, and he'd buried what blame he'd placed on God, if there was one. Maybe it was less buried than forgiven. His trip to Nod had made him realize that even though he'd done bad things, he wasn't a bad person, and he supposed that way of thinking extended to the Laudners and to Paris. He let it all go.

Deep within the darkness of the tunnel, he thought about his life. He'd convinced himself there was no God because of the evil in the world and certainly that evil was real; it filled the Watcher church around his body. But as he thought of Gideon, Dr. Silva, and his mother, it was just as clear that every force, every action, had an equal and opposite reaction. If evil existed, then an equal degree of good existed somewhere, too. It existed in them, in the fact that they were willing to die to protect him. It existed in their willingness to fight, to die, rather than become part of the evil.

What if believing was not about the good in the world? What if people had faith not because of what some superior being could do for them, but what they could do when the light of something bigger than any one individual awakened within them—for the sake of others? If evil had been here since the dawn of time, maybe goodness was also here. Maybe, his mistake was thinking it was about him, his own future, his own soul, and not about this: the world needed the good that was in him.

He reached the end of the tunnel. Jacob could make out a pair of boy's feet and the hem of a rag sack just like he was wearing. He looked down at himself and wondered if the light was some sort of reflection, like a giant mirror. What he could see looked just like him. But the white radiance burned his eyes and he struggled to tip his head up to see the boy's face. Shielding his eyes with one hand, he reached out his other and stepped forward. Before he could touch the image, a voice rang out, "Not yet, Jacob."

In a rush of wind, power, and will, he fell back into his body. The pain was gone. All he could feel was the pressure of Malini's touch. He looked down at the tops of her bloody hands, and then pushed them aside. Through the burnt hole in his rag clothing, he could see fresh pink skin. The wound was completely healed.

He needed to save Malini. It was his job, his purpose. He knew it at that moment as surely as he knew his name was Jacob Lau. This was war and it was time for him to choose a side. For all the pain his name had caused him, for all the agony over his mixed blood, every experience he'd ever had brought him to this place.

"Oh my God, Jacob … Jacob you're healed," Malini said, staring at the blood on her hands.

But he wasn't listening. He was watching Mordechai turn toward them, another fireball forming in his palm. Jacob crawled in front of Malini, blocking her body with his. On his knees in front of her, he knew what she'd said was true. He did get her into this mess and he would get her out of it.

He kneeled before Mordechai knowing he was a Horseman. He was a protector, connected to the universe with a unique purpose, and he would not fail. The quickening came without warning or the hum of water that had always accompanied it in the past. His thoughts moved so fast that everything else seemed to slow down. The strings inside his body tightened.

Jacob's reasons were not the same as Malini's, or John's, or even Dr. Silva's, but he made his peace with God in that moment. It had nothing to do with religion or church or a specific name for who He was. He didn't sign his name to anything or chant a special prayer. In his head, he sent a yes into the universe, an invitation to whatever force for good existed. For the first time, he wanted to be a part of it. He was willing and he was there.

In that moment, he believed.

There was no water left. The bottle lay empty at his feet. He had no idea what the strings inside of him were connected to, but as the fireball moved from Mordechai's hand, and the sound of Malini praying behind him reached his ears, he prepared to release.

He circled his arms and let go. The push that came was not from his own strength but from beyond. It was a push from a place of deep realization that he was a warrior, a Horseman, for everything good. The ground shook, the walls shook, and as the fireball exploded above his ducked head, water poured in from all directions. It was as if every pipe in the church had burst simultaneously, only there was no water in Nod. This water came from somewhere else.

"It will kill me, Jacob!" he heard Dr. Silva scream. He willed the deluge to flow around her. It washed forward, sweeping Mordechai through the door. His melting form thrashed wildly against the water until he dissolved into a puddle of black ooze. Auriel had taken to the air. She flew out the window, screaming for help, the drops of water burning her like acid. The pieces of Turel dissolved with the blue bindings and washed away.

When they were gone Jacob willed the water back. It went out the way it came in, flowing around Dr. Silva as if she were in a bubble.

"There will be more," she yelled, grabbing her backpack and the extinguished candle from the circle.

Gideon headed out the door first, the light from his body all they needed to run full speed down the twisting path toward the garden. It was also enough to catch the attention of a host of

Watchers who had emerged from the city of Nod. Unearthly howls and beating wings bit at their heels.

They reached the tree just in time. Gideon grabbed Lillian's hand and disappeared through the bark. Dr. Silva clasped Malini with one hand and Jacob with the other and followed. The transport was slower this time, because of the weight of the three of them being pulled up through the ground by her magic. But in minutes, Jacob was in the sand in front of Oswald, panting. He had never been so grateful for the nausea that wrenched his stomach. The nausea meant they were free. They had escaped Nod.

Chapter 45
Homecoming

When he'd finally recovered from his journey through the tree, Jacob sat up in the sand and looked around him. Malini was still on her side, holding her head. It was only her second time through Oswald. He scooted over to her and scooped her up into his arms.

"Thank you, Malini, for coming for me."

Malini hugged him tightly and kissed him softly on the lips. She buried her face in his chest.

Gideon stood in front of the tree in his angel form, chanting something Jacob couldn't understand.

"What's he doing?" he asked Dr. Silva, who had pulled her knees into her chest and looked both sad and tired.

"He's blessing Oswald so that his soul will leave the tree and go to heaven."

"Well, that's terrific, isn't it?"

"It means the tree won't be a portal anymore. Oswald's soul was what made it work. He's closing it off so that the Watchers can't use it to get to us."

"Do we need the portal? For the work that I'm supposed to do?"

"No, not really. There are other ways. Better ways actually. I'm just going to miss Oswald."

Then he remembered what was at stake. "The garden—it was Oswald's magic that kept this place alive, wasn't it?"

"Yes."

"And, all of this will die when he goes?"

"Yes."

"I'm so sorry, Dr. Silva. This is my fault."

"No, Jacob. There were problems before you ever came along. Why do you think I had a gate?"

And then another hand was on his shoulder, a hand he never thought he would see again.

"Mom!" he yelled and hugged her as hard as he could.

"Jacob, I missed you so much." Lillian's eyes were full of love and tears.

"But how long have you known? That you were a Horseman, I mean?" he asked. As much as he was glad to see her he was a little put off that she'd never told him.

"Since your dad died. That was my trigger."

"But why didn't you tell me?"

"After Charles died, I noticed changes. I would be chopping vegetables at the kitchen counter and the knife would become like an extension of my arm. Someone would startle me after work and my body would move instinctively. I was faster, stronger than ever. Any weapon I touched, I knew how to use like an expert. But I didn't know what was happening to me. I didn't have a Helper yet."

"So what happened?"

"Don't you remember? The bruises, the arrests ... I got into fights just to try out my skills, to learn what I could do. I purposely put myself into dangerous situations. I wanted to be attacked—for the exercise."

Jacob remembered her strange behavior, how it had gotten worse those last weeks. They'd fought the day of the accident. He'd thought she was on drugs or something. She wouldn't tell him what was going on or where she was going. That's why he'd followed her.

"One night, I wandered into a martial arts academy called the Red Door. I saw weapons in the window, ones I'd never tried before. Sure, I could wield a knife and shoot a gun; these were intuitive. I wanted to know if I could fight with something I'd never touched before, a mace or a staff. Master Lee met me at the door. He said that he was my Helper and I was called to fight evil. Of course, at first I didn't believe, but after a few meetings he had me convinced. He taught me the basics about fighting Watchers. The box and the throwing knives were my graduation present.

"When those women went missing in Manoa Falls, I thought it was the work of Watchers. Master Lee called in a team of Horsemen to investigate. My first mission would be to help hunt the thing down and kill it before it murdered anyone else. I was too anxious. I didn't think I needed the help of the other Horsemen, so I went to Manoa Falls myself. I found the Watcher on instinct, but I was taken."

"Why didn't you tell me?"

"Would you ever believe it, if you weren't one yourself? If you hadn't seen what you've seen?"

"Maybe. You could've tried me."

He stared at her for a long time. The picture of his past had been fractured and his brain was snapping the pieces together in a different pattern, a whole different past, as he reinterpreted the events that he'd defined himself by for so long. Lilly hadn't been a messed-up and irresponsible widow, she was a Horseman struggling to understand her power, just like him. The accident that had changed his life forever was no accident at all. His memory rang true.

"When you are taken to Nod, Jacob, the despair of that place overwhelms you. All you can think about is the worst thing you've ever done. You try to resist but eventually you convince yourself that you belong there. You convict yourself and, believe me, a person is their most unmerciful judge. When I was in that cage, Jacob, I was a prisoner to one thought, one terrifying offense. I had abandoned you. I left for Manoa Falls knowing that I might never return. I left you with nothing, no means to survive."

"You thought you'd be successful. You didn't mean to."

"It doesn't matter, Jacob. I'm so sorry."

"I think you've suffered enough. I forgive you. Just don't let it happen again." He smiled knowing a weight had been lifted with his words.

"But how will we explain this? What story will we tell for how she got here?" Malini asked. "Nobody is ever going to believe what really happened."

"I don't know." Lillian looked at Dr. Silva. "But we'll think of something."

"It's more than Lilly we have to explain," Dr. Silva said. "You two have been gone for three days."

"Three days!" Malini and Jacob yelled together.

"Yes, unfortunately time in Nod is different than time here. You've been gone three Earth days. Lilly, you've been gone almost a year," Dr. Silva said.

Lillian covered her face with her hands.

"But what will I tell John?" Jacob asked.

"Or my parents?" Malini added.

"Oh, we will think of something. The most important thing, Jacob, is that now you are a true Horseman. I'll connect you with others like you so that you can work together. You will apprentice with a team and participate in your first mission. Your mother being here is a blessing. She can help," Dr. Silva said.

"But I don't understand. I never finished my training."

"That, Jacob," she said, pointing to the tree, "was the advanced course."

Jacob wasn't sure he was comfortable with that answer but he turned toward his mother, another question pressing against his lips. "Are we going back home?" He'd assumed she would want to go back to Oahu, to pick up where they'd left off.

"It's not safe, Jacob," she said. "Right now, this is the safest place on Earth. There just isn't that much here to entice the Watchers to attack. Now that the portal is closed, it will be more difficult for them to get to you."

"Plus, you need Malini," Gideon said. He'd finished at the tree and now faced them, his green eyes twinkling in the late afternoon sun. "You two have been brought together, spirit to spirit, for a reason." He stopped when Dr. Silva shot him a sharp glance.

"Jacob, you need to know, difficult or not, they will come for you. You killed two of their top leaders. Mordechai and Turel were very powerful, what you might call vice presidents in your world. We can slow them down, but I'm afraid there are more Watchers in your future. Both of you."

He glanced toward Malini. He hated that he'd dragged her into this. Picking up a handful of sand, he watched it run through his fingers, thinking about the day, about everything he'd learned.

"Why didn't you just tell me what you were?" Jacob asked Dr. Silva.

"Would you have trusted me if you knew I was a Watcher?"

Gideon shook his head, his green eyes resolute. "You're not. You are not the same as them, Abigail. I wouldn't be here if you were." He was beside her in an instant. He didn't actually touch her but sat less than an inch away, his wing sheltering her in its protective arc. Even in the daylight, his glow was undeniable.

Malini nudged Jacob's shoulder and shot him a look. He hadn't meant to hurt Dr. Silva's feelings.

"I guess it doesn't matter what you are, Dr. Silva, but who you are," she said. "You're our friend. You saved us today."

Malini always knew just what to say.

"I think that honor goes to Jacob," Dr. Silva replied. "Why don't we all go back to the house and have some tea? Then we can talk about what to do next."

"I think I've had quite enough of your tea, thank you," Malini said.

"Whatever you'd like then," she answered with a laugh.

Malini and Jacob led the way out of the cactus maze, through the field, and up the twisting forest path. Lillian followed closely, but Dr. Silva and Gideon lagged behind. As they entered the forest, stepping from stone to stone through the blood dragons, something started to nag at Jacob, a thought, a piece of the puzzle that didn't quite fit. He told Malini to take his mom to the gate and quietly backtracked to the edge of the glade.

Gideon and Dr. Silva had stopped in the meadow, the setting sun a red halo behind them. His hand hovered within an inch of her cheek, his body as close to hers without touching as possible. Under the shadow of his wings, it looked as if he would kiss her at any moment. His lips were so close to hers Jacob could feel the tension between them. It was a level of intimacy that made Jacob blush. He knew he shouldn't be watching their private moment but for some reason, he couldn't turn away. Even a bystander could feel the love there, as intoxicating as fairy dust.

After what seemed like an eternity, their lips finally touched— only they didn't. At the moment of contact, Gideon transformed, folding in on himself until only the red cat remained. Jacob could see it then, the sadness between them, hanging like a lead weight around their necks.

Dr. Silva turned for the path and Jacob didn't bother to hide. He was too affected by what he'd seen. He swallowed the lump in his throat and waited for them to join him on the trail.

"So, it seems like you are doomed to experience one more form of hell today," she said softly. Then she held a hand out toward Gideon. "Witness, the curse of the angel who fell in love with the Watcher."

The big red cat ran ahead, making a sound like a cry.

Chapter 46
Gideon's Challenge

They huddled in the parlor of Dr. Silva's home and helped each other recover. Being in the presence of evil, true evil, sticks with you. It hangs off a person like the stench of sewage and takes more than its share of your thoughts. The original elation of being free from Nod settled into quiet contemplation. Dr. Silva insisted each of them have cookies with tea or milk and only discuss their happiest memories for at least an hour. She said it wasn't safe to go out otherwise. A person shouldn't take those feelings of grief and hopelessness into the world with them.

"Jacob, you and your mom can't go home dressed like that. Go cut some chrysanthemums from the back of the house and I'll build you an illusion," Dr. Silva said.

He nodded. He was still wearing the grotesque rag from Nod. He walked through the sunroom, out the back door, and was about to cut a handful of burgundy flowers when Gideon joined him in the flowerbed.

Jacob glanced up in time to see the cat transform. The process was gruesome, the cat turning inside out on itself, skinned alive. But in the end, Gideon looked no worse for it. He ran his hands through his auburn hair and stretched his wings to their full span before folding them neatly behind his back. He wore jeans and a black T-shirt Jacob assumed was an illusion since the cat hadn't had any clothes. Still, he was thankful for that much. More comfortable than staring at a naked man with wings.

"Does that hurt?" Jacob asked.

"Mildly. Kind of like vomiting your own shoes."

"Oh." He took in the glow around Gideon. "Then, why did you change?"

"Because I need to talk to you."

"About what?"

"I want to tell you about Abigail and about why I'm here."

"Okay."

Jacob took a seat on the garden bench and Gideon leaned against the fountain. His movements were quicker than a human's and the turn of his head was reminiscent of a bird.

"Before the beginning of time, we angels lived with God. Angels do not marry the way that humans do but we do have families. Abigail's family decided to follow Lucifer when he challenged God for power. He and all of his followers were cast from heaven, including Abigail. I knew her then, before it happened. We had spent an eternity together.

"Abigail never agreed with what Lucifer did. She went along blindly, following her family group. She regretted it immediately. While the others established Nod and preyed on humans, Abigail lived among men peacefully. She knew she was cursed, like the rest of them, but she refused to give up. She wanted to return to heaven. So, she left her family and lived a solitary life for thousands of years.

"Then she met Oswald. She loved him, as much as any human has ever loved another. He believed she was human of course. She tried to tell him about her past, but he interpreted her words to mean that she had done some things wrong when she was young. He encouraged her to be baptized because he believed it would redeem her. She did it in good faith, not knowing what effect it would have."

"Wait a minute," Jacob interrupted. "You guys are angels, you've been to heaven, and you've met God. How could you not know what effect it would have?"

"I can see why you would think that, Jacob, but angels are servants of God. We don't have any more answers than you. In fact, humans have been promised more from God than angels ever have. Your future, your soul, is more a certainty than ours."

"But don't you know? I mean, who's right? All of these religions on this Earth … you've been to heaven and back! Are you telling me that even *you* don't know who is right?"

"No, I don't. But I can tell you that where I come from, in the presence of God, it is less important who is right than what is right."

Jacob tried not to look disappointed. Here he was, a new believer, and not sure what exactly believing meant for his life. He'd hoped that knowing Gideon, he would know for sure what to believe, what the truth was. He tried to bring himself back to the story. This was obviously important to Gideon.

"So, you were saying, that Dr. Silva was baptized?"

"Yes, she was. When Oswald died, I knew that God had plans for her when He allowed the portal to grow. To allow that kind of power in her hands—God trusted her. And then, I was called."

"Called?"

"Yes. When God has a job for us, we hear it in our head and we obey. My job was to offer Abigail another chance. I was the messenger. I came down to her in the garden and I told her what God told me. Soon, a boy would come who would be important to the battle between good and evil. If Abigail proved her allegiance by successfully helping this boy, then she would be rewarded."

"Am I the boy? Will she get to go back now that I'm a believer?"

"Yes. You are the boy and no, she cannot go back now. First, because your purpose is far from complete. There is much for you to learn and do. And, second, because going back is not her reward. At least not in the same form she left."

"What do you mean?"

"If Abigail fulfills the Lord's will, He will make her human. He will give her a real soul, a mortal body."

Jacob stopped himself from asking why an angel would want mortality. He didn't want to be rude.

"You are wondering why she would want this?" Gideon filled in.

"Yes," he admitted.

"You, silly human, have free will. You have a soul. And, God does not call you a servant like He does the angels, but a friend. When you die and go to heaven, angels will serve you."

"Oh," was all he could muster.

"You haven't asked me the obvious question," Gideon said with a grin.

"What should I ask?"

"Why am I still here?"

"Why are you still here, Gideon?"

"Because when I came to deliver the message, I fell in love with Abigail. I suppose, I have always loved her and will always love her."

"But what does that mean for you? If she becomes human…"

"I asked, I begged the Lord, if I could help her, if I could stay … and He said, 'yes.' If Abigail succeeds, then I will be made human also. We will be able to be together like no two angels could ever be."

"You can't be together now?"

"I can't even touch her in this form. She has a Watcher's skin, a cursed body. This stuff that I am made of cannot make contact with it. Only as the cat, can she touch me."

"So, that's what she meant by the curse. You have to stay with her now, because of your agreement with God, but you can never really be with her, until she succeeds in her quest. Until I succeed."

"Yes."

"And, I am her first? She's never been a Helper before, has she?"

"You are her first and only chance at redemption."

"Suddenly, I feel a lot more pressure to be good at this Horseman thing."

"I thought you should know."

"Thanks. I think," Jacob said. "Can I ask you one more thing?"

"Sure."

"Auriel told me that Watchers lose their power above ground. How does Dr. Silva do it?"

Gideon smiled. "She never ate flesh. Watchers who feed on flesh are cursed and must continue to do so or lose their power. Abigail has maintained a vegetarian diet for her entire time on

Earth and thus was never cursed in this way. It's another reason she's different from them."

Jacob nodded. "Well, I better get inside."

He leaned over to cut a handful of chrysanthemums and tried not to watch as Gideon folded in on himself.

Epilogue

It was amazing how fast news traveled in a small town. Jacob stood in the atrium of St. Mary's Catholic Church with the Laudners amidst a sea of whispers and sideways glances. Truth can be a fuzzy concept in the best of circumstances. His story was less than perfect.

When his mom returned with him to the Laudners' home, he wondered how Uncle John and Aunt Carolyn would react. Dr. Silva, Malini, Lilly, and Jacob had talked for hours about what story they would tell. What explanation could there be for her disappearance on Oahu and reappearance in Paris?

They told Uncle John that Malini and Jacob had decided to drive to Florida and back, just for fun. Jacob said he'd found Lillian on the side of the road on their way back. Lillian's appearance certainly upheld the story. She was gaunt, bruised, and her clothes were torn.

For her part, Lillian said she couldn't remember anything but being held in a dark warehouse. Dr. Silva had given them a place to say they had found her, a place of great evil. It turned out the FBI knew that place was frequented by human traffickers, and told Lillian she was lucky to have made it out alive. They had no idea.

Although Aunt Carolyn wasn't happy about it, Uncle John invited Lillian to stay in the Laudner home until she could get back on her feet. With Katrina gone, they gave her room to Lillian so she could be close to Jacob. They even gave her a job working in the flower shop. Jacob asked to work there too and Uncle John seemed ecstatic to finally have him on board. In truth, he did it to make up for lost time with his mom, but he was glad it made John happy anyway.

He had no excuse for why he hadn't called John. The Laudners were beside themselves with worry and had called the police, as had Malini's parents. Although, Uncle John did admit he'd talked to Jim Gupta the first day after the pumpkin chuck and they had guessed something like this had probably happened. It didn't lessen their punishment. Both of them were grounded until further notice, maybe forever.

Dr. Silva's garden slowly died as winter moved in. With Oswald's soul departed, the tree did not have the warming effect on the environment around it. Jacob tried to help Dr. Silva collect seeds and roots for her greenhouse, but many varieties were lost during the first freeze.

Once Jacob returned to school, there were dozens of stories about what had happened between him and Dane. He'd been in pretty bad shape. Dane's official story was that he was mugged in the parking lot by three large men but didn't get a good look at their faces. Jacob stuck with his story about finding him beaten in the parking lot. They never spoke of what really happened, but

Dane completely changed his treatment of Jacob and Malini. It was too early to say they were friends, but the idea wasn't as crazy as it used to be.

All of this gave the people of Paris more than enough to gossip about as Jacob slid into the Laudners' usual pew. He stared at the crucifix that hung at the front of the church. He couldn't help but be reminded of the last church he'd been in and the last pew he'd sat in, the one in Nod. He was never so happy to be in a real church as that moment, a real church with holy water that hummed to him from every corner, waiting to be a weapon if evil came his way. The ceremony itself didn't make much sense to him. It wasn't his way of believing. But that was okay. Because, as he looked at the crucifix, at his mom smiling next to him, and at his own hands, he had something better than confidence. He had hope.

* * * * *

The Christmas tree in the corner of the Laudners' living room was the biggest Fraser fir Jacob or his mom had ever seen. They'd helped to decorate it with red and gold glass balls of various sizes. Clear glass icicles dangled from the branches behind silver snowflake garland. Early Christmas morning, Uncle John had finished the tree by laying fresh red poinsettia flowers on the branches.

Jacob's favorite part was the angel on the top, which looked nothing at all like Gideon. When there was no one else in the room, he and his mom laughed about how the flowing blonde locks looked more like a Watcher than an angel. He understood now that the reason Dr. Silva had looked so much like Auriel was that they'd borrowed the same image, from the Swedish woman, in slightly different ways. He wondered what the real Dr. Silva would look like, if she ever became human.

"This one is from all of us," he said to his mom, handing her a square package. The Laudners had already opened their gifts and John and Carolyn were looking on, smiling. Katrina was home from school but still pouting about having to share a room with Jacob's mom.

Lillian peeled back the red and gold paper and pulled the top off the box. Under the tissue was a framed picture of her and Jacob, posing in the front bay window.

"I thought it was about time we added you to our wall," Uncle John said.

"Thank you, John. It's beautiful." She stood up and gave him and Aunt Carolyn a quick hug. Her eyes were misty and Jacob knew it wasn't just because she liked the picture. It was what it represented. Lillian Lau had finally been accepted by the Laudner family.

Jacob handed her a second gift. "From me," he said.

Underneath the gold paper was a scrapbook. The first several pages were already filled with pictures of Jacob, Malini, and the Laudners with a few of her mixed in.

"So that you can start a new history," he said, and then leaned over to whisper in her ear. "There's a knife in the binding."

She glanced down and saw the glint of silver nestled in the spine. "It's exactly what I wanted, Jacob. Thank you." She hugged him hard. "Now you."

He took the box from her hand and removed the paper in one rip. As he opened the lid, he saw a watch with five time zones.

"In case we ever travel," his mom said, smiling, and then discreetly motioned to look under the watch. Jacob didn't take it out but in the bottom of the box was a thin flask with a strap. It

was the kind you could wear around your ankle or wrist. He knew
without checking that it was full of water, he could hear the hum.
With this, he would never be without it.

"Thanks, Mom. It's perfect," he said and then reached for the
picture of the two of them. "Let's go hang our picture."

She was on her feet too quickly and Jacob hoped the Laudners
didn't notice her lightning-fast reflexes, but they were too busy
picking through a plate of Christmas cookies. Jacob followed his
mom up the stairs, only speaking when he was out of earshot.

"The flask was brilliant, Mom," he said, hanging the picture on
the hook John had made ready on the wall the night before.

"It's important for you to protect yourself."

They turned with a start when a sound like a firecracker came
from Jacob's room down the hall. Jacob looked back at his mom.
She placed a finger over her lips and motioned for him to follow
her. Silently, they crept toward the room, his mom pulling the
knife from the binding of the album. Her dark eyes spoke volumes
as she kicked open the door.

Malini stood in the middle of the room clutching her chest.
"Jeez, Lillian, I think you stopped my heart." She was leaning on a
thick wooden staff.

"Everything okay up there?" Uncle John yelled from below.

"Yes, John," Lillian called toward the stairs. "I just dropped my
album."

"How did you get up here?" Jacob asked Malini, looking at his
locked window.

"So, you haven't opened your gift from Dr. Silva and Gideon?"
Malini asked.

"No." But then he saw it. A long, wrapped gift leaned up
against the corner of his room. He ripped the paper off and saw a
wooden staff, identical to Malini's.

"It says something in Aramaic. Can you read it to me, Jacob?" Malini asked.

"Sure," he said, turning the staff in his hands. "It says *anywhere.*"

"If you read the card, it says Gideon made these from the branches of the tree. Oswald has moved on but Gideon has enchanted these. They'll take us anywhere we need to go, at any time," Malini said. "I was surprised she gave me one."

"Do you think there's one for me?" Lillian asked and excused herself to go look in her room.

"Dr. Silva says she's going to help me figure out what I am," Malini said.

"I have something that will help." Jacob handed her a box from his nightstand. She unwrapped it carefully and pulled off the lid.

"The stone!" she said, putting her head through the cord and holding up the red disc between her fingers.

"It can tell the future. I think, at this point, you need it more than I do."

"Thank you, Jacob. And something for you." Malini handed him a tiny box from her pocket. He ripped into it and found a thick silver ring engraved with Sanskrit. He slid it onto his finger.

"Did you know this says 'Water,'" he asked.

"Yes, I had it engraved. So, now you read Sanskrit?"

"I guess so," he shrugged. "I love it, Malini." He leaned forward and kissed her, their lips starting out gentle and soft and ending in something that made his heart beat faster. He pulled away when he realized the door was still open. "I imagine you're not supposed to be here."

"Nope. As far as my parents know, I am in my room putting away my Christmas gifts. I believe I'm officially grounded for life."

Jacob tossed the staff back and forth between his hands. "Then I suppose this gift is even more important because I can't be away from you for that long."

Malini rewarded him with a smile he knew was exclusively his.

"Does it have the same side effects?" he asked her.

"No. I felt fine coming over here," she said. "Maybe we should go next door to say thank you."

"Great idea. I want to give Dr. Silva the gift I got for her, anyway." He grabbed a wrapped box from his closet.

"What is it?" Malini asked.

"A pink cable-knit sweater."

"What? Have you ever seen Dr. Silva wear anything but black?"

"No. But I thought it was time she started dressing for her future."

"Very sweet, Jacob. I'm sure she'll love it." Malini kissed him again, this time on the cheek. "How do you think she stays here? I mean, if she doesn't age, why hasn't anyone in Paris noticed?"

"She never told me but I think I figured it out. My uncle once said that her grandmother lived in the same house. Obviously, Dr. Silva has never had a grandmother. I think she ages herself by illusion, and then comes back as her own daughter. She doesn't come out much. It wouldn't be hard for her to fool everyone," he explained.

"It must have been hard for her to live her life in a lie like that, no one ever really knowing who she was," Malini said.

"Well now she has us," Jacob said. He held up the staff. "So, how do these work?"

"It's easy, you just think about where you want to go and tap them on the floor," Malini said.

"Now?" he asked, tucking the gift under his arm and interlacing his fingers with hers.

"Yes, Jacob, I'm ready," she replied and he believed she was, for anything. There was a deep trust in her eyes that hadn't been there before. Not ever. Not even before he had tried to force her to go through the tree. Not even on the beach. Something had changed. They were bound to each other in an almost magical way.

"Together then," he said.

They raised their staffs and looked out the window toward the gothic Victorian, together to anywhere.

Other Books in The Soulkeepers Series

Weaving Destiny (Book 2)
Malini Gupta thought Jacob Lau was her destiny. But after months of failing to decipher how she fits into the Soulkeepers, frustration threatens to tear their relationship apart. And it doesn't help that a new Soulkeeper named Mara is ready to stop time itself to earn Jacob's love.

When Malini faces her worst fears, and even death, she learns a funny thing about destiny. Fate is a tapestry of choices, and she has the power to weave hers.

Return to Eden (Book 3)
Dr. Abigail Silva has waited over 10,000 years for redemption and a chance at a real relationship with the angel she loves. But when you're made from evil itself, it's hard to remember if salvation is worth the wait. With Lucifer's plan coming to fruition, she must decide if God's offer of humanity is all it's cracked up to be, or if a deal with the devil is the more promising solution.

Soul Catcher (Book 4)
Dane Michaels has been to Hell and back and isn't interested in repeating the experience. But as a human caught up in the Soulkeeper's world, his life isn't exactly his own. No one can explain why Dane was allowed through the gates of Eden, but it's changed everything. Now, the only one who can make him feel

safe is Ethan, the telekinetic Soulkeeper with a dark past and a heart of gold.

When Malini asks Dane to be part of a mission to find the last Soulkeeper, Cheveyo, more than one team member thinks she's tempting Fate. But Malini suspects Fate has had a hand in Dane's life for some time and that he could be the key to unraveling Lucifer's latest plan of attack.

Lost Eden (Book 5)
Rules. Balance. Consequences. War.

When Fate gave Dane the water from Eden to drink, she did more than save his life. She changed his destiny. Since the beginning, a covenant between God and Lucifer has maintained a tenuous peace, balancing Soulkeepers and Watchers and the natural order of things. Dane upset that balance the day he became a Soulkeeper. Fate broke the rules.

Now, Lucifer is demanding a consequence, requiring Fate to pay the ultimate price for her involvement. God intervenes on the immortal's behalf but in order to save her soul must dissolve the covenant and with it the rules, order, and balance that have kept the peace. A challenge is issued. A contest for human souls begins. And the stakes? Earth. Winner take all.

The Soulkeepers are at the center of a war between Heaven and Hell, and this time nobody, anywhere, is safe from Lucifer's reach.

The Last Soulkeeper (Book 6)
The end is near.

Just when the Soulkeepers think they've established a foothold in the war between Heaven and Hell, the playing field shifts. Enraged by Cord's disappearance, Lucifer replaces his right-hand man with the Wicked Brethren, three Watchers so formidable even their own kind fears them.

The Soulkeepers struggle to survive in an increasingly deadly world while continuing to defend human souls. How far will they go when saving the world means sacrificing their most precious team member?

Other Books By G. P. Ching

Grounded
A seventeen-year-old girl discovers she's the product of a government experiment, when her father's illness causes her to leave her isolated community.

Weaving Destiny (Excerpt)
The Soulkeepers Book 2

Chapter 1
Closer

Katrina Laudner ached to be noticed. Within the crowd of college students in the living room of Sigma Nu fraternity, she danced, careful not to spill the contents of her red plastic cup. Her denim skirt scarcely hit her upper thigh. Her cami scooped dangerously low. And the thump-thump of the music the DJ blasted from the corner pounded its way out of her body in a rhythm of invitation. No one noticed. Even half naked, she was wholly invisible.

"What are you drinking?" a velvet voice asked. He was close, close enough for her to hear over the deafening music, close enough to feel breath on her earlobe. Katrina stopped dancing and turned. A boy stood between her and the wall.

"The red juice from the back," she answered.

He was exceptional in his stillness. The strobe light made the rhythmic mass of people to their left and right jerk with the illusion of disconnected movements. But like an inanimate object, the light had no effect on his image. Every flash was the same.

"Are you here alone?" he asked.

"Yeah. I was supposed to meet my roommate but she never showed."

"You're not alone anymore." He stepped in closer. Navy blue eyes, almost purple, set off his pale skin and black hair. The overly confident smile on his lips did as much to entice her as did the hard line of the jaw it was attached to.

She took another sip from the red cup. The juice she'd scored from the man in the back was spiked with something that burned her throat on the way down. She hoped it made her nice and numb. Maybe then she could play it smooth. Guys could smell desperate a mile away.

"Do you know there's alcohol in that?" he asked.

"Are you a cop?"

He laughed, a dark, hollow sound that caressed her ear like a lover's kiss. "No."

"Then I can safely say that if I didn't know it was spiked before, I sure as hell know now. I'm pretty sure this stuff could remove nail polish." She drank again, but couldn't stop herself from peeking over the top of the cup. Wide shoulders, pierced eyebrow—he was rock-star, chiseled-by-the-gods gorgeous.

He wrapped his hand around her upper arm and pulled her forward, bringing his lips to her ear again. "It's just ... you look underage," he said.

"I'm old enough." The heat from the spot where his skin touched hers was almost too much to bear. She went back to dancing a little, breaking the connection.

"Hmm. A lawbreaker, I think. What should I call such a reckless and wild one?"

"Katrina."

"Do you have a last name or am I to assume you're so infamous that you don't need one?"

She tilted her head to the side and smiled. "Laudner. Katrina Laudner. What's yours?"

"Cord."

"Cord like what you open the drapes with?" she teased.

"No." His expression darkened. "Cord like what you strangle someone with."

Katrina took a small step backward. She thought about leaving altogether but then his face relaxed into a teasing smile. He was trying to be funny.

She shrugged off a foreboding weight that had settled on her chest. That was the problem with growing up in Paris, Illinois. She wasn't used to anyone different. She was too cautious. "Do you have a last name, Cord?"

"No," he said. The corner of his mouth tugged upward as he looked over the bump and grind on the dance floor. "Infamous."

"Nice. I'm beginning to think it begins with a B and ends with astard."

The smile melted from Cord's face, replaced with an intensity she'd never seen before—well, maybe in some wild animal show where the predator was about to eat the prey.

Katrina crossed her arms over her chest as if the position could deflect the raw power he'd turned in her direction. An intoxicating scent drifted over her, cinnamon, sandalwood, a dark forest. Closing her eyes, she breathed deeply through her nose. She was about to compliment him on his cologne when Cord's touch made her eyes flip open.

He'd moved in closer. While her eyes were closed, he'd stepped forward until the back of his hand brushed the bare skin above her elbow. The contact made her ache to close what little space was left between them. It stirred something deep within her. Every inch of her became super sensitive, her flesh reaching out for him, knowing he was the source of some unknown thrill.

A hot blush crept across her cheeks. She distracted herself by lifting her cup to her lips again, but it was empty. Had she drank it all so quickly?

"Can I get you a refill?" he asked.

"Yeah."

He lifted the cup from her grip, never breaking eye contact. "I'll be back in a moment. Don't move, Katrina Laudner."

She didn't. He slid gracefully between the gyrating students toward the back, giving her a delightful view of the taper of his hair down his neck, wide shoulders, and dark jeans that hugged the curve of his hips. She wasn't going anywhere. In fact, if he asked her to stand there all night, she might comply.

A new song thumped from the speakers and the crowd went nuts, throbbing to the industrial rhythm. She joined in, arms reaching toward the ceiling.

"I like this music. What's it called?" Cord was beside her again.

Startled, she stopped dancing. "Oh my God, you scared me. Shit, you were fast."

Cord handed her the red cup, full now. "Do you know this music?" he asked.

"I think it's from the nineties. Um, 'Closer' I think. Yeah, it's called 'Closer.'"

"I like it."

She sipped her drink, aware that his purple eyes scanned every inch of her as if he were trying to see under her skin. Unnerved, she shifted away from him.

"Hey is this the same punch? It tastes different ... like cinnamon or something." Katrina took another sip and felt the burn travel all the way to her toes.

Cord shrugged. "Where are you from, Katrina?"

The room began to sway and she reached out a hand to steady herself against the wall. "Paris, I'm from Paris, Illinois."

"Paris?"

"Yeah, I know. Don't blink or you'll miss it."

"Oh, I like small towns. I've been meaning to visit Paris."

"Really? Why?" A foggy weightlessness caused her to lurch forward.

"Are you okay?" he asked.

"I think I've had enough. I better quit while I'm still sober enough to find my way home."

"That sounds ultimately responsible. Was I wrong about your reckless and wild ways?"

She laughed. "I have my moments."

In front of her, his muscles shifted beneath the drape of his shirt. It was some kind of silky cotton, not too tight, not too loose. The gray fabric beckoned her to reach out and run her hand up his abs and across his chest. Thanks to the red cup, inhibition had packed its bags. On impulse, she rested her palm on his stomach. She swayed on her feet.

A hand caught her lower back. Cord pulled her into his body, effectively holding her up. Taller, he had to lower his chin to meet her eyes.

"You smell good," was all she could manage. The room floated away. He was her tether to the Earth.

"May I walk you home, Katrina Laudner?"

There was no hesitation on her part. She wanted to fall into him, to press every part of herself up against his hard body. She wanted to cover herself in that delicious smell. "Sure, that would be nice."

He reached for the empty cup in her hand, nesting it inside his own before setting it on the floor near his feet. Something about the action bothered Katrina and she found herself staring at the cup. A headache bloomed at her temple.

"Are you going to leave that there? I mean, I could find a garbage can. It's rude." Her voice sounded muffled, like she was hearing herself through a thick wall of glass.

"Don't worry about it. It's okay just where it is."

Katrina was normally obsessive about neatness. It bothered her that he wouldn't pick up after himself. But at the moment, she had more pressing issues. "Whoa," she said, weaving toward the door. "Whatever was in that drink went straight to my head."

Cord half carried her through the crowd. Once they were out the door, the fresh air revived her. A moment of clarity came halfway across the deserted walkway of the quad.

"What was in that drink?" She shook her head and inhaled the crisp night air, stepping away from Cord, whose cologne suddenly seemed overpowering. Disoriented, she stumbled toward the gnarled trunk of an oak tree, planting her hand on the rough bark.

"Stay close to me, Katrina," Cord said. "Girls shouldn't walk alone. You never know who or what could be lurking in the shadows."

Much clearer now, Katrina blinked her eyes and focused on Cord. In the lamplight, the black hair and purple eyes, so sensual at the party, looked menacing. The shadow of the tree she leaned against seemed to reach for him, like his presence was a magnet to the darkness. The silhouettes bowed and stretched, rippling under the illumination of the lamppost. Shadows weren't supposed to bend that way. The air wasn't supposed to ripple.

"I think I'm hallucinating," she said from the harbor of the tree's branches. "I think there was something other than alcohol in that drink."

She closed her eyes and shook her head again. Had he drugged her? She'd heard of boys slipping things into girls' drinks. Every college girl had. She was so stupid. What was she thinking, leaving the party with a stranger?

"Relax," Cord said. His arm snaked behind her shoulders.

When had he moved so close to her? He'd closed the gap between the walkway and the tree in what seemed like the blink of an eye.

"Wait. I need to get home, Cord. I'm not feeling well."

"Lie down right here, Katrina." He lowered her slumping body to the grass.

Part of her wanted him. He smelled good. He felt good. But a larger part of her knew something was wrong. She'd been drugged, that was for sure. The hard, cold ground cut unevenly into her back.

"Wait," she said, her voice barely a whisper. "Let's go back to my dorm."

With his arm still behind her shoulders, he leaned over her, his face hovering with the promise of a kiss. "No, Katrina," he said. His purple gaze cut the darkness. "I want to talk to you. I want to know all about you. I want to be closer."

From behind heavy lids, she tried to respond, but she was transfixed by the curve of his lips. She closed her eyes and tipped her chin, an invitation for him to finish what he started.

Nothing.

When she opened her eyes again, Cord was gone. She was lying next to the tree, the glow from the lamppost illuminating an empty walkway at her feet. She sat up, wondering if she'd hallucinated him all together. Man, what was in that drink?

On autopilot, she stood and walked back to her dorm. Her brain felt fuzzy. Exhausted, she let herself into her room and stumbled through the darkness toward her bed.

"Ohmygod, Katrina. I've been so worried about you!" Mallory said. Katrina heard a click and the soft glow of her roommate's lamp made her blink. "First, I couldn't find you at the party and then you weren't here when I came home. Where the hell have you been?"

"What time is it?"

"Four in the morning."

"Four? Really? Shit, I don't know, Mallory. I think someone slipped something into my drink. I feel weird."

"Into your drink? What, like a roofie? Are you okay? Do you need me to walk you to health services?"

Katrina thought about it for a minute. "No. I feel okay. I don't think anything happened. I just need to sleep it off."

"Well, the good news is it's officially spring break, so you can sleep as long as you want."

"Yeah, spring break. I'm supposed to go home to Paris tomorrow ... I mean today, later. Hell, I've gotta get some sleep."

Katrina didn't bother to undress. She slipped beneath the covers of her bed and closed her eyes. She was asleep before Mallory turned off the light.

About the Author

G.P. Ching is the bestselling author of The Soulkeepers Series and Grounded. She specializes in cross-genre YA novels with paranormal elements and surprising twists.

G.P. lives in central Illinois with her husband, two children, and a Brittany spaniel named Riptide Jack. Learn more about G.P. and her books at www.gpching.com

Follow G.P. on:

Twitter: @gpching
Facebook: G.P. Ching
Facebook: The Soulkeepers Series

Sign up for her exclusive newsletter at www.gpching.com to be the first to know about new releases!

The greatest compliment you can give an author is a positive review. If you've enjoyed this title, please consider reviewing it at your place of purchase.

Acknowledgements

Special thanks to the following people for saving The Soulkeepers from the recycle bin.

First, I have to thank my late father-in-law, Bob Ching, who inspired much of this story. I miss our conversations.

To friends Michelle Moore and Rhonda Kasper, thank you both for believing in my work when nobody else did. Michael Brennan, Jeff Smith, and Robin Ferrier, thank you for providing fresh eyes when mine were very tired.

Thank you to my parents, Yvette and Joe, for supporting my reading habit as a child and my writing as an adult. And Jon Hall, Annette Wirth, Sue Hall, Joe and Monica Pommier, and Aaron for reading early versions of the manuscript and encouraging me with your enthusiasm for the story.

Thanks to fellow authors Dawn Malone, Scotti Cohn, Michelle Sussman, and Karly Kirkpatrick for helping to polish the manuscript to a high gloss.

Thanks to Adam Bedore of Anjin Designs for the amazing cover art and Jon Hall, Eric Hall, and Kimberly Pommier for their opinions on the art.

Finally, a big thank you to the #fridayflash community who helped give my writing a voice. All of you are special to me.

Book Club Discussion Questions

1. Do you think forgiveness came easily to the characters in The Soulkeepers? Do you think it would be easy to forgive if similar events happened to you?

2. Are the prejudices of past generations more forgivable or understandable than those of today? For example, do you find it easier to gloss over a racial slur said by a grandparent than a peer?

3. Why do you think the concepts of faith, religion, and spirituality are avoided in most young adult literature?

4. Uncle John asks the question, "Do you think a person is only as good as the worst thing they've ever done?" How do you feel about this question? Are there certain actions that define a person's character permanently?

5. Mysterious biblical history plays a pivotal role in the plot of The Soulkeepers. Are there parts of the bible (or your particular holy text) that you find disturbing or paradoxical? How do you reconcile that with your faith?

6. How do people create their own prisons in their life? Do you think an individual can be his or her own harshest judge and jury?

7. Is there an evil force in this world that can push otherwise good people over the edge?

8. What do you think about the way God is depicted in The Soulkeepers?

9. How do people growing up in rural communities have a different reality than those in urban or suburban settings? Do you think this upbringing effects how they think about moral choices?

10. Do you think our culture is obsessed with our physical appearance, what we wear, and how we smell? Do you think the focus on outside beauty is an attempt to capture something else?

62239433R00213

Made in the USA
Middletown, DE
19 January 2018